HELEN COX

A Body
in the
Bookshop

Quercus

D0334276

First published in Great Britain in 2019 by Quercus
This paperback edition published in 2020 by

Quercus Editions Ltd
Carmelite House
50 Victoria Embankment
London EC4Y 0DZ

An Hachette UK company

Copyright © 2019 Helen Cox

The moral right of Helen Cox to be
identified as the author of this work has been
asserted in accordance with the Copyright,
Designs and Patents Act, 1988.

All rights reserved. No part of this publication
may be reproduced or transmitted in any form
or by any means, electronic or mechanical,
including photocopy, recording, or any
information storage and retrieval system,
without permission in writing from the publisher.

A CIP catalogue record for this book is available
from the British Library

PB ISBN 978 1 52940 223 0

This book is a work of fiction. Names, characters,
businesses, organizations, places and events are
either the product of the author's imagination
or used fictitiously. Any resemblance to
actual persons, living or dead, events or
locales is entirely coincidental.

10 9 8 7 6 5

Typeset by CC Book Production
Printed and bound in Great Britain by Clays Ltd, Elcograf S.p.A.

MIX
Paper from
responsible sources
FSC® C104740

Papers used by Quercus are from well-managed forests and other responsible sources.

For all those who have kept in touch
with the child in their heart.

ONE

Evie Bowes took short, timid steps along the frosty pavement York council had not seen fit to grit. Though it was only half past five it had been dark for more than an hour. Between the early December dusk and the large hood on the royal blue winter coat she'd invested in last month, the facial scars from her ordeal in October were invisible to passers-by. In the eyes of cyclists with tyres intimidating enough to slice through the ice and dog walkers hopping about on the spot to stay warm, Evie looked like just another person huddling away from the pre-Christmas chill.

The scars were hard proof that she really had been kidnapped by a murderer six weeks ago, surreal though it still seemed. Evie's doctor had prescribed silicone sheets designed to improve the appearance of the marks, but so far she could see little difference. The special make-up available worked pretty well most of the time, but even so she could still see the unsightly ridges along her temple and jaw. Because of all this, and the number of double-takes from strangers she experienced in the average day, Evie had come to consider the darkness a dear friend.

Taking a right, turning away from the river and up Ouse View Avenue, Evie watched her breath rise in a whisper towards the sky. Despite everything that had happened, despite the face that didn't look like her own any more, she was still breathing and that was something.

Walking up the path to number thirteen and smiling at the lush green wreath hanging on the door, Evie rang Kitt's bell. There was the usual shuffling and shoving as her best friend tried to work the stiff door out of its overly snug frame.

'Evie?' Kitt's voice called from the other side.

'Guilty as charged,' Evie called back.

'Give it a kick, will you?'

'All right,' Evie said. 'One, two, three.' She kicked the door near the bottom, giving it the extra push required to release it, and then Kitt appeared. She had braided her long red hair into a plait that snaked around her shoulders. There was a time when Kitt would still have been in her work clothes but she'd been a bit better about making time to relax in the last month or so and was instead wearing a pair of jeggings and an over-sized sweatshirt emblazoned with the slogan: *What happens in the library stays in the library.*

'At least we know we're safe from any undesirables lurking around, I suppose,' said Evie. 'Not like they could get at us if they tried.'

Kitt put a hand on her hip. 'If you're going to be funny you can stay on that side of the door.'

Lifting her hands in mock-submission, Evie stepped into Kitt's living room and lowered her hood. Just how obvious would her scars look now she didn't have the veil of darkness to protect her? The room was fairly dim, lit only by the fairy lights arranged around the mantelpiece, the open fire and two small lamps. Evie looked sidelong at Kitt, wondering if her friend had guessed how sensitive she was over her new appearance. Certainly, Kitt never put the big light on when Evie came to visit any more.

'Couldn't you get Inspector Halloran to take a look at your door?' Evie asked. She began unbuttoning her coat to reveal the leaf-patterned A-line skirt and mustard cardigan she had changed into after finishing work at the salon, both from vintage clothes shops.

'We're, ugh ... taking ... things ... slow,' Kitt said, huffing and puffing at the door until it shut.

'So?'

'So, we're not at the "will you take a look at my stiff front door?" part of our relationship.'

Evie giggled. 'Not what I've heard.'

'Don't start with that.' Kitt pressed her lips together in what looked like an attempt to ward off a smile. 'And will you please stop calling him Inspector Halloran? I don't know why you think it's funny.'

'That's his name . . .'

'Not amongst friends.'

'Well, I can't call him Mal.'

'Why not?'

'Because I've heard the way you say it to him.'

Kitt crinkled her nose. 'What's that supposed to mean?'

Evie crossed her arms and fixed her eyes on her friend. 'When you say his name your tone goes all throaty and you sort of . . . wrap all the sounds around your tongue.' She lowered her voice as though someone with sensitive ears might be listening. 'You make it sound like a naughty word.'

Kitt's cheeks burned and she gave her friend a playful slap on the arm. 'Ooh, will you give over? I've never heard anything so daft.'

Evie continued to chuckle to herself as she went to sit in her usual armchair. At once she remembered how difficult a spot it was to leave once she had arranged herself there. She could never be sure if it was the chair itself, its proximity to the open fire or the company that made it so comfortable, but she suspected it was the latter. Next to her, Kitt's black cat Iago was playing a game of chicken with the fire: lying as close to the flames as he possibly could without being burned alive.

Evie breathed in the scent of cheese baking in the oven and thought she might burst with hunger.

'That lasagne smells amazing,' she said. 'Lunch feels like forever ago.'

'What did you have?'

'Just a supermarket salad,' Evie said with a shrug.

Kitt bristled. 'I don't know how you can. Especially on a cold winter's day. It's hardly salad weather.'

'You never think it's salad weather,' Evie teased.

'Mercifully, I never have to. I'm not the one who insists on squeezing herself into an endless array of vintage dresses, most of which were made in an era when people were living off tongue and tripe and bread and dripping.'

'I know, I know, I've heard the monologue before,' said Evie, inwardly wishing carbs weren't quite the decided luxury they were in her life.

Kitt walked out to the kitchen muttering under her breath about beauty standards and feminism and returned a moment later with two plates piled high with lasagne and garlic bread. 'Here we go.'

'Have I ever told you how much I love you?' Evie said, her mouth watering as she watched steam rise from the plates.

'Between the almost incessant mockery, I believe it has come up once or twice,' Kitt said, placing a plate on the folding table by Evie's armchair. 'Say you'll have some wine with me?'

Evie tilted her head at her friend. 'It's only Thursday. The weekend come early?'

'No, but I spent three hours in a budget meeting this afternoon . . . with Michelle,' Kitt said.

'I thought you'd decided you weren't going to let her get to you any more?'

Kitt pouted. 'Three hours. Three long hours.'

Evie laughed. 'All right, pour me a glass. Some of your most entertaining moments happen when you're inked.'

Kitt sighed. 'I have no intention of getting inked, an expression that surely hasn't been used since the turn of the twentieth century.'

Evie stared at the fire and smiled. Vintage words, vintage anything in fact, brought her a pleasure she had never quite been able to explain. Perhaps it was because the past always seemed simpler than the moment you were living in now.

'You know,' she called out to the kitchen, 'there might be some kind of award you could nominate Michelle for. Maybe World's Grouchiest Boss?'

'Dreariest Disposition of the Decade? She'd win that one, no contest,' said Kitt, returning with two glasses of what was most likely to be Pinot Grigio.

'You're so lucky having a boss like Diane,' Kitt said, referring to the owner of Daisy Chain Beauty, the salon where Evie was employed as a massage therapist.

'Yeah.' Evie sighed and took a big gulp of her drink. 'She's been good to me.'

'True, she didn't exactly leap to your defence when you

were accused of murder six weeks ago, but she didn't suspend or fire you either. Which she could've done.'

Evie noticed a frown cross Kitt's brow.

'What?' Evie asked.

Kitt shook her head. 'I shouldn't have mentioned the murders, I'm sorry.'

All of a sudden, Evie's face felt too hot, even taking the open fire into account, and her green eyes filled with tears. Panic gripped her as she tried to blink them back. 'You can't spend your life tiptoeing around me. It happened.'

Kitt put down her fork. 'Doesn't mean I have to harp on about it, I know you're still recovering.'

Evie offered her friend a shaky nod. She hadn't expected to talk about this. She had done all she could since the incident not to think about it at all, but every now and then, the pain she'd been trying to push down resurfaced.

'I'm sure I'll get there. It's just . . . I just feel – ' she began, but she was interrupted by a knock to the front door.

Kitt tutted and stared wistfully at her plate. They had yet to dig in to that dreamy, cheesy lasagne and, when it came to food, Kitt didn't take kindly to delayed gratification.

'You'd better get that,' said Evie, her tone betraying her relief that someone had interrupted the outpouring she'd been holding in ever since the doctors had told her that her facial disfigurement might never fully heal.

'I'm not answering it. It'll likely be the Jehovah's Witnesses. They always call at teatime.'

7

'No it won't, they don't call on you at all any more since you started gifting them with copies of *The God Delusion*.'

'You're just saying it like that to make me sound tart,' said Kitt. 'In fact, it was a mutually agreed exchange of texts. They handed over reading material to broaden my horizons and I did the same. I was genuinely interested in their thoughts on the strengths and limitations of the arguments presented by Dawkins.'

Evie smiled. 'So what you're really saying is, you've managed to turn unsolicited doorstepping into an opportunity to start a book club?'

The librarian opened her mouth to issue a retort but was interrupted by a voice from outside.

'Kitt, you in there?' came Inspector Halloran's call, followed by the buzzing of the bell.

Kitt winced and Evie's smile broadened at her friend's predictable reaction. She hated the sound of that bell and always told people to knock instead. It seemed she and Halloran had yet to have that discussion. They really were taking it slow.

Frowning, Kitt walked over to the curtains and pulled them back to get visual confirmation that it was her new boyfriend before opening the window ajar. 'I can't let you in. The door's stuck.'

No sooner had the words left Kitt's mouth than the door groaned open as Halloran pushed through it.

'You need to lock this,' he said, closing the door behind him. 'Anyone could get in.'

8

'Not unless they work out as much as you do,' Kitt said, closing the window.

Her tone dripped with sarcasm but her eyes, Evie noticed, traced the lines of Halloran's dark grey winter coat in a manner that suggested she was more than OK with what was underneath it.

Kitt pushed up on her tiptoes to kiss Halloran and he leant in to oblige her. Evie averted her eyes to the fire for some time before she heard Halloran say: 'Evening, Evie.' He nodded and she nodded in return, thinking that it seemed such a formal way of greeting someone who was dating her best friend, someone who had saved her life, but she'd only met Halloran on a handful of occasions and they still hadn't found that comfortable state of friendliness. Perhaps in part because the first time they crossed paths Halloran had all but accused her of murdering her ex-boyfriend. Or perhaps it was because the sight of each other made them both remember things they would rather not. Such as how the shock of cold river water can pull all the air straight out of your lungs.

Kitt cleared her throat and addressed her cat, who was still lying flat by the fire and had turned just his head to evaluate the latest visitor. 'Iago. Look who's here.'

Iago gave the librarian his yellow-eyed stare for a moment before turning back to the fire in the most unimpressed manner.

'I wouldn't take that personally,' Kitt said to the inspector.

'The only person that cat has ever really been a fan of is himself.'

It was true. In the eight years Evie had been friends with Kitt Iago had only approached her on a handful of occasions and in every instance she'd had some kind of fish on her plate.

'Anyway,' said Kitt. 'We're having a girls' night in here. Unless you want your toenails painting, you'd best be on your way.'

'I might not be completely averse to having my toenails painted . . . depending on the colour,' Halloran said.

'Oh right, in that case I'll pop upstairs and break the manicure set out,' Kitt said with a smile.

'I'm not sure a pampering session should be my first priority,' said Halloran. 'The thing is, something's happened.'

'Nothing serious, I hope?' said Kitt.

Halloran's face hardened and the lines around his eyes that betrayed his years deepened.

'It – it concerns Banks, and I don't know what to do.'

Evie sat up straighter in her seat. In the aftermath of the murder case, Halloran's partner, Detective Sergeant Charlotte Banks, had been very good to her. Not least, Charley had been adamant that the scarring on Evie's face wasn't off-putting. For some reason, she was the only person Evie came close to believing on the matter.

'Banks?' Kitt repeated.

'Is she . . . all right?' asked Evie, her heart beating faster as the look on Halloran's face grew sterner.

'This mustn't go any further. It's very difficult for her and I'll be for it if my superiors find out I've said anything to anyone.'

'What's gone on?' Evie asked, with greater urgency this time.

'Banks has been suspended from duty effective immediately, pending an investigation into her alleged assault of a suspect. At the moment it looks like her career as an officer may be over.'

TWO

Evie blinked hard, wondering if she'd dreamt those words. 'That can't be right. Charley wouldn't do that.'

Halloran didn't quite flinch when Evie used Banks's first name but it was clearly odd for him to hear it. He was probably most comfortable thinking about the sergeant in a professional capacity. Evie, however, had seen a softer side to the officer in the hospital last October, at a moment when softness was what she had needed most.

'Suspended for assault . . .' Kitt said, shaking her head. 'Hard to believe of an officer who has, in my limited experience, been nothing but by the book – perhaps even a bit too much so.'

'I know,' said Halloran. 'It's . . . It's a difficult one.'

'Difficult how?' asked Evie, staring harder at the inspector. 'You don't think she actually did it?'

Halloran's jaw tightened. 'I don't want to believe she did it. She's never shown any sign that she would.'

'So, why doubt her?' Evie asked.

Halloran glanced at Kitt and then turned his attention back to Evie. 'Let's just say I've had some ... experience with people who haven't seemed capable of anything like that and proved me wrong.'

Kitt gave a deep, sympathetic sigh and stroked the inspector's arm. It was then Evie remembered what Kitt had told her in confidence a few weeks back: that one of Halloran's ex-colleagues had murdered his wife. It was understandable that he had a hard time trusting anyone after that.

'But you will try and help her, won't you?' Evie said, with some doubt given the expression on the inspector's face.

'I'll do what I can to help those investigating it get to the truth,' Halloran replied.

Evie felt a knot forming in her stomach. That wasn't very reassuring. Didn't Halloran care that his partner had been wrongfully accused? Didn't he want to prove her innocence?

'Her case won't be helped,' he continued, 'by the new superintendent who is soon to take over from Detective Chief Superintendent Percival.'

'Oh yes,' said Kitt. 'You did mention her, what's her name? Ricci, right?'

'That's her. She's only been with us three weeks but I got the impression from the off that she and Banks didn't really get along, and she hasn't leapt to Banks's defence. She was straight on the phone to the Independent Office of Police Conduct.'

'I thought coppers were supposed to stick together, present a united front,' said Evie.

'Matters like these have to be thoroughly investigated either by the IOPC or the Professional Standards Department,' said Halloran. 'I thought her pristine track record might have won Banks a little faith with Ricci, but apparently not.'

'Put yourself in Ricci's shoes though,' said Kitt. 'She doesn't know Banks. She's only just started at the station and the first thing she has to deal with is one of her officers being accused of assault.'

'Poor Charley,' said Evie, hugging her arms around herself. Perhaps she could engender some sympathy for the officer, persuade Halloran to fight her corner. 'Surely her statement counts for something? A police officer's word against the word of someone suspected of burglary?'

'That's part of the trouble,' said Halloran. 'If it was just the suspect's word against Banks it probably would have been quicker to get to the bottom of it all. But there's hard evidence that Banks was the culprit.'

'Hard as in forensic?' asked Kitt.

The nod Halloran made was almost imperceptible.

'What evidence?' asked Evie, remembering all the evidence that had been stacked against her just a few weeks ago. That experience had taught her just how deceiving evidence could be.

'Her fingerprints were found on the weapon used in the attack,' said Halloran.

'What was the weapon?' Evie could tell by the inspector's slow responses that he wasn't comfortable giving away this much information but all she could think about was how gentle Charley had been with her when she was pulled out of the river after the incident. She had even sent her the occasional encouraging text message since, wishing her back to health and suggesting the pair go for a drink when she was feeling better. That sort of kindness was surely above and beyond her duties as a police officer.

'It was a hammer. Banks has identified it as belonging to her. Said she kept it in the tool box in her garage and when she checked it was missing. Obviously, her finger-prints were on it but the attacker was wearing gloves and smudged some of them, which offers us some hope. It puts a question mark over whether Charley was the last person to handle it. But it's not conclusive. The partials belong to her. The weapon belongs to her, and it's covered in the victim's blood.'

'What about the victim? Are they all right?' asked Kitt.

'He's in hospital,' Halloran said. 'Looking very black and blue in the face, but still just about conscious.'

'Crikey, this is brutal!' said Evie. 'But can't he clear this up? He must have seen the attacker.'

Halloran shook his head in a way that indicated at least some remorse. Perhaps he cared about Banks more than he was letting on.

'The attacker was wearing a balaclava. But the height,

build, accent and gender description is a match to Banks and he says the attacker was shouting at him about the case. About how he'd better confess to the crime or else they'd come back to finish him off.'

'What kind of case was it?' asked Kitt.

'Relatively low-key,' said Halloran. 'Some rare books were stolen from Bootham Bar Books two weeks ago.'

'Oh yes,' Kitt said, her blue eyes lighting up in the way they only ever did when she was talking about books. 'The second I read about that I paid a visit to the shop to check in on Donald and Shereen.'

'Why am I not surprised that you know bookshop owners by first name?' Halloran teased. 'And I'm sure your concern for the staff was your only reason for paying a visit to the bookshop.'

'I might have purchased one or two volumes while I was in there. It only seemed right to put my hand in my pocket. The books that were stolen were worth no small amount of money, you know.'

'How much?' asked Evie.

'Fifty grand,' Halloran replied.

'Crumbs!'

'So Banks has been working on this case?' Kitt asked.

Halloran nodded. 'With the cuts and all that, we don't investigate all burglaries now but because the items were worth so much, it suggested something bigger might be going on there.'

'Didn't know books could be worth that much,' said Evie.

'They were no ordinary books,' said Kitt. 'They were all first editions. *The Big Sleep, Endymion, Jamaica Inn.* Not to mention a first edition copy of *Goodbye to Berlin* by Christopher Isherwood. I'd given that one many a wistful glance through the glass cabinet. It was beautiful. Donald let me touch it once.'

'I hope his wife doesn't find out,' Evie said before she could stop herself. Her eyes darted at once towards the inspector. She wasn't used to Kitt having a boyfriend. As far as Evie was concerned Kitt had spent the last ten years being married to Edward Rochester, of *Jane Eyre* fame, in her head. Halloran, however, only let out a rich, deep laugh that filled the whole room, a laugh Evie had never heard from him before.

'Can't you let even one opportunity for innuendo go by?' Kitt said, sighing in her friend's direction.

'Seems like such a waste,' said Evie.

'In fact, those weren't the only things stolen from the bookshop,' said Halloran. 'But the other things weren't of high value so we didn't release them to the press. Thought they might be a means of catching out the burglar in interview.'

'What else was taken?' asked Kitt.

'An Enid Blyton book and one of the soft toys that are sold at the counter.'

'Which Enid Blyton book?' Kitt pushed – when it came to books she wanted no detail spared.

'*Secret Seven Mystery.*'

'Another first edition?'

Halloran shook his head. 'That book wasn't worth anything.'

'Clearly it was to the thief,' said Kitt.

'What about the soft toy?' said Evie, ignoring Kitt's knowing look. Evie had told her how much reluctance she had shown to giving up her childhood soft toys. Her dad had said adults didn't have teddy bears, but she had secretly always missed the comfort of them. Consequently, every now and then she would try and convince Kitt to visit the Teddy Bear Tea Rooms in town, and every now and then Kitt obliged even though she always made out she didn't think it was a fitting place for two women in their mid-thirties to have tea. Despite her protestations, however, the pair always had a lot of fun there.

'It was a large Peter Rabbit toy sitting in a display by the counter,' said Halloran.

'Yes, I've seen those. What a rum thing for a thief to take though,' said Evie before pausing and thinking for a moment. 'This beating. The hammer and all that, wouldn't Banks have known that all this evidence pointed to her? She would never do anything that stupid, surely?'

'On the surface it doesn't add up, no,' said Halloran. 'Don't get me wrong, she is strong and physically capable of doing something like this – she can hold her own. But intellectually and professionally Banks has always relied on the letter of the law. She's ambitious. Her goal is to work her way to the top of the policing ladder. It seems unlikely she'd jeopardize that for anything, let alone a small case like this.'

'So, you think someone is setting Banks up?' Kitt said.

'That's what I'd like to believe, yes. After all . . .' The inspector tailed off and glanced between Evie and Kitt. 'Recent events have made me think twice about the places evidence can point to.'

Evie gave the inspector a grudging smile. In his own way, he was saying that he trusted both her and Kitt, or at the very least wanted to.

Her thoughts slid back to Charley. She knew what it meant to be accused of something unforgivably brutal. She knew how alone that could make a person feel.

'What's going to happen to Charley? Will she really lose her job?'

'I'm sorry to say, at this point that's looking like a best-case scenario.'

'What do you mean?' asked Evie.

'The role of a police officer is to protect the public, and any breach of that is rightly taken very seriously. It's likely the Professional Standards Department will task an anti-corruption unit to investigate and if they find Banks at fault, she'll stand trial for her actions.'

Evie swallowed hard. When she'd been accused of murdering her ex that had been one of the things she had feared most. Standing in a courtroom, surrounded by people who were staring at her and judging her for something she hadn't done. Everyone believing her to be a criminal.

'So, Banks could actually go to prison for this?' said Kitt, her eyes widening.

'If they gather enough evidence to take this to trial that's almost a certainty,' said Halloran.

'A police officer in prison . . .' said Kitt. 'It doesn't bear thinking about . . . what they'd do to her.'

'Banks is a survivor,' said Halloran. 'But she'd have to be to get through it.'

'Where is she?' Evie asked, glancing briefly at her watch.

'I don't know, she was dismissed from the station earlier this afternoon.'

'Well I've got to go and see her, now,' Evie blurted out.

Kitt raised her eyebrows and Evie admitted to herself that she wasn't so sure why she had to go and comfort a person she had only met on a few, albeit somewhat momentous, occasions. Perhaps because Charley had been so kind to her in the hospital after her near-death experience. She wanted to return the kindness and be there for her.

'You and Banks have kept in touch?' said Halloran.

'Here and there,' said Evie. 'She's been very kind to me since, well, since what happened. I hate to think of her going through this alone.'

'I see,' Halloran said. 'I did call at her house before making my way here, to check in on her, but she wasn't there.'

'I'll find her,' said Evie.

'How?' asked Kitt.

'I don't know, York isn't that big. I'll drop her a text message or call her or something.'

'She hasn't been picking up her phone to me,' said Halloran, thinking for a moment before speaking again. 'Perhaps she will respond to you though . . . someone who has nothing to do with the job. Maybe that's what she needs right now.'

Evie rose from the armchair and began putting her coat back on.

'But what about . . .' Kitt began and then paused, looking at Halloran. She wasn't going to say anything outright about Evie's wobbly moment earlier on, but a concerned frown lined her forehead. 'What about your tea?'

'I'll be all right,' said Evie, with only a slight note of regret. That lasagne did look delicious but there were more pressing issues. She looked into the blue eyes of her friend and squeezed her arm. 'Halloran can have mine.'

'Well, text me if you need to,' said Kitt.

'I will.'

'And tomorrow's my late shift at the library, promise to swing by and see me?'

'It's a date,' said Evie. She tugged at the door. It budged an inch but no further.

'Allow me,' Halloran said, gripping the handle and pulling the door open in one swift movement.

'Show-off,' Kitt said to him, and then quickly followed it up with, 'Evie, stay safe.'

'I will,' Evie called back. She and Kitt knew there was no real danger in walking the streets of York, especially this early in the evening, but after recent events the pair had, perhaps understandably, become even more protective over each other's safety.

Evie scuttled along the path and pulled up her hood, smiling at the sensation of once again being sheltered in the deepening, masking darkness.

THREE

In less than an hour, Evie was scanning small friendship groups lolling on the wooden benches set up in Parliament Street as part of the St Nicholas Fair – an annual Christmas market that dominated the city centre throughout the winter months. At this time of day, the fountain at the centre of the square twinkled in the glow of red and green fairy lights and the scent of roast chestnuts hung in the air. Most of the stall-holders were busy packing away plum-scented candles and star-shaped Christmas decorations woven in wicker, sprayed silver and gold. Though the market was winding down, the food trucks were still very much open for business, selling mulled wine and sloe gin to shoppers wanting to rest their feet and take the edge off the cold. It took her a moment, but Evie soon spotted Charley, right where she said she'd be: perched on one of the benches on the periphery of the seating area. The multicoloured Christmas lights dazzled around her while she bowed her head towards a polystyrene cup.

Walking towards her, Evie thought back to the first time she had come into contact with the officer. Then, it had seemed as though her hair had never been unwound from that tight knot at the back of her head. But here was evidence to the contrary as it hung loose in dark waves across her shoulders. On their first meeting, Evie remembered too how Charley's work suit had somehow been pressed in a manner that gave it distinct, angular lines. Now, there was nothing outright scruffy about the black leather jacket she had thrown on over a dark grey hoodie and jeans but somehow she looked more vulnerable in civilian attire.

'Now then. Want some company, young lady?' Evie said, and at once regretted it. Where did that idiotic comment come from? Nervousness, she supposed. She had never had to talk to someone who had been suspended from their place of work before, and it was difficult to know what to say.

Charley turned her mouth up at the edges, just a fraction, perhaps to suggest she appreciated the attempt at cheering her up. Either that or it was a smile of sympathy just wide enough to imply she understood how awkward this was and was willing to overlook any goonish behaviour.

Evie sat on the bench opposite Charley, brushing her hair over her face so it might cover the edges of her scars.

'I didn't know if you'd reply to my text,' she said, shuffling about on the bench to try to get more comfortable. It didn't seem to have been built with the human form in mind. 'Halloran said he hadn't been able to get hold of you since this afternoon.'

'I know he means well, checking in on me,' Charley said in her sharp Glaswegian accent. 'But I couldn't face talking to him just now. Even over the phone. It's just too embarrassing.'

'I can understand that. But I'm grateful you didn't brush off my messages too.'

Charley's charcoal eyes stared into Evie's. 'You're quite a hard person to ignore.'

Evie permitted herself a short, edgy laugh. 'You make that sound like much more of a compliment than Kitt ever does when she says it.'

'That works out well, because I meant it as a compliment.' A soft smile appeared on Charley's lips but was at once eclipsed as she took a sip of her drink.

Evie toyed with one of the curls nearest her face while wondering if it was possible for a person to physically feel a heavy heart growing lighter. 'I'm so sorry for what's happened,' she said, remembering why she'd come.

Charley sighed and covered her face with her hand. 'I don't know what the hell to do.'

'We'll figure something out.'

'I'm not talking about the bigger picture, I can't even start thinking about that,' Charley said, bringing her hand down on the wooden picnic table between her and Evie. 'I mean, I literally don't know what to do, from one moment to the next.

This afternoon I went to the pictures and watched the latest Transformers film. On my own. Because I didn't know what else to do with myself. Do you know how depressing that is?'

'That does sound pretty dire; there are better films out at the moment.'

'Probably some subconscious form of self-inflicted masochism,' said Charley.

'You shouldn't be punishing yourself, even subconsciously. You've done nothing wrong.'

'I know.'

'But it's natural to feel disorientated. You've had an outrageous shock. Trust me, I know what that feels like.'

Charley looked at her. 'Yes, you do, don't you? This is what you went through when we accused you of murdering Owen.'

'Well, that's all water under the bridge,' said Evie. 'Quite literally.'

Charley bit her lower lip and Evie told herself it was to hold back a smile. That her little joke had made a difference to the way Charley was feeling, just as Kitt's little jokes did whenever she was in a jam or feeling down.

'I don't want to believe this is happening,' Charley said. 'I keep thinking maybe I'll wake up. Except I don't. I just feel . . . helpless.'

Evie crossed her arms and rested them on the table. 'There's got to be something we can do. Isn't there some proof that the weapon was stolen from your house?'

Charley took a gulp of whatever was in the polystyrene cup. 'There's no sign of tampering with the garage lock, but there is a window that's easy enough to jimmy if you know how and if that's how they got in there's a chance some forensic evidence was left behind. But it'll take time for them to investigate it.'

'So it's a waiting game,' said Evie, putting her hand on Charley's arm and squeezing it. The gesture was perhaps a bit forward, but she couldn't resist offering some sign that she was there if Charley needed her.

The officer looked down at Evie's hand and then up at her face before smiling. It was a forced smile, an attempt at gratitude. Evie returned the smile but wondered if there was something more she could do here than simply reassure. When Owen's murderer was at large, she had felt just as helpless. So much so that she had to find a way of doing something, and Kitt had helped her do that by running her own little investigation. Perhaps she could do the same for Charley? All Kitt had done in real terms was go around the city and ask a few questions. How hard could that be?

'I'm not sure if you can bear to think about it,' she said slowly, 'but do you have any idea who might have wanted to set you up?'

'With the number of people I've put away, the list is long,' Charley said, frowning. 'But . . . the likelihood is it's someone connected to this burglary case. I mean, they'd have to know all the ins and outs of it.'

Evie wanted to smile, but held it back. It was obvious she was thinking, and thinking was without a doubt better than moping. Her plan was already working . . .

'What about the suspect himself?' Evie said. 'He might have set it up to make it seem like he was being unfairly treated by the police to help his case.'

'Yeah, that's a possibility,' Charley said. 'I wouldn't put anything past him. Except maybe having enough sense to know what he'd stolen was valuable.'

'How do you mean?'

'Well, I take it Halloran told you where the burglary took place?'

Evie nodded. 'Bootham Bar Books, though I knew about it anyway. If it's to do with books, Kitt doesn't miss a thing.'

'That I can believe. So, you know that the books that were stolen were the most expensive in the shop?'

'I'm not sure it was quite put in those terms when we were talking about it earlier,' said Evie. 'But what does that mean?'

'That it wasn't random or opportunistic. The people behind it had in-depth knowledge about the stock in that shop and knew exactly where to find the most valuable items.'

'And you don't think the suspect who accused you of assault has that kind of knowledge?'

'Not on your life.'

'Then why is he a suspect?'

Charley looked down into her drink. 'Forensics swept the place and it's a shop so obviously there were a million different fingerprints and DNA samples but only one matched a person with a criminal record, parking tickets aside. So we called him in for questioning. He was as defensive as ever – this wasn't his first visit to the police station.'

'Does he have an alibi?' Evie asked.

Charley gave a wry smile. 'Spot the girl with interrogation room experience.'

'On the wrong side of the desk,' said Evie.

'Hopefully you feel you were treated fairly.'

'Considering you thought I'd killed a person you were pretty cordial.'

'I never thought that,' Charley said with an urgency in her voice. 'I just wanted to get to the truth, like I do now.'

'I know.'

'Made more difficult when you're suspended from duty. It's so frustrating because before this it was shaping up to be a straightforward conviction.'

'Did you manage to get him to profess his love for Peter Rabbit and the Secret Seven?' Evie giggled.

'Halloran really spilled his guts then?' Charley said, shaking her head. 'You know he can get into real trouble for that?'

Evie smiled. 'From the way him and Kitt look at each other I'd say they're both in trouble.'

'Aye,' Charley said with a smile. 'He needs to check

himself though – if Percival or Ricci find out he's been sharing information with civilians, he'll be stuck with the Saturday night shift at York train station until the end of time. It's not pretty, I can tell you.'

'I've witnessed what goes on there on a Saturday night first-hand once or twice,' said Evie, offering Charley a mischievous smile. 'But now that I know most of it, can it really hurt to tell me a little bit more?'

'In my case I'm already in so much trouble I don't suppose it will make much difference, so long as you don't go broadcasting it around town.'

'I'm not much of a public speaker,' said Evie. 'So, did your suspect have an alibi?'

'Oh aye, his mother, for God's sake.'

'And he didn't strike you as the kind of person who'd spend his evenings knitting with dear old Ma?'

'Not with his record. And if you'd ever met his mother you wouldn't want to spend much time in her company either. But he's just a patsy at the end of the day.'

'How's that?'

'As I said, Enid Blyton aside, the books that were stolen were very specific. Someone must have put him up to it. Someone with a knowledge of rare books.'

'And . . . you were hoping the threat of prison might make him talk about who was really behind it?'

Charley nodded. 'I put a bit of pressure on him – within the bounds of the law – and I just thought he'd crack and tell me who it was. But instead the next thing I know he's been beaten up and I'm being summoned to a meeting with my Police Federation rep in tow. Superintendent Ricci did nothing to defend me and I was suspended from duty in a snap.'

The sadness, which had for a few moments left Charley's eyes, returned.

'If this suspect was put up to the job by someone in the know, it's unlikely he's feeling very warm towards them right now, lying in hospital beaten almost to a pulp.'

'Probably not. So?'

'So, maybe he's on the brink of realizing he's bitten off more than he can comfortably chew. Maybe he can be reasoned with enough that he'll offer up a name?'

'Maybe, but I can't do anything about it. I can't go anywhere near anyone or anything connected with the case, not if I want a chance of ever getting my job back.'

'No, you can't,' said Evie. 'But I know a certain detective inspector who might be of assistance. Especially if his girl-friend asks nicely.'

Banks shook her head. 'I can't ask Halloran to get involved with this. It could be his career too if he's not careful. I'm his partner. If they suspect me of being corrupt, they might suspect him too.'

'Well then maybe there's – '

'Evie . . . I appreciate you want to help. But there's nothing to be done right now. I've been shut down. With a bit of luck the forensics will come back from the garage with a lead. Possibly even Alim's DNA.'

'Alim?'

Charley held a finger to her lips and lowered her voice. 'Alim Buruk, the suspect.'

'Something about that name seems familiar.'

'You've probably read it in the local headlines at some point. He has been involved in multiple theft incidents. In and out of juvenile correctional facilities more times than the wardens.' Charley paused then, and her stare became harder. 'I doubt you'd go to the kind of places he frequents but don't, whatever you do, go around chanting his name. If someone in his circle recognizes it they might think you're involved with him somehow, and he's got enemies.'

'I won't say a word about him,' said Evie, choosing her words carefully to ensure that even though a plan was hatching in her head, she wasn't telling a lie.

'Good,' said Charley. 'Because I know you mean well, but right now I've got enough to worry about without worrying about you too.'

Evie watched as the biting northern breeze blew strands of Charley's hair back from her face. She stood up from the bench and walked round to sit next to her. She told herself that she put her arm around Charley purely in the spirit of reassuring her but deep down she knew that it was partly selfish. It was partly to enjoy that physical contact that she had shied away from since the incident. For some reason she couldn't quite put her finger on, she didn't want to shy away from Charley.

'You don't need to worry about little old me,' Evie said, giving Charley a squeeze and revelling in the smell of her leather jacket more than she'd expected to.

'Old?' Banks said with a smirk. 'You've got some catching up to do with me before you can go about saying that.'

'How much catching up?' asked Evie, narrowing her eyes in mock suspicion.

'I've got a good three years on you, and it's showing. Bloody shift work.'

'You look beautiful to me,' said Evie, and then, feeling a blush creeping into her cheeks, added, 'I mean, I don't think it shows at all.'

Charley smiled and opened her mouth to say something but was interrupted by the shrill chirp of her mobile which she retrieved from her inside coat pocket.

'Sylvia?'

Sylvia? Evie listened for any clues as to who Sylvia might be while Charley talked to the caller in what seemed like deliberately general sentences. As she spoke, Charley cast the odd sideways glance over at Evie before eventually sighing and hanging up the phone.

'That was my Police Federation rep.'

'Oh.' An involuntary smile formed on Evie's lips, the only outward sign of the strange relief she was feeling.

'She wants to meet with me.'

'Now?'

Charley smiled and stood up from the bench. 'Out of hours is our normal hours. She wants to run through some possible scenarios and come up with a plan of defence in each instance.'

'Will you keep me posted, on what happens?'

Charley looked at Evie thoughtfully for a moment but then nodded. 'I'll let you know if there are any breakthroughs.'

'And if you need someone to talk to ... well, I'm sure you've got people to talk to but if you want to talk to me, I'd be happy to listen.'

'Noted,' Charley said with a vague smile. 'Thanks.'

With that the officer turned on her heel and began a quick march out of the market. Evie watched her disappear into the night with a strange emptiness growing inside. A feeling she decided to put down to the fact that she hadn't had any tea.

FOUR

Before she found herself at the entrance of York General Hospital, it had never occurred to Evie just how useful those unwanted scars on her face might be. She approached the reception desk make-up free, with her hair pinned back so the true extent of her scarring was in full view. It was the first time she had worn her hair like this since she'd got the scars, and on the way to the hospital she had counted the number of double-takes and wary stares she'd received from strangers who passed her by.

Twelve.

''Scuse me,' Evie said to a man behind the reception desk who was busy stamping a high-rise stack of papers. 'I'm visiting Alim Buruk – can you tell me which ward he's in?'

The receptionist looked up and studied Evie's face for what felt like an eternity, even though it couldn't have been more than a few seconds. She dropped her eyes and ran an idle finger over the scar that cut along her jawline, making a show of looking awkward. It wasn't a difficult act to pull off. She had to resist behaving this way every time somebody looked at her directly, even friends. In fact, especially with friends, as they knew that she hadn't always looked like a horror show and probably couldn't help comparing the old face with the new. At last she had an excuse to behave how she really wanted to, deep down.

'Just a moment,' the receptionist said in a gentle tone before tapping a few buttons on his computer. 'He's been moved to the Acute Admissions Ward. Just follow the yellow line on the floor, and you'll find it.' He gave Evie a sympathetic smile.

Evie nodded and as directed began to follow the yellow line painted along the polished cream flooring. The scent of hand-sanitizer and disinfectant was so strong she could almost taste it as she turned five antiseptic corners and pushed through a set of double doors to reach the Acute Admissions Ward.

Walking along the corridor, she scanned each room for the man she had looked up on Facebook at lunchtime. This was the moment when her disfigurement was really going to serve her in her mission. Even sans hospital gown, people would believe she was on her way to see a specialist about the nasty scars on her face. The chances of anyone questioning her cover story were slim.

Evie passed by seven doorways before she spotted the man she believed she was looking for. He didn't look exactly like his Facebook profile picture, but then just now neither did Evie.

Unlike most people who simply didn't match their profile picture because they'd gained a few pounds or a few wrinkles, Alim Buruk's whole jaw area was red and swollen. One eye was part closed and he looked small, much less alive than he had in the photo she'd seen of him in a nightclub, his dark skin illuminated with strobe lighting like an extra in a nineties music video.

Taking a deep breath, Evie swung open the door. Visiting hours had started half an hour ago so there were already a few people dotted about the beds, eating the grapes they had brought for the sick or making small talk about the quality of hospital food.

Alim was lying in the fourth cubicle along on the right-hand side. Despite the fact that Charley had mentioned Alim's mother, there were no visitors present to comfort him. The blue curtain that ran in an ellipse around his bed was pulled back. He had been staring at the ceiling but as Evie entered he looked towards the doorway and she immediately averted her eyes. She had to make out like he was the last person she was looking for. Like any exchange between them was purely accidental – the kind of coincidence that could only happen in a small city like York.

'Sorry to bother you all, but has anyone seen Dr Cornfoot?' asked Evie, swaggering up the aisle between the two rows of beds, safe in the knowledge that nobody would have seen Dr Cornfoot on account of the fact that he was a figment of Evie's imagination.

One by one, the people in their beds shook their heads.

'Sorry, haven't seen any doctors. Just nurses,' said a man in a grey anorak who was visiting another man lying in bed with a cast on his arm.

'Which one's he?' asked the gentleman lying in the bed next to Alim. He too was without any company. Seizing the opportunity, Evie walked over to the space between his bed and Alim's. She took great care to keep her eyes fixed on the man who had addressed her. He had tough, wrinkled skin that reminded Evie of a rhinoceros.

'Well, he's tall. Bald. Quite a pointed nose. Walks with a bit of a limp,' said Evie, her eyes darting at the man to check if her accidental literalism about the 'corn foot' had aroused suspicion. But the man was looking up at the ceiling, deep in thought.

'Not ringing any bells. Are you sure he's in this department? It's a big hospital, you know?'

'I was directed to this department by the front desk,' said Evie, which wasn't a lie.

'The front desk,' the man in the bed spat out the words. 'Left hand doesn't know what the right's doing.'

'Mmm. You're probably right,' said Evie. Though that wasn't her impression at all she needed to get the room onside. 'I'm sick of being messed around by these doctors. Do they think I like running around town with these?' She drew her fingertips first over the scar at her right temple then again over the one at the left side of her jaw.

The man in the bed looked down at his hands, which worked over the satin trim of his blanket. 'How'd you get them?'

Evie wanted more than anything to smile. She knew morbid curiosity would get the better of somebody in the room sooner or later but she crossed her arms over her chest and frowned, doing all she could to contain her satisfaction. 'Believe it not, a policeman did it.'

Again, not strictly a lie.

'Coppers?' Alim growled.

FIVE

Evie started, as though she hadn't noticed Alim lying there. Her GCSE drama skills were really coming to the fore this afternoon.

'Sorry,' she said, 'I didn't catch that.'

'You can't trust coppers,' Alim half-grunted, and then winced. He was hooked up to several bags hanging from a silver stand behind him including an IV which probably meant he was finding it difficult to eat or drink; talking couldn't have been much easier.

Evie offered the man in the bed next to his a brief smile before turning away and sidling closer to Alim.

'Your experience of them as bad as mine?' Evie said.

'Wh-who do you think put me here?' Alim croaked, and began coughing.

'Are you able to take a bit of water?' asked Evie. Alim nodded and continued to cough while she circled her way to his bedside table. There, a cup of water with a straw in it was sitting on top of some car magazines. Wondering if Alim just had a passing interest in cars or whether he read the magazines to make sure he only stole the most valuable vehicles, Evie reached over and held the straw to his lips. Each gulp was coupled with a wince but she still noticed the gratitude in his cinnamon eyes.

'Sorry if I brought that on,' she said when he signalled he'd had enough. 'Didn't expect to meet someone in the same boat as me when it came to the law.'

'How'd they get you?' Alim asked, ignoring Evie's apology.

Evie looked around the room to check that everyone else had gone back about their business. Everyone had, save for the man in the next bed who was leaning in their direction, trying to overhear. She kept her voice low. 'Well, I was under suspicion for murdering my ex-boyfriend.'

Alim, following Evie's lead on the volume, and perhaps to make it less painful when he spoke, whispered, 'Did you do it?'

Evie smirked in what she hoped was a sinister fashion. 'Of course not, I'm innocent.'

Alim smirked too, or at least tried to. There was a big welt on the left-hand side of his mouth that had partly immobilized his lips.

'So the coppers attacked you, eh? Tried to get you to confess?'

'Not exactly. I was kidnapped in the back of the car, which my kidnapper drove into the river.' Evie tried not to dwell too long on the words coming out of her mouth. If she wasn't careful she would feel it again; that almighty gush of the footwell filling with icy water. Her face smashing against something blunt and hard. The panicked thuds and moans of desperation from her captors in the front seat. The moments she had spent trying to hold her breath while Halloran broke the car window and pulled her to safety. 'My kidnappers only drove the car into the river because the police backed them into a corner. If that inspector had known what he was doing, it never would have happened.' Evie threw that last part in for good measure. She had to keep up the pretence that she blamed Halloran for what had happened to her face. For some reason, however, blaming him didn't feel difficult. She frowned at the realisation. Did part of her blame Halloran for the person she saw in the mirror?

'So this copper was a bloke?' Alim said, regaining Evie's attention.

'Yeah. He did pull me out of the car though. Suppose that means I owe him my life.'

Alim did what he could to shake his head. 'You can't trust them. Any of them. Was probably doing all he could to shock you into confessing.'

'The thought crossed my mind, but I'm too smart for that . . . Wait, you said a copper did this to you too?' Evie made her eyes a little wider at this juncture. The more surprised and oblivious she could come across, the better.

'She was wearing a balaclava, yeah, so I didn't see her face. But I recognized the Scottish accent. She beat me . . .' Alim's voice failed him but he swallowed hard and found it again. 'She beat me with a hammer and was shouting at me about some burglary she was working. Telling me I better confess, or else.'

'Crikey. Do you know her name? Sounds like someone to steer clear of.'

'Banks, crossed paths with her a few times. She's always fingering me. She'd have me for every burglary within five miles if she had her way.'

'Banks . . .' Evie said, letting her frown deepen for effect. 'I think I know who you mean. She was there the day they pulled me out of the river.'

'The way she went at me . . .' said Alim, in a voice that suggested that his lower lip would have wobbled, if only it could.

'I can see you took a good beating,' Evie said, looking at his face and shuddering at the thought of that hammer meeting bone and flesh. 'I'm sorry you had to go through this.' Alim may not be an angel, but he didn't deserve to be in this situation which, given how young he was, Evie suspected wasn't entirely of his own making.

Alim lowered his eyes. The conversation was going to come to a natural end here unless she found a way to prolong it, and she hadn't quite yet achieved what she'd hoped for.

'This Banks, have you reported her?'

Alim gave a small nod. 'The police say they are investigating it. Apparently they found her fingerprints on the hammer.'

'The police told you that?'

Alim's mouth turned up at the corners. 'We have an inside source.'

Evie's heart quickened. Somebody on the local force was leaking information to the Buruk family? And who knows who else. She needed to find out more about this but now probably wasn't the time. If she pushed, he might guess her agenda. Best to keep him onside and see if she could weasel something out about that later.

Evie sighed. 'What a mess, I'm sorry. But on the bright side, this Banks woman probably will get caught out sooner or later. She's clearly not very smart.'

'How do you mean?'

'Well, you're a police officer, yeah? So you know how criminal investigations work. You go to the effort of disguising yourself and even put on gloves. You go round to the house of someone who you like for a burglary, you threaten them, beat them up enough to hospitalize them, then leave the assault weapon with your fingerprints all over it where anyone could find it.'

'It was dropped on my bloody doorstep.'

'What an idiot. I mean that's a fine way to get yourself caught. Can't even bully someone right.'

Alim's face was crinkling in thought. But then his stare wandered in the direction of the door and in an instant his eyes widened enough for Evie to read the fear in them. She followed his gaze and saw a woman stomping towards them in a black long-sleeved maxidress that left very little of her pasty flesh on show. Her brown frizzy hair clung to the sides of her jaw and she seemed to be sweating with the effort of moving. The few wrinkles around her eyes indicated that she was somewhere in her early forties. There was something about the woman's squarer-than-average face that left Evie feeling uneasy .

The woman's stare darted between Evie and Alim and Evie frowned as she approached.

'Who's this?' she asked, speaking to Alim and pointing at Evie.

Evie's shoulders clenched. She had hoped not to get so far as giving out her name. She had hoped to breeze in and out like a good fairy, plant the seeds of doubt over Charley's guilt in Alim's mind and never be seen or heard of again.

'She's just a patient at the hospital, Mum,' said Alim.

So this was Alim's mother?

Evie knew it was wrong to judge someone by their appearance but it wasn't just the woman's features that unnerved her. Her manner made it clear she was not a woman to be trifled with.

Evie's shoulders lowered at Alim's deflection. She might yet get away with remaining anonymous.

'A patient at the hospital?' Mrs Buruk repeated. 'Who you've been talking to, when you don't even know her name?'

'Just got talking, it's boring in here, you know?' Alim croaked.

'And what have you been talking about?' asked Alim's mother. Her eyes were still fixed on her son. She was concentrating every ounce of energy on a hard stare that made Evie shudder and it wasn't even directed at her.

'Nothing,' said Alim. 'Just, you know. This and that. She was looking for a doctor and then we got talking about coppers.'

'What about the coppers?' The woman scowled at Evie.

'I didn't mean to disturb you at this difficult time,' Evie said, conscious of the fact that if Alim said one more word he was likely to give away their whole conversation and, given his mother's suspicious disposition, that wouldn't end well for her. 'Your son was just being kind and trying to help me find a doctor I was looking for, I'll go now.'

'Kind?' The mother repeated, as though this was more suspicious than anything else.

'Yes, so kind, thank you so much.' Evie was speaking so fast that each word almost ran into the next. She began walking towards the door.

'I'll see you out,' Alim's mum said. Evie swallowed hard. Being followed by the mother of a known criminal wasn't exactly a positive turn of events.

She contemplated making a run for it but that would likely cause more trouble. Best that she just tried to stand her ground as best she could and then get out of there as quick as possible. She was in a public place, after all. With witnesses. There was only so much this woman could do to her . . . right?

The moment the pair were outside the room, the woman turned on Evie and backed her up against the nearest wall. 'Listen to me,' she said poking a finger into Evie's right shoulder. 'My son thinks he's streetwise, thinks he's clever. He hasn't got a clue but I know. I know how the world works.'

'So lovely to hear of a mother looking out for a son, not enough of that about these days.' Evie wanted to believe she sounded casual but the fact that she half-stammered these words undermined any hope of acting breezy.

'What were you really doing in there with my son?'

'Really, I was just trying to find the doctor. About my scars, you see?' Evie tilted her head at an angle that – she believed – made her scars look the most unseemly.

'Who are you?'

'Me?' Evie said, with a nervous chuckle. 'I'm . . . I'm nobody, really nobody worth bothering about at all.'

'What's your name?' Mrs Buruk asked through gritted teeth.

Evie couldn't give her own name. It wasn't just about the consequences for Charley if anyone found out she had been here, though the thought of that was bad enough.

47

She was useless at handling high pressure situations. She had to be someone else, someone who could handle situations like this.

'My name is Kitt,' she heard herself say, and then her eyes widened. Oh God no . . . why had she said that name? Now Kitt could be in danger.

'Kitt what?' Evie didn't think it was possible for the woman's face to get any closer to hers but somehow she managed it.

'Kitt . . . Schmartley,' Evie said, deciding that she was probably going to hell for this. She couldn't count how many times Kitt's friendship had saved her and now, here she was, throwing her to the wolves.

'Schmartley?' Alim's mum repeated.

'Yes,' Evie said, assuming Kitt's strait-laced posture and pushing the woman back out of her way. 'That's right. And being a highly educated woman, I have looked up every possible regulation on assault and if you're not careful I will press charges. Good day to you, madam.'

Evie turned on her heel the way she imagined Kitt might in this situation and strutted down the corridor towards the nearest exit. Just before she pushed through a set of double doors, Evie heard Alim's mother call: 'You better watch yourself. I'll be looking out for you, Kitt Schmartley!'

SIX

Despite a somewhat calamitous end to the afternoon, Evie managed to remember her promise to visit Kitt at the library on her way home. She took the quickest route to Kitt's place of work, through Rowntree Park and down to the river front, being sure to keep her eyes on the path as she neared the water.

The river Ouse had once been one of Evie's favourite things about living just outside the longest medieval town walls in England. Not any more. Looking at the river now gave her flashbacks to the moment her kidnappers' car had splashed into it. At this time of year the river always flooded, swallowing certain sections of the city whole, and even catching the submerged steps up to Skeldergate Bridge in her peripheral vision was enough to make Evie shudder.

She turned her back on the river completely and looked towards the front entrance of the Vale of York University Library. The exterior lights were a pure white, and shone upwards, illuminating the five-floor, mock-Tudor building in all its glory. Black beams stretched towards a gable roof. Above the doorway, the university motto was inscribed into a golden plaque in tall letters: *The mind is its own universe.* Evie had always rather liked this phrase and when it came to Kitt it was definitely a truism. There sometimes seemed no bounds to the things she held in that head of hers.

Hopping up the steps and pushing through the solid oak doors, Evie was at once overcome by that familiar, dusty scent of aging books and began her usual route across the ocean of blue ceramic floor tiles, past the rows of computers and up the spiral staircase to Women's Studies, the section that Kitt was responsible for. On reaching the second floor, though, she found that Kitt wasn't behind her desk. This was odd. Evie scanned the rest of Kitt's desk, looking for the 'Back in 5 minutes' sign the librarian always scribbled out if her duties, or her somewhat concerning tea habit, took her elsewhere. But there wasn't one. Evie frowned. Her friend was always so keen on making sure the students knew help was close at hand. Evie walked along the end of the bookshelves, assuming she would catch sight of Kitt, refiling one of the volumes off the returns pile, or showing a student where a particular book was, but as it was so late there were only a few students milling about. The rest had gone home to Uber a McDonald's to their house and watch the latest TV box set.

Evie headed towards the second-floor office where she

presumed her friend was making herself an emergency cup of Lady Grey while hoping that Michelle's spies weren't watching her take an unscheduled break. She was no more than six paces away from the door, however, when a sickening feeling settled in her stomach. She could hear something faintly unfurling under the doorway. It was Kitt's voice, and from the tone of it she was in some distress.

Evie swung open the door and was greeted with three faces wearing a variety of expressions.

Two of the faces she recognized. Kitt was standing next to the table in the centre of the office. Her arms were folded but her face seemed to relax a little on seeing Evie walk through the door. Halloran stood to the right of Kitt in a dark grey suit. He was frowning and his lips were tight and thin. In his hands, Evie noticed a pencil hovering above a notebook, poised to take notes on whatever had been going on just before she opened the office door. Then there was the woman on the left, who Evie had never met. She too was dressed in a suit, though hers was brown. She was wearing a turquoise silk scarf around her neck, knotted like a tie. She was as tall as Halloran and had shoulder-length wavy hair, black as a starless night.

All three of them were surrounded by piles of papers and books; the second-floor office wasn't the most organized of environments.

'S-sorry to interrupt,' Evie said, though from the weak smile crossing Kitt's lips, it seemed the librarian was glad she had. 'It sounded as though Kitt was in trouble, or upset. That's why I rushed in.'

Kitt opened her mouth to speak but the unknown woman got there first.

'Who are you?' she asked. She seemed to be scrutinizing every cell in her body.

'I'm . . . Evie. One of Kitt's friends. That's why I dashed in here. I thought there was something wrong.'

'There is something wrong,' Kitt said with a sigh. 'Quite a few things actually. Superintendent Ricci here believes that I've been interfering with this bookshop burglary case. She's accusing me of paying a hospital visit to somebody I've never even heard of.'

Evie swallowed and hoped it didn't sound like an audible gulp. For a moment she wasn't able to breathe as her brain connected the ever more alarming dots.

Alim's mother must have put in a complaint and Halloran had been dragged down to the library immediately with a superior in tow to ensure Kitt didn't do any more snooping around. Except, Kitt hadn't done any snooping.

'Please, Ms Hartley, don't act the innocent,' said Ricci. 'I know all about your interference with the murder case in October.'

'Strange,' Kitt said, her tone bone dry, 'I wouldn't have expected a police officer to think that a civilian hunting down a wanted murderer was interference.'

Halloran didn't utter a word but Evie noticed his shoulders

tighten. Though he and Kitt had only just started seeing each other Kitt had suggested Halloran was more than a little bit protective of her.

'Regardless,' said Ricci, folding her arms across her chest. 'It's clear you've got a few ideas above your station along the way. Criminal investigative work is not your place, police business is not your business. It seems you need to be reminded of that. Your little charade this afternoon is going to cost us dearly in both paperwork and reputation on an already complicated case.'

This was the moment, Evie thought, when she should explain that it was she who had been to the hospital, not Kitt. But when she opened her mouth something stopped her from making a full confession. It wasn't just fear of the consequences – though Evie couldn't deny that was a factor – it was more the fear that if she confessed now then she would be on Ricci's radar just as much as Kitt and who knew how much more covert investigation it would take to get Charley off the hook? On top of that, Kitt was the curious type and for all Evie knew, even if she hadn't been down to the hospital herself she could have been doing a little bit of investigative work on the sly. Best to see how this situation panned out before offering up incriminating information.

'I've told you,' Kitt said. 'I haven't been to the hospital this afternoon. I've been at work.'

'And you haven't taken any breaks?' said Ricci. 'The hospital is just a short taxi ride from here.'

'Oh good grief,' said Kitt. 'No, I have not taken any breaks or taken a taxi to the hospital. If I had done that, I would have mentioned it when you asked me if I'd been to the hospital this afternoon.'

Ricci glared at Halloran, glanced back at Kitt and then turned her attentions to Evie. 'What about you? You say you're friends with Ms Hartley?'

Evie nodded. 'Best friends.'

'The same best friend that was arrested for murder a few weeks back?'

'Wrongfully arrested,' said Evie, without quite being able to look at Ricci directly.

'And are you familiar with the Bootham Bar Books burglary case?'

'Yes . . . I've heard about it.' Evie chose her words with as much care as possible – above all else she couldn't lie to a police officer. That would only lead to more trouble. That said, there was something about Ricci that put her on edge, that didn't encourage a person to be forthcoming.

'And how did you find out about it?' Ricci pushed.

Evie told herself sternly she mustn't even glance at Halloran otherwise he really would spend an eternity working the Saturday night shift at York train station. 'In the news at first, and Kitt's a semi-regular customer in that bookshop. So we have naturally chatted about how awful it was, as anyone would when there's been a local burglary.'

'And there's nothing else you want to tell me in relation to this case?' said Ricci.

Interesting wording, thought Evie. She wouldn't want to tell Ricci about anything, if she could avoid it.

Evie shook her head. Again, not quite willing to tell an outright lie in case it came back to haunt her later.

Ricci took a step closer to Evie and nodded at her face. 'Those scars look quite new.'

All oxygen left Evie's body and a numbness started to creep in.

'How did you get them?' Ricci asked. Her tone wasn't as hard as it had been before but the question still felt like a punch to the gut. Evie was so taken aback that this time she couldn't help shooting a glance at Halloran. The lines on his face remained hard and stern but there was a certain sadness in his blue eyes. A sign that indicated he wished his superior had asked any question except that one. Ricci looked between the two of them for a moment before Kitt broke what was becoming a thick, heavy silence.

'You don't have to answer that.'

Ricci kept her eyes fixed on Evie. 'But you can, even if your friend might prefer you didn't,' she said. 'If you've been pulled into a difficult situation, I might be able to help.'

'I'm not sure asking somebody with facial scarring intrusive and cruel questions is helping them,' Kitt said.

Evie wanted to smile at Kitt, to let her friend know she appreciated her yet again leaping to her defence – especially when Ricci was only sniffing around because of something Evie had done. But after Ricci's question there was no hope of a smile. It was taking all of her effort to hold back tears. She had become accustomed to the wary sidelong looks but nobody had had the gall to perform a mini-interrogation as Ricci had just done.

Ricci sighed and looked back at Kitt. 'We will be looking at CCTV footage of the hospital entrance to glean whether you paid a visit this afternoon. You'll make this a whole lot easier on yourself if you just admit it now. Halloran will take notes on it and then we'll arrange a follow-up statement at the station.'

The librarian took a deep breath and very slowly exhaled. Kitt had quite a temper on her sometimes so Evie could only assume it was Ricci's superiority that was saving her from a proper scolding. 'If I was going to pay a visit to a suspect in a criminal case and didn't want to leave my real name I'd come up with something a lot more ingenious than "Kitt Schmartley". You insult my intelligence, and I will tell you now that looking at that video footage would be a terrible waste of police time.'

'I'll decide how best to use my officers' time, Ms Hartley,' Ricci said in a tone that made Evie feel at once cold to her core. 'If they find anything in that video footage, you'll be hearing from me again. Picking you out shouldn't be hard. We already have your photograph on file from when you were arrested for murder six weeks ago.'

'Like Evie, wrongfully arrested,' Kitt said through her teeth.

Ricci nodded. 'Just so we're clear, I recommend that you stay away from this case, and any others currently being worked by the North Yorkshire Police. If I find any evidence at all to suggest you've been interfering with our duties, there will be serious consequences.'

Without another word Ricci turned and began walking towards the staircase, giving Evie one last look up and down as she passed.

'Coming, Inspector Halloran?' Ricci said, as she realized Halloran wasn't following her.

The inspector looked at his watch and then back at Ricci. 'It's gone seven o clock, ma'am. I'm off duty now. I'll make my own way home.'

Ricci sucked her teeth, presumably put out that Halloran was uninterested in helping her put on a show of solidarity, but then nodded and marched out of the door.

Halloran went as far as the doorway and looked down the row of bookshelves, craning his neck to check that Ricci really had made an exit. Once satisfied, he turned back to face the most unforgiving hard stare Evie had ever seen Kitt administer.

SEVEN

'I know what you're going to say,' said Halloran. He walked slowly back into the room, approaching Kitt like a zookeeper might approach a tiger. Slow steps. Both hands raised.

'Do you now?' said Kitt. Her tone was as cold as it always was when the librarian felt hard done by, but Evie noticed a watery film had also formed over her blue eyes.

'Don't look like that, pet. I did what I could to put her off coming down here but I'm not in a position to oppose the professional judgement of a senior ranking officer. If I'd pushed any harder, Ricci would likely have put me on desk duty for the insubordination – if I was lucky.'

Kitt didn't say anything. Instead she let out a steady sigh and continued to stare at the inspector.

'You don't know the trouble I could get into for the things I shared with you when we were investigating those murders back in October. And although I'm reserving judgement on this whole case right now, I want to be in a position to help

Banks should I need to and if I'm on desk duty that won't be possible.' He paused and a smile flickered at the corner of his mouth. 'It's difficult to do anything productive when you're bound to a desk.'

The corner of Kitt's mouth twitched, seemingly desperate to join her lover in his smile. 'Well, I suppose that depends on how creative you are,' Kitt replied, staring into Halloran's eyes.

Evie could feel the heat between the two of them. Were they really talking about getting up to no good on Halloran's desk? In front of Evie? Shameless. Ordinarily she would have had a field day with this kind of exchange but just at this moment she had a confession to make.

She cleared her throat and Kitt jumped as though she had completely forgotten her friend was even in the room.

'There's something I need to say,' Evie said, looking between the two of them but unable to meet their eyes.

'Are you all right?' asked Kitt, taking a couple of steps towards her friend.

Evie worked her hands one over the other. 'Yes, I think so, but I might not be in a few seconds.'

'Why do you say that?' asked Halloran, folding his arms.

'Because I'm about to tell you that it was me at the hospital this afternoon . . .'

There was a moment's silence as Kitt and Halloran digested this information and then Kitt rubbed her brow, her hand obscuring her expression. 'Oh, Evie, what on earth were you thinking?'

'I'm sorry, I'm so, so sorry. I think it's safe to say I wasn't thinking at all. I didn't plan on crossing paths with Alim's mother. Charley hinted that she was bad news.'

Halloran frowned. 'Banks knows about this?'

'Oh no,' said Evie, shaking her head harder and faster now. 'If Charley had known what I had planned she would have stopped me without a doubt but I . . . I just had to do something so when she mentioned Alim's name in passing I thought it couldn't hurt to . . .' She couldn't say any more. She was too distracted by the thunderous look on Halloran's face. He didn't shout or bark or snap, he didn't have to. It was perfectly obvious what he thought of her actions.

'I have to admit, I thought this had Grace's name written all over it,' said Kitt, referring to her library assistant who was known for impersonating Kitt just for the fun of it and could be quite mischievous at times. 'Evie, you can't just go around interfering in police business. Especially when an internal investigation is under way. You do realize Ricci might suspect Banks of putting somebody up to a hospital visit to put more pressure on the victim of her alleged assault?'

'I . . . I hadn't really thought of that,' Evie said, her voice growing quieter.

'When Mrs Buruk called the station she made it clear she would be reporting this incident to the IOPC, she's probably got them on speed dial,' said Halloran.

Evie bit her lip, thinking for a moment before she spoke again. 'That's not the best news. But I don't think they're going to find Charley at fault. It's so obvious from what Alim said that she isn't responsible for the attack.'

'What do you mean?' asked Halloran, his curiosity finally overcoming his annoyance.

Keen to distract Halloran and Kitt from any anger they might be feeling towards her just now, Evie explained. 'Alim said the assailant wore black gloves, and then ditched the assault weapon.'

'Yes, I was already aware of that detail,' said Halloran.

'What does that prove?' asked Kitt.

'It doesn't prove anything, but it is contradictory behaviour and one of the key elements of the case that suggests Banks is being set up,' said Halloran.

'I suppose you're right,' said Kitt. 'Were there any signs that the weapon had been wiped down to remove prints?'

Halloran shook his head. 'There wasn't any mention of that. But remember the fingerprints were partial, smudged, which already calls into question whether she was the last person to handle the weapon.'

'Even so, if it was Banks who committed the assault, it would be lunacy to leave the weapon at the crime scene,' said Kitt.

'Not just at the scene, Alim said it was left on his doorstep,' said Evie.

'Ricci didn't mention it had been left on the victim's doorstep,' said Halloran pondering.

'Why wouldn't she tell you that?' Kitt asked, narrowing her eyes.

'I don't know. If she's holding specific details back it might be a sign that she doesn't trust me. That she thinks I might be in on it with Banks. But even she must know that Banks wouldn't be so stupid as to leave that weapon on the victim's doorstep knowing it would lead straight back to her.'

'What does that mean?' asked Evie.

'It means Ricci could be looking at this only from an angle that suits her,' said Halloran.

'I'm a bit confused about how a corrupt officer in the ranks could be to Ricci's benefit,' said Kitt. 'Wouldn't it be more beneficial to her to cover it up so her officers didn't suffer a damage to their reputation?'

'She could be counting on accolades for hunting out a corrupt officer,' said Halloran. 'That would buy her a lot of favour with people even higher up in the force than she is.'

'And there's no way this could be a personal vendetta?' Kitt asked, looking at Halloran. 'You did say that Ricci wasn't exactly a fan of Banks.'

Halloran shook his head. 'Ricci's dad was a highly respected copper in his day and she comes recommended by Percival. He's given thirty years of his life to the force and can tell a good apple from a bad one. If he says she's on the level, she's on the level.'

'All right,' said Kitt. 'We'll rule that out for now. The weapon was left there to implicate Banks so the bigger question is, who would benefit from having Banks suspended from duty?'

'The people she suspected of committing the Bootham Bar Books burglary,' said Evie. 'I certainly wouldn't put it past Alim's mother to frame an officer for a crime if it got her son off the hook. That woman was beyond creepy.'

'All right, that's one idea for the pot,' said Kitt. 'Anyone else?'

'Banks has a lot of enemies,' Halloran said. Whenever you put people away for something, there's always a chance they'll seek you out one day, looking for payback. The list of people who might want to hurt either of us isn't short.'

'But the people who know enough about this case to orchestrate this is quite short, isn't it?' asked Kitt.

'Well, probably,' said Halloran.

'Only probably?'

'Alim or his mother could have bragged to anyone about pulling off the burglary, or made it known that Banks liked them for it.'

'Considering everything he gave away to me at the hospital, and how suspicious his mother was about what he might have let slip to me, Alim didn't strike me as the most discreet person on the planet,' said Evie.

'But did he strike you as a book expert?' asked Kitt.

'Not particularly,' said Evie. 'Though unlike you, I don't

start up conversations about books so easily, so I didn't really get him onto that. Charley seemed to think Alim might have been a pawn and someone else was behind it. Someone with that kind of specialist knowledge.'

'A book expert . . . yes,' said Kitt, clasping her hands. '*The Burglar in the Library*.'

'What? Where?' Evie said, her eyes widening as she looked behind her.

'No, no, no, it's the name of a book by Laurence Block.'

'Of course it is,' said Halloran, with a grudging smile.

'I don't know why I didn't think of it before,' said Kitt. 'The central character in that book is a man called Bernie Rhodenbarr – he's a bookseller and burglar and he sets out to steal a very valuable copy of *The Big Sleep* by Raymond Chandler.'

'Wait, wasn't that one of the items stolen from Bootham Bar Books?' said Evie.

'That's right,' said Kitt. 'It was a first edition too – just like the one in Laurence Block's story.'

'Much as I enjoy your parallels between fiction and reality,' said Halloran, 'please don't tell me you're suggesting somebody is acting out that book for real. Because I'm not sure that thieves are usually interested in that kind of rigmarole.'

'That's not exactly what I'm suggesting,' said Kitt. 'In that book, Rhodenbarr wants the book because he believes it has a rare inscription to another author – Dashiell Hammett?'

'Never heard of him,' said Halloran.

'*The Maltese Falcon*?' Kitt tried again, a note of incredulity in her voice.

Evie and Halloran stared at Kitt blankly.

Kitt tutted. 'Never mind. But what if there's something special about these books besides their face value?'

'Special how?' asked Halloran.

'I . . . well perhaps there's something hidden between the pages. The details of a drug meet or the code to a safe at a mansion or . . . Oh! Maybe the book itself provides the solution to some kind of code that leads to a lost treasure.'

'Surely any old copy of the book would do, in that case?' said Evie.

'Not necessarily, each edition of the book is typeset in a particular way and –'

'Hang on a minute,' said Halloran, his voice growing sterner. 'I see where this is leading. You're thinking about looking into this, aren't you?'

'I might consider it,' said Kitt, a note of defiance flaring in her tone.

'Ricci just warned you off.'

Kitt shrugged. 'The way I see it, if I'm going to get into trouble for investigating things I haven't been investigating, I might as well investigate them, especially when it relates to the serious matter of stolen books.'

'I don't think that's a very prudent way of thinking,' said Halloran.

'It wasn't prudent for Ricci to come to my place of

employment and make accusations, but she did it anyway,' said Kitt. 'It would be worth investigating it just to see the look on her face when I uncover those books before she does.'

'Before you launch yourself headlong into the Revenge Book Recovery trade, maybe you should consider the fact Banks's job is on the line here, and possibly even mine too.'

Kitt crinkled her nose, thinking. 'All right, that's a fair point.'

'But . . .' said Evie, looking between Kitt and Halloran, 'isn't that even more reason to investigate it? The more people working for justice on this case, the better, right?'

Kitt bit her lower lip as the arguments of her best friend and her boyfriend battled it out in her head.

'I'm not suggesting we make a nuisance of ourselves,' said Evie.

'Bit late for that, isn't it?' Kitt said.

'Yes, well. That was when I was left unsupervised. You know how to be more discreet about these things. So Ricci never has to know, if we're careful. And who better to trace a set of stolen antique books than you? It's a book case. A book CASE. Get it? Come on, you cannot resist that kind of symmetry.'

Kitt nodded. 'My knowledge of the book market is a distinct advantage in this case, it's true.'

Halloran surrendered to a smirk at Kitt's unexpected boasting.

Making the most of the advantage, Evie turned her attentions on Halloran. 'I promise you, I'm not doing this for the thrill of it. I'm genuinely concerned. It's obvious that something's not quite right about this story and when I saw Charley yesterday she was in a right old state over it. We can't just leave her to suffer, can we? Especially when it's so obvious she didn't do it.'

Halloran rubbed the back of his hand along his beard. 'Ricci has assigned this burglary case to Wilkinson in Banks's absence which is a sure sign she doesn't feel she can rely on me to be objective.'

'Wilkinson?' said Kitt. 'Do cases like this usually get handed to a PC?'

'In the absence of an available detective constable or detective sergeant to investigate them, it's not completely unheard of,' said Halloran. 'He's made no secret of the fact he wants to progress up the ladder as quick as he can. He's keen to take his exam to become a trainee detective so he might even have stepped forward and pushed to work on the case.'

Evie and Kitt exchanged a look of mild surprise. In their previous dealings with PC Wilkinson, he hadn't seemed ambitious or even that competent.

'The point is,' Halloran continued, 'Ricci has made sure this case hasn't landed on my desk so there's not much I can do for Banks at present.'

'Charley seemed to think that Alim's mum might be masterminding it,' said Evie, slowly. 'But there's no way of approaching her directly after today—'

'And you shouldn't be even thinking about it,' said

Halloran. 'She's connected to some seriously sick individuals and is more dangerous than you know. That said, there are ways and means of trained police professionals acquiring sensitive information, if we really need to.'

'How's that?' asked Evie.

'I could pull in a favour with one of the other officers and ask them to run a financial check on Alim's mother. If they've been paid for that job, the likelihood is the money went into her account. Banks probably already thought of this when she was leading the investigation but maybe they delayed paying in the money so it couldn't be traced back to the crime. If someone else looks into it on my behalf, Ricci won't see anything untoward if, or more likely when, she checks my computer logs.'

'Won't you get into trouble if she finds out?' said Kitt, taking a step towards Halloran. 'It's one thing for us to look into things without your help but by pulling a favour like that you're going against a direct order.'

Halloran sighed. 'It's not ideal, but ever so occasionally these measures are necessary. Like if your superior officer shuts you down over something you've got a hunch on. Sometimes, you have to keep things under wraps. I don't want to make a habit out of it, but I could do it, this once. For Banks.'

Kitt nodded. 'Good, because I don't think I can just stand by and do nothing.'

'Not when there are first edition books to recover,' said Halloran.

Kitt smiled a sheepish smile. 'Now, tomorrow is my Saturday off and since I'm the best person to recover these books – at least from a civilian perspective – I don't think it would hurt for us to pay a visit to Bootham Bar Books. Find out if they've had any visits from rival shop owners or antique dealers lately. If they have, they might have taken the opportunity to case the joint.'

'Case the joint?' Evie repeated with a smirk on her face.

'I'm not sure the day that you've impersonated me without permission to a known felon is the day to poke fun of anything I say.'

'Point taken,' said Evie.

'Now wait a minute, I thought you might do a bit of research into this but I'm not sure it's a good idea for you two to go straight to the scene of the crime asking questions,' said Halloran. 'Ricci might have someone tracking your mobile and dispatch an officer if she sees you approaching the bookshop.'

'Well that's easily solved,' said Kitt. 'We'll just make it seem like we're on a book shopping spree rather than going to Bootham Bar Books in particular.'

'And how will you achieve that, exactly?' asked Halloran, a sparkle glinting in his deep blue eyes.

Kitt smiled. 'By visiting every bookshop within the city walls, of course. I'm sure you'll agree, Inspector, it's the only way to be safe.'

EIGHT

Evie stifled a yawn as Kitt chatted with the shop owner at Tower Street Books, a small second-hand bookshop just a hop from Clifford's Tower – or as the tourists knew it, York Castle. This was the seventh bookshop the pair had been in and Evie had forgotten just how long Kitt was able to talk about books for when she met a fellow enthusiast. None of their visits so far could have been described as swift or seemingly that helpful to the inquiry. Everyone thought it was a real shame about the burglary at Bootham Bar Books but nobody had been able to offer any information Evie and Kitt couldn't have read on the local news websites.

Kitt's current conversational partner was a black man called Derek who wore small glasses with oval frames. The hair on his head was snow white and it matched the curly beard that covered his chin from ear to ear. He wore an oversized grey sweater with holes in it here and there and was nodding along to Kitt's current monologue about her visit to the Cornish town of Fowey, childhood home of Daphne du Maurier.

Derek picked up a mug of tea, the contents of which looked almost as grey as his sweater, and nursed it in his lap. 'I've never been, myself, long drive to Cornwall from here, but I've seen pictures. It's supposed to be picturesque from what I understand.'

'Oh, it really is just the quaintest place you can imagine. The house Du Maurier grew up in overlooks the river there, and the Jamaica Inn that inspired her book isn't far away either.'

Evie smiled to herself. Although a great deal of Kitt's chatter about books might have been considered unnecessary to their quest, she had found several different ways of working the titles of the stolen books into conversation. In the previous bookshops, once the topic of the stolen books had been raised, they hadn't hung around long. Kitt had explained she didn't want to push her luck too much in case she asked the wrong person too many questions – and Evie very much hoped the swift departure policy would be put into effect at Tower Street Books too. The vintage kitten heels she'd put on this morning were starting to pinch her toes, and she could do with a sit down. The shoes were usually more than comfortable, but when deciding what to wear this morning she hadn't realized Kitt had been literal about visiting every last bookshop in York.

After eight years of friendship, she should have known better.

'Yeah, I've not read *Jamaica Inn*, actually,' said Derek. 'Just *Rebecca*, *My Cousin Rachel* and *The Scapegoat*. She's got quite a back catalogue to work through, Du Maurier.'

'You're not wrong,' said Kitt. '*Jamaica Inn* is a goodie. Mind you, it's a sore subject at Bootham Bar Books at the minute.'

'Oh yeah,' said Derek, not looking directly at Kitt. 'Terrible business that burglary. It's put all the bookshops on edge, double-checking they've locked the doors at night, looking into alarm systems, and all that. Most of us don't bother usually – people don't think of books as worth stealing.'

'I suppose in this case it wasn't books stolen off the pound shelves out the front,' said Kitt, picking up a Harlequin romance novel from a nearby shelf and reading the back of it in an attempt to act casual.

'I heard the books were worth £50,000 in total,' said Evie, trying to do her part in the investigation and also trying to hurry the conversation along so she could rest her sore feet.

'That's what people are saying,' said Derek, running his finger around the rim of the mug and still failing to look directly at either Evie or Kitt.

Kitt narrowed her eyes at Evie, and then returned her attentions to Derek. 'Whoever did it must have known a bit about the value of those books, and they knew just where to find them.'

Derek shrugged one shoulder. 'Probably a burglar posing

as a customer. If someone took an interest in my first editions I'd let them take a good look in the hopes of making a sale.'

'I suppose you're right,' said Kitt, but Evie noticed a suspicious note in her voice and she had to admit there was something off about Derek's manner. 'I'm sorry to hear it's put you all on edge. From what I understand from the news the police haven't made a formal arrest.'

Derek remained silent.

'Don't suppose you've heard anything about the burglary on the grapevine, have you? A person who loves books as much as I do has a special interest in seeing justice dished out.'

Derek at last looked up at her but still didn't say anything.

Kitt put the romance novel back on the shelf and frowned at him. 'You seem a little quiet today, Derek. Are you worried about something?'

Derek's spare hand was tapping the counter but it didn't seem to Evie that he was aware of it.

'It's just a rumour,' he said after a lengthy pause. 'I'm not convinced I should repeat it.'

'We're no gossips,' said Kitt. 'You might as well talk to us about it. Whatever it is, it seems to be getting to you.'

'I don't know . . .' said Derek. 'I don't know Donald and Shereen Oakes personally but I know a couple of people in the business who do. And they've been concerned for a while about the financial state of their business. They say

Donald's been complaining for a long time about poor takings in the shop.'

Kitt nodded. 'It's not easy for bookshops now, online and all that.'

'Not to mention Brex – ' said Evie.

'Please don't say that word. Not in my place of worship,' Kitt said, gesticulating towards the rows of paperbacks surrounding her. 'I'm sick to the back teeth of hearing about it.'

'You and me both,' said Derek, shaking his head. 'But the thing is, in somewhere like York you can do pretty well in high tourist seasons. People are pottering around and spending their holiday money on luxury items – trying to forget the headlines. But all through the summer when most of us were seeing an uplift, Donald was apparently complaining to his friends about a downturn.'

'You heard him say this yourself?' said Kitt.

Derek shook his head. 'I didn't, like, it was one of the other booksellers in town. I'd rather not say who, they told me in confidence. I don't know where they heard about it.'

'If business hasn't been good, this robbery won't have helped matters, I imagine,' said Kitt.

'Well, actually they'll probably be all right one way or another – they were insured for those books,' Derek said, the whites of his eyes growing wider the longer he fixed his stare on Kitt and Evie.

Kitt tilted her head to one side. 'You're not suggesting . . .'

'I didn't say anything,' Derek said.

Evie frowned. 'What?'

'I think Derek is suggesting Donald and Shereen were behind the burglary,' said Kitt. 'Orchestrated the whole thing . . . to get the insurance money?'

'No . . . I don't know what to think,' said Derek almost before Kitt had finished her last syllable. 'As I said, didn't hear it from Donald or Shereen themselves, not the kind of thing you can just bring up in casual conversation anyway, but there have been rumours.'

'But Donald is such a sweet old man,' said Kitt. 'I've known him years now.'

'It's probably not true,' said Derek with a dismissive wave of his hand. 'It's town gossip. You know what people can be like for gossip.'

'Yes . . . but just supposing for a minute they did orchestrate it,' Evie said, thinking about Charley's point that Alim had no understanding of rare books, 'they'd be able to tell the burglar which books to take and exactly where to find them.'

'That's true,' said Kitt. 'It's just . . . I've been buying off Donald for such a long time I find it hard to believe he'd go this far even if his business was in trouble. It doesn't seem like the man I've come to know. Not at all.'

'I shouldn't have said anything,' said Derek.

'No, no, I'm glad you did,' said Kitt. 'But you'll forgive me for hoping it's not true, and at the same time for being grateful that in any case it hasn't played out the way it does in all my favourite mystery books, where a spouse is almost inevitably killed off for the insurance money.'

'Aye, we've got to be grateful we're not living *Double Indemnity* all right,' said Derek.

At that moment, the door to the bookshop swung open and a girl with long dark hair, dyed purple and blue at the ends, walked in. After she had closed the door, she grabbed the length of her hair and twisted it around her hand in a sort of awkward gesture.

'Can I help you?' asked Derek, standing from his stool and putting down his mug of tea.

'Vintage sci-fi?' said the girl. 'Got any?'

Derek opened his mouth to speak but Kitt interjected. 'Oh, you'll find that down the third aisle over there,' she said, pointing. 'There are at least six shelves' worth for you to look through. And some real classics too.'

'Thanks.' The girl gave a thin smile before following Kitt's direction.

Derek grinned at Kitt. 'You after a job here, or what?'

'No, sorry, force of habit,' said Kitt. 'Helping people find books is what I do.'

'Well, I'd better go and see if I can help any further,' said Derek. 'Donald Oakes isn't the only one who could do with making a few sales.'

'Right you are,' said Kitt. 'We'll leave you to it.'

Evie could almost feel the relief in her toes as Kitt said

this. True relief wouldn't come until the weight had been completely taken off.

She turned to open the shop door and the moment she did an icy blast blew in. She threw Derek an apologetic look before hopping outside and tightening her scarlet scarf around her neck. Kitt jumped out just behind her and glanced over towards the queue for Clifford's Tower. 'Who in their right minds wants to go up there on a day like today?'

Evie knew Kitt wasn't expecting an answer. It was part of the local shtick to express a sense of wonderment at the often perplexing behaviour of tourists. The same tourists who bottlenecked the quaint, cobbled street of Stonegate every year, even though York was in no shortage of quaint, cobbled streets if that was what they were after. The same tourists who queued for an hour on a summer Bank Holiday to have lunch at Betty's Tea Room – delightful as it was, both Kitt and Evie agreed that a sixty-minute wait to even order food was not their idea of a relaxing dining experience.

'All right if we sit down for a scone somewhere? My shoes are starting to pinch.'

Kitt glared at Evie's feet. 'I thought those were your comfortable shoes.'

'They are,' said Evie. 'But we have walked quite a distance between here and Micklegate, you know? And we've been standing for hours.'

Kitt looked at her watch and gave a firm nod. 'All right,

yes, let's stop before we go on to Bootham Bar Books. I could do with a cuppa and I . . . I've got something I need to talk to you about anyway.'

Evie looked at Kitt sidelong. 'What?'

The librarian shook her head. 'I can't talk to you about it without a cup of Lady Grey in hand.'

'Sounds serious,' said Evie, frowning at her friend, but Kitt's expression offered no clues at all.

NINE

Due to Evie's protests about how far they had already walked, Kitt headed straight to the silver service tea room opposite Clifford's Tower called, rather quaintly Evie thought, Tea by the Tower. The interior was just as sweet as its name. It was wallpapered in white and pink candy stripes, had a small vase of silk white roses on each table and a large sign hung near the door that read: Tea Junction: Give Way to Biscuits. Evie found puns almost as irresistible as innuendo and thus couldn't help but smile at this. Kitt had once passed a comment that given her sense of humour Evie would get on well with William Shakespeare but somehow, even though Shakespeare was one of the most revered writers in the English language, Kitt had managed to make this sound much more of an insult than a compliment.

No sooner had Evie and Kitt ordered a cup of tea and a scone apiece than Evie raised her eyebrows at her friend and fell silent, waiting.

'Shall we not wait until the tea arrives?'

Evie gasped. 'You must be joking. You're not keeping me in suspense any longer.'

Kitt's jaw tightened. 'It's you, lady, who's been keeping me in suspense.'

'What do you mean?'

'I mean, something was bothering you the other night, and with Ricci's visit and our investigations, I've not had time to find out what's going on with my best friend in the world.'

'Oh, that,' said Evie. Tiny chills prickled all along her arms. She had forgotten she had given away that anything was even wrong.

'Yes, come on. Out with it. I won't have you struggling with something on your own like this,' said Kitt.

'It's nothing to worry about really, it's just about my job at the salon. I don't think I can keep doing it.'

'Has something happened?'

'Yes,' said Evie. 'This.' She pointed at her face, or more specifically to her scars.

Kitt tilted her head in the same manner as a dog trying to decipher its owner's words. 'Are they painful?'

'Not physically,' said Evie, staring down at her hands, 'but in so many other ways, yes. I just . . . I don't think I can keep working in the beauty industry when I look like this.'

'Oh Evie, you don't really feel that way?'

Evie glanced back up at her friend. 'You should see some

of the looks I get from customers. And those who *can* control it, I know deep down what they're thinking.'

Kitt blinked as she took in what Evie had just said.

'Tea and scones, ladies?' said the waiter, appearing without warning at their table before taking an inordinate amount of time to set out each item of crockery and cutlery.

'But you love your job. Love making people feel better about themselves,' Kitt said, once the waiter had whirled away to talk to an American tourist who wanted to know if the tiny pots of jam they used were for sale to customers.

'I used to. But that was when I felt pretty good about myself. I mean, at least on the outside. Now I'm ... well, look at me.'

'I am,' said Kitt, her brow furrowing as she concentrated hard on her friend's face. 'I don't see anything so disconcerting as you're suggesting.'

'I think some of the other staff members want me to quit too.'

'They've said this to you?'

'No, but sometimes they say little things that make me think they're hinting at it. I'm not exactly the first-choice face for a beauty salon.'

'Well, I disagree,' said Kitt. 'How many clients have you had over the years that have had low self-esteem and while chatting to you during the massage let it slip that they thought themselves far from beautiful?'

Evie shrugged. 'More than I can count.'

'And what have you always said to me about people like that?'

Evie didn't reply.

'You say they're all beautiful, they just can't see their own beauty; and it looks as though the same is now true for you. You are still beautiful. You've just forgotten how to see it in yourself.'

Evie smiled but she knew it was too quick a smile to be believable. 'I don't know if I can go back to seeing myself that way.'

'Well I'll be happy to help you, any way I can. It might be best to give yourself some space to breathe before you make any rash decisions about your job. The healing qualities of time are a cliché for a reason,' Kitt said with a smile. But then her phone buzzed in the pocket of her cardigan. Sighing, she whipped it out and held it to her ear.

'Grace? Well, you are in my contacts but I also know you can't really resist interrupting me when I'm trying to have a cup of tea.'

Evie half-smiled as she cut into her scone and started lashing on the butter. Kitt was a fan of tough love when it came to dealing with her assistant, but given Grace's penchant for winding Kitt up at every opportunity, this perhaps wasn't a surprise.

'That's right,' Kitt said, 'I would search nationwide if I were you.'

There was a pause then as Kitt listened to what Grace had to say next.

'Yes, eBay too. OK. Let me know if anything turns up. Until soon.'

Kitt hung up the phone.

'Another library emergency?' Evie joked before taking her first mouthful of scone.

'Not quite.' Kitt looked around, leant forward and lowered her voice. 'Grace is doing her Saturday shift on the rota today. If there's a few quiet minutes here and there I've asked her to look up auction sales of rare books. I still haven't ruled out my theory that there's something special about those books. Some greater interest the criminal element might have in them, but I can't rule out the possibility that they were stolen for their monetary value alone.'

Evie nodded along to Kitt's explanation. 'So, you're expecting them to turn up at some kind of auction? Is that right? I don't know. I've never had any rare books to sell, myself.'

'Honestly, I think that might be a bit risky because those kinds of places do checks but it's worth keeping an eye out anyway. eBay is another possibility, however. If they don't turn up on any of the listings, if the thief is hanging on to them, it might suggest there really is something special about those editions.'

Evie frowned. 'Or that they're hanging on to them until the fuss over the robbery has died down.'

'If they do that, our chances of catching the culprits are much diminished so I'm very much hoping if it's the money they're after, they are too desperate to wait around for it.'

'Isn't there a chance that they've sold the books through some kind of dodgy back channel?'

'Yes, I thought about that but I asked him and Halloran said that the books have been registered on the Stolen Arts Database due to their cultural value,' said Kitt.

'What will that do?'

'Anybody acquiring articles of cultural value has certain due diligence checks to go through. One of them is checking databases of stolen cultural items. Even if initially the books are sold on through some dodgy back channel, the odds are that before long someone will try and sell them through a reputable method in order to make the most they can from the sale. Whichever way they go about it, we'll know about it before long.'

Evie sighed. 'Of all the things to steal. There's an art gallery full of expensive works just sitting right around the corner and these particular cultural thieves decide to nick three second-hand books.'

'I agree, this isn't making much sense to me as yet,' said Kitt. 'But I suppose breaking into an art gallery might be more intimidating than breaking into a bookshop. I'm not sure how high security is at the gallery but perhaps Bootham Bar Books was in part selected because it was deemed an easy target.'

'Or . . . there is something to this rumour about the insurance scam?' said Evie.

'Oh, I really don't want to give that theory any credence,' said Kitt. 'But if we're to get to the truth of the matter, I suppose I have to keep an open mind about Donald and Shereen's involvement. Certainly, I'll be watching their movements very closely. The insurance story might be the most logical solution but I'd much rather discover some outlandish plot than see the pair of them go to prison.'

'If it's outlandish you're looking for, I'd say you're in luck. This whole case is a bit weird.'

'Which is why we're just the right people to solve it, don't you agree?'

Evie giggled and took another mouthful of scone.

'Right,' said Kitt, 'now for the serious business of getting this tea down us. No time to waste. The next one is the big one: Bootham Bar Books.'

TEN

Daylight was already fading by the time Evie and Kitt were strolling the curve of St Leonard's Place, past the city art gallery, towards Bootham Bar Books. Evie smiled as Bootham Bar came into view. It was one of the four entry points built into the city walls that once led into a Roman fortress. She had always thought they had majestic lines about them but, at this time of year, they looked especially enchanting come nightfall as the council draped them in tiny blue lights. Passing through the structure in the winter months felt like passing into a magical land.

As the pair walked towards the gateway, Evie noticed Kitt looking around in more directions than was necessary to cross the road. Before she got a chance to ask her about it, however, the pair were interrupted.

''Ello, loves,' said a familiar voice. Kitt and Evie turned to see Ruby, an elderly lady who frequented the library and, much to Kitt's eye-rolling scorn, believed herself to be psychic.

'Hello, Ruby,' Kitt said. 'Bit late in the day for you to be out and about, isn't it? I thought you'd be at home by the fire by now. As all sensible people should be.'

'On me way to do a tarot reading for one of me regulars,' Ruby said, her short curly hair, dyed the colour of Irn-Bru, bristling in the low wind. 'The offer still stands for me to read your cards if you want to know how to hold on to that policeman friend of yours.'

Evie tried to hold back a chuckle. Though Kitt was more than happy to suspend disbelief for any kind of story caught between the pages of a book, once the book was put down she was a woman wedded to logic and practicality. The idea of having her tarot cards read, especially by Ruby, was a surreal image to say the least.

'I deal my own cards, thank you,' said Kitt with a little snap to her voice. 'I doubt those cards will tell me anything about myself I don't already know.'

'Yes, but sometimes we need reminding that we know what we know,' said Ruby.

Despite her, at times, zany clothing choices and left-field conversational topics, Ruby was not so green as she was cabbage-looking, and Evie wondered if, on occasion, Ruby deliberately said silly things to tease Kitt. Which, in fairness, was pretty much standard among Kitt's circle of friends.

Kitt raised her eyebrows at Ruby, a signal of infuriation that Evie wagered the old woman was well acquainted with.

'Oooh, eyup. I'm getting a feeling . . .' said Ruby, grabbing Evie's arm.

Kitt brought a hand to her temple. 'Oh good grief, here we go.'

'An ending, there's an ending coming. And . . . fear. So much fear. I can feel it.' Ruby's eyes were closed, her face contorted and she held her head at an angle as though it were an antenna trying to pick up some kind of signal.

Evie wanted to ask Ruby exactly what she could see but before she had a chance the old woman released her grip on Evie's arm and opened her eyes again.

'No, that's it, I'm afraid. Something scary and final. That's all I can tell you.'

Evie looked at Kitt with wide eyes but the librarian just shook her head.

'I think we'd best be getting along the road, Ruby,' Kitt said, her tone a bit gentler than it had been before. 'We've got a few jobs to do before the shops shut.'

'Oh, aye, all right,' said Ruby, casually, as though a moment ago she hadn't been gripped by some psychic presence, and perhaps she hadn't. 'But mind my words and think about the cards eh, love? I'll be in at the library next week.'

Kitt and Evie watched Ruby amble off in the direction of Clifton, waving at the odd passer-by.

'Mad as a snake,' Kitt said with a sigh.

'Don't you think what she said was a bit ominous?' said Evie.

Kitt snorted as they set off again towards the bookshop. 'Something final and scary? That kind of prediction could be applied to tonight's episode of *Coronation Street*.' And then her attentions were returned to the environment directly around them. Just as before she looked in all directions, examining the crowds and stopping on occasion for a second look.

'Everything all right?' asked Evie.

'Yes, thank you,' said Kitt, but still her eyes narrowed at someone or something she was staring at off to her right. Evie followed her friend's stare but couldn't see anything out of the ordinary. Just the usual pre-Christmas shoppers and tourists who were trying to get their cameras to take night shots in the looming dusk.

Evie looked back at her friend. 'What are you up to?'

Kitt, still looking into the surrounding crowds, spoke in a low voice. 'This morning, Halloran told me to be vigilant about anyone following us on our approach to Bootham Bar Books. He's still worried about Ricci tracking us and said we should only risk going into the shop if the coast was definitely clear.'

'This morning?' Evie said, with a smirk. 'So Halloran is staying over then?'

'Oh, must you pick up on every detail of my personal life?' said Kitt. 'Yes, he slept over but it's not what you think. I told you, we're taking it slow.'

'All right, all right,' Evie said, crossing the street and

trying to keep stride with Kitt even though her shoes were still pinching a bit. 'But how will we know if someone's following us?

'If it's an officer, they'll probably be in plain clothes and probably know how to stay under the radar. But of course after your escapades at the hospital yesterday there's also a chance Mrs Buruk has got people watching the shop too.'

Evie's shoulders tensed. 'You don't think so, do you? That woman gives me the heebie-jeebies.'

'It depends how involved she really is and how worried she is that the truth might come out. Halloran said to look behind us when we set off from our point of origin – in this case the tea room.'

'I didn't notice you do that,' Evie said with a frown.

'That's because you were too busy cooing over that Labrador puppy that was walking into Tower Gardens.'

'Oh yes,' said Evie. 'He was so cute, did you see the little bandana he was wearing? It had pawprints all over it.'

'Yes, adorable,' Kitt said, quickly and without any feeling. 'Halloran then advised that I check again five minutes later, which I did whilst we walked along Coney Street. Halloran then told me to wait ten minutes and check again for any familiar faces. That's why we've come the long way round, avoiding the cut through High Petergate.'

'Oh,' said Evie, her eyes widening in realization. 'I just thought you wanted to take the scenic route to burn off some of the scone we just ate.'

'Yes,' said Kitt, her voice Martini-dry. 'That's me, always so concerned about building a workout into my day.'

'Mmm. OK, point taken. I must have been projecting,' said Evie, already wondering about how she was going to manage her festive eating and still fit into the vintage Chanel coat dress she liked to wear once a year on Christmas Day. It was the most luxurious shade of red but the cut didn't allow for the extravagance of scones or mince pies which made pre-Christmas social functions a bit of a minefield. 'So, is the coast clear? Do you recognize anyone?'

Kitt took one last look into the crowds. 'Halloran said that if I saw the same face twice that might be a coincidence, but if I noticed them three times, we should abort the mission and not go into Bootham Bar Books.'

'And have you?'

'I don't think so. I saw one group of people twice but they were a family and if there are people following us they are likely to be on their own, according to what Halloran said anyway. Even if there is someone following us though, they'd have to prove that we were there purely to talk about the burglary which, given the fact we've visited almost all of the bookshops in town today, and that we've still a couple left to visit after this, would be hard to prove.'

'We're going to more bookshops after this?' Evie half-wailed.

'We haven't been to Fossgate Books or The Little Apple Bookshop yet,' said Kitt. 'We have to keep up our cover.'

'I suppose you're right,' said Evie as the oval sign for Bootham Bar Books swung into view. 'The last thing Charley needs is us creating any more trouble for her than she's already in.'

And at the thought that they might be helping out the officer, Evie forgot about how much her feet were hurting.

'We'll be careful. Let me lead and we should get by OK,' said Kitt, pushing open the door to Bootham Bar Books.

Evie looked back along High Petergate and caught another glimpse of Bootham Bar. She remembered something she had learned at school: the bar hadn't always been adorned with such pretty trinkets as twinkling Christmas lights. In the sixteen hundreds, it was used to display the decapitated heads of traitors. A symmetry between this image and the drama surrounding this little bookshop formed in Evie's mind. Between the burglary and potential insurance fraud, there was plenty of treacherous behaviour going on and Evie could only hope that this dark situation wasn't going to result in more bloodshed.

ELEVEN

The second they were inside, Evie was overwhelmed by the sheer number of books before her. The other bookshops they had visited were modest, almost poky venues but Bootham Bar Books was something else. It was no surprise that Kitt was such a good customer here. The walls were floor to ceiling with volumes on every imaginable genre and the shop extended way back in a seemingly never-ending corridor of books. The bookcases were fitted with several of those ladders on rails that enabled you to reach the upper shelves or move from one side of the shop to the other with ease.

Though it was approaching teatime on a Saturday and it was almost closing time, there were still a couple of punters at the back of the shop, running their fingers along the spines of books and picking the odd volume off the shelf to take a look at the first few pages.

The air was filled with the homely smell of second-hand

books. A sort of mustiness with hints of vanilla. A soothing fragrance, even if Evie's muscles were tensing at the thought of what they might find out from Donald and Shereen Oakes about the recent burglary.

'Hi, Olivia,' said Kitt, greeting a girl who couldn't have been much over the age of twenty given her flawless caramel skin. Her long, chestnut hair flowed down her back like a shampoo advert. Evie betted herself that she didn't buy off the shelf in Superdrug but spent all of her money earned at the bookshop on products only sold by professional hair salons. Olivia's tight, white T-shirt was thin enough to show a black bra underneath and to Evie's mind was totally out of sync with the current weather, especially given it stopped just above the waistband of her skinny jeans, showing off a taut tummy.

'Oh, hi, Kitt,' said Olivia, who was standing behind a small counter stacked with bookmarks, badges, pocket city guides and other tourist-driven paraphernalia. The girl offered Evie a genial nod. They had never met but, it seemed, any friend of a book-lover like Kitt was a friend of hers.

Kitt rested her trilby on a nearby bookshelf, pulled off her gloves finger by finger and shoved them in the pockets of her coat. 'I was just passing with Evie here and, well, you know I can't really walk past without coming in for a bit of a browse.'

Olivia let out a squeaky giggle that, to Evie's ears, sounded somewhat forced. 'I'd be the same if I didn't work here.'

'Yes . . .' Kitt emitted a fluttery laugh that sounded just as forced as Olivia's. 'Being a librarian you'd have thought the novelty would have worn off. But I'll still take any excuse to talk to bookish people. Speaking of which, Donald and Shereen not in today?'

Olivia looked away and she started fiddling with a Snoopy figurine in one of the sale baskets. 'Not today. They . . . had some jobs to do and left me in charge until closing.'

'Oh,' Kitt said, glancing at Evie out of the corner of her eye. 'I'm a little surprised at that.'

Olivia frowned. 'Why? I've worked here for more than a year now. It's not like I can't look after the shop on my own.'

'Of course you can,' Kitt soothed. 'I was just thinking one of them might have stayed with you for safety reasons. To look after you.'

'Safety?' said Olivia. The hard note had left her voice but her frown remained.

Kitt's face was at once a picture of concern. 'Well, they still haven't caught whoever it was that broke in here. What if the burglars came back for round two? And you'd be on your own, young girl like you. I hate to think of it.'

'I don't think that's going to happen,' Olivia said, with a small, tight smile.

'Oh?' said Kitt. 'Has there been a breakthrough of some sorts?'

Olivia's face froze just long enough for Evie to notice, and she would bet her life on it that it hadn't escaped Kitt's attention either.

'No . . .' Olivia said. 'But whoever it was, they already have the most valuable books in the shop. There's nothing really worth coming back for, is there?'

Evie glanced over at the soft toy display standing to the left of the counter. Particularly, at the large Benjamin Bunny, Mrs Tiggywinkle and Jemima Puddleduck toys that lined the top shelf. All of Peter Rabbit's friends were in attendance but he was noticeably missing. Adorable as the toys were, Evie was inclined to agree with Olivia on this one. The burglar seemed unlikely to return to collect the rest of the set.

'You're right, of course, silly me,' said Kitt.

Evie smiled at this comment. The last word Kitt would ever use to describe herself was silly, unless she wanted Olivia to think of her as silly, a façade that must be nothing short of torture for someone as well-read as she. What was Kitt's plan?

'Anyway,' Olivia added, 'Donald and Shereen said it was important, something to do with their insurance broker.'

'I see,' said Kitt. 'With a loss like that I can understand they'd want to make that trip a priority.'

'Exactly,' said Olivia, in a haughty tone.

Evie really wasn't sure what to make of this young woman; her manner seemed to run from hot to cold in an instant. But, Evie conceded, perhaps she had become so vintage at heart that she was now completely detached from the next generation.

'Such terrible luck, the whole business,' said Kitt seemingly unruffled by the young girl's tone. 'Except, I suppose it wasn't really luck, was it? The burglars somehow knew exactly where to look for the most expensive items in the shop.' She took a step closer to the counter and eyed Olivia in a manner that would put anyone on edge.

Olivia crossed her arms over her chest, and the sharp note returned to her voice. 'What are you saying, like?'

'That whoever it was who stole from you knew exactly where to look and that means they had probably been in the shop before the robbery.'

'Well, I don't know about that,' said Olivia, her eyes looking anywhere but at Kitt.

'I hadn't thought of it before,' said Evie, in mock-surprise. 'But I think Kitt's right. If they knew where to look they must have been in the shop.'

Olivia squirmed on the spot before controlling herself and shrugging.

'You've got a wonderful knowledge of the customers who are in and out of here,' Kitt said in the most sugary voice Evie had ever heard her use. 'Did anyone ask about the books that were stolen in the last few months? If so, you might be able to pass on their descriptions to the police. I'm sure they'd welcome any help finding the culprits.'

'I already talked to the police about that. Nobody I served asked after them. But Donald said he'd had a couple of enquiries a few months back. He told the police what he could remember.'

'I see. Sorry if I'm stating the obvious, I just feel so badly that this happened to my favourite bookshop,' said Kitt. 'At least Donald was able to offer the police a lead. I do just think it's a horrible shame.'

Olivia smiled then. 'You're right, it is. And it's not like Donald and Shereen haven't got enough to worry about right now.'

'Oh?' said Kitt. 'I'm sorry, I didn't realize they had more strain happening on top of that.'

'Well, they don't like to let on. Small town. Word gets round a bit too easy.'

'Too true,' said Kitt.

Slowly, Olivia looked Kitt up and down. There was something about the gesture Evie didn't like, though it was difficult to put her finger on what it was. 'But I'm sure, given you're such a regular customer, only looking out for them and that, they wouldn't mind me saying to you that business hasn't been too strong lately.'

'Really,' said Kitt, glancing over again at Evie just for a moment. 'Oh, that is sad news. Have things been slow?'

Olivia shrugged. 'I don't know the exact ins and outs. But I've overheard one or two things that suggest they haven't been exactly raking it in lately. I wondered if they were going to cut my hours because of it, but they haven't yet.'

'This robbery must have been the last straw with that already hanging over them,' said Evie.

'Tempers have been short around here,' said Olivia,

and took pains to lower her voice before continuing even though the customers scuttling around at the back of the shop were definitely out of earshot. 'About a week before the robbery, Donald and Shereen had a proper blow out in the back room.'

'That's not a good sign,' said Kitt. 'Were they arguing about money? Financial trouble does put a lot of strain on relationships.'

'That was a big part of it,' Olivia said, looking down at the counter.

Kitt tilted her head to one side. 'There was something else?'

'I . . . I could be mistaken, but I thought I heard Donald accusing Shereen of having an affair. When he said that she completely went off on one. Screaming back at him, denying it.'

'An affair? Shereen?'

'That's what it sounded like. But it was quite difficult to make out every word. They were so angry it was all a bit garbled. She got so mad at one point she . . .'

'What?'

'She shouted at him that if he didn't shut up about it she was going to kill him.'

Evie swallowed hard. People made idle threats like that every day. Six months ago she wouldn't have thought twice about it. At some point she must herself have idly suggested she would do someone in if they didn't stop whatever they might be doing to irritate her. But after the events of recent months, the idea of murders taking place in York, of bodies turning up in the places that you once thought of as safe and homely, wasn't so fantastic an idea.

'Oh, I'm sure she didn't mean it,' said Kitt. But Evie could tell from the waver in her friend's voice that she was thinking along the same lines. 'People say a lot of things when they're angry.'

'You're probably right,' said Olivia. 'I've heard them getting at each other a couple of times since I started working here. I've just never heard them go at each other like that before.'

Evie wanted to ask who Donald suspected his wife was having an affair with. She didn't know exactly how but it seemed like the robbery and the affair might be connected. Both of them spelled trouble for Donald and Shereen. But given she didn't know the bookshop owners herself it might be considered prying a bit too far and Evie couldn't risk rousing Olivia's suspicions.

Evie's thoughts were interrupted as the door to the bookshop swooshed open and she heard Kitt say, 'Donald, Shereen, there you are. How are you keeping?'

Donald was a short man, or at least a good foot shorter than his wife. After closing the door he took off his flat cap to reveal a heap of grey, wild, wispy hair. 'Back again, are we? Always good to see you,' he said.

Shereen was busy removing a pair of sheepskin gloves

but once she had she gave Kitt a broad smile. 'How are you doing, my love?' she asked, squeezing the librarian's arm on her way past. Olivia was looking down at the counter again, rather than making eye contact with her employers. Probably feeling a bit guilty for talking about them behind their backs.

'All's good at my end of the bookshelf,' said Kitt. 'I was just passing and couldn't resist popping in. This is my friend, Evie.'

Evie's heart stopped for just a moment. She hadn't expected to be formally introduced. Hastily, she arranged her curls around her scars as best she could and then offered both Donald and Shereen a smile.

Donald returned her gesture with a quick 'hello there'. Shereen, however, did a small double-take when she looked at Evie's face and then tried to avert her eyes. Evie's whole body sagged. She tried not to look back at Olivia but she could feel the young girl's perfection taunting her in her peripheral vision.

'Ee, what a mess,' Shereen said, looking into a small, round mirror that was hanging just to the side of the counter as she flicked sections of her bobbed black hair into place. 'It's getting a bit wild out there.'

'Any excitement this afternoon?' Donald asked Olivia.

Olivia shook her head. 'Nothing earth-shattering. We have run out of pricing labels though.'

Donald gurned. 'Yes, well. We've decided to move away

from pricing labels anyway. We're just going to write the price in the inside cover in pencil so customers can rub it out afterwards if they want. It's more cost-effective.'

Shereen sighed at this but then looked at Kitt and Evie, seemingly remembering she was in the presence of customers, and said no more about it.

Kitt stared at Evie and Evie stared right back. Had things got that bad? That they were unwilling to even stretch to the basic equipment required for running a shop? What about the insurance money that was due to them? Surely that would have calmed any financial fears? Unless, for some reason, the insurance money wasn't forthcoming . . .

'I know you must be sick of hearing this question after all that's happened in the last couple of weeks,' Kitt said to Shereen, 'but is there anything I can do for you?'

'You can catch the burglar the same way you caught that murderer a few weeks back, if you're offering,' said Donald. He had a strange look on his face. Evie couldn't tell whether he was joking or not.

'I think the police have the matter well in hand,' said Kitt.

'They seemed to 'ave it in hand to begin with,' said Shereen. 'But some new officers have taken over the case for reasons unknown. They were in here this morning and I didn't think much of either of them.'

'Watch what yer saying, love,' said Donald. 'Kitt'll have her boyfriend after you.'

Evie did all she could to fight a smirk but Kitt's face was

locked in its most unimpressed expression, which always made her want to giggle.

'As a tax-paying member of the community I daresay you're permitted an opinion on the efficiency – or otherwise – of the police force,' said Kitt. 'But just out of interest, which officers paid you a visit?'

'Can't remember the name of the young PC that came knocking,' said Donald. 'But I won't forget the woman who was with him in a hurry. She was in 'ere throwing her weight around. Said a violent crime case was now linked with the burglary.'

'She asked us if we knew some lad – Alim something,' said Shereen.

'But it didn't sound like much of a question, not the way she said it,' Donald added.

'Did you know this . . . Alim person?' asked Kitt, doing a good job of making it seem like she had never heard the name before the Oakeses mentioned it.

'No,' said Shereen, with a defensive note in her voice. 'They showed us a picture of him but we'd never seen him before.'

At that juncture, one of the customers who had been browsing walked up to the counter. Olivia began serving the woman, who had a halo of tight, ebony curls and carried a shopping bag with the phrase 'I don't own my cat, my cat owns me' printed across it. An uneasy silence fell on the others as the customer paid for several Georgette Heyer novels, packed them into her bag and exited the shop.

'I'm so sorry you haven't got those books back, and that they haven't caught the culprit,' said Kitt. 'But I am sure the police are doing everything they can, and in a worst-case scenario hopefully you'll get some insurance money?'

'Hopefully,' Donald said, his jaw tightening.

Just as Evie was wondering if they were outstaying their welcome, Kitt cleared her throat and looked at her watch: 'Ooh, I hadn't realized it was quite so far into the afternoon. I'm sorry, I've got to go and check in at the library before my assistant goes home for the weekend. I'm going to have to come back next week to do my browsing.'

'No problem,' said Donald, his face brightening a little. 'We'll be pleased to see you as always.'

'We're always pleased to see our best customer,' Shereen said, with a thin, weak smile.

'It was nice chatting with you,' said Olivia.

'See you anon,' said Kitt, pushing open the door.

Evie said goodbye to Donald and Shereen and offered Olivia a polite nod, taking pains not to look at her perfect face straight on, before following Kitt out into the biting winter twilight.

TWELVE

Evie had been bold enough to hope that Kitt had meant what she said to Donald Oakes about needing to dash to the library but her friend had insisted on visiting the last two bookshops on her list 'just to keep up their cover'. Evie hadn't been that convinced by this but given it was her idea to do some digging around on this case she could hardly complain, even if she was cringing at how swollen her feet would be when she took off her shoes later.

'I take it you were playing a little game with Olivia, when you called yourself silly,' Evie said to her friend.

Kitt smiled but didn't slow her pace. 'I was trying to emulate Miss Marple.'

'You're a bit young for that comparison, at least in physical years spent on the planet.'

'Yes, thank you for that backhanded compliment.' Kitt sniffed. 'But that's not what I meant. Miss Marple is underestimated by many a character over the course of her time as an amateur detective. It was in my interests for Olivia to think of me as a bit dotty so she might do the same.'

'Well, it seemed to have worked,' Evie said, hopping up the stone steps to the large oak doorway at the front of the library. 'She had plenty to say for herself.'

'Didn't she just,' came Kitt's response. 'Here's hoping Grace has one or two things to say for herself too.'

The pair smiled at each other and marched their way through the ground-floor reception area. Evie had to walk double-time to keep up with Kitt as she darted up to the Women's Studies section.

Grace was sitting at her desk, which was just next to where Kitt usually sat. Grace's short, black-brown curls swayed to the rhythm of her vigorous typing action. Though she was seated, Evie could still admire the turquoise silk of the dress she was wearing over her jeans. She always seemed to opt for garments in rich, deep colours, a choice that Evie thought must be at least part-inspired by her Indian heritage. Clothing from India had always struck Evie as so exotic and graceful; she would love to wear something like that herself but it didn't seem all that appropriate when you had the skin tone of a person who had never seen the sun. Nor for a person who hailed from the small market town of Thirsk. Tweed jackets and wellington boots were much closer to the accepted dress code there.

'Everything all right, Grace?' Kitt asked, eyeing her

assistant as she placed her trilby on her desk and hung her crimson winter coat over the back of her chair.

Grace jumped and then put her hand over her heart. 'Oh God, for a second there I thought you were Michelle. I didn't have a chance to do much research at home before I left for my shift this morning and I couldn't stand to wait till I clocked off to catch my next criminal but she's made three checks of this floor in the past three hours. It's like she can smell the fact that I might be using library resources for something other than bona fide university business.'

Kitt smiled. 'Well if anyone had the ability to sense that it would be her. I didn't mean to startle you. I just don't think I've ever seen you typing that fast.'

'I type fast enough usually, thank you very much,' Grace said with a playful note in her voice.

Kitt smirked and then, as her attentions turned from her assistant to her desk, did a double-take.

'Grace ... what is that?' she said, pointing at a plush green Christmas tree ornament complete with a pair of goggle eyes, a scarf made of tinsel and a Santa hat perched at a jaunty angle where one might traditionally expect a star or a fairy to sit.

Evie bit her lip as she examined it, wondering what mischief Grace had cooked up this time.

Grace smiled, stood from her desk, leant over to the tree and flicked a switch at the base. At once the tree jumped to life, the plush material writhing to a high-pitched version of 'I Saw Mommy Kissing Santa Claus', which sounded like it was being sung by a trio of chipmunks.

Kitt folded her arms, her gaze torn between the dancing ornament and Grace, who was mouthing the words to the song whilst doing her own little jig. All this distraction meant that Kitt hadn't noticed quite how hard Evie was laughing. By the time the last note of the song sounded out, Evie was wiping tears from her eyes.

'And what, may I ask, have I done to deserve this high-brow festive treat?' Kitt asked.

'Just been the best boss in the world, that's all,' said Grace, giving Kitt a playful punch on the arm.

'I dread to think what you'd give the worst boss in the world. No time to hunt down criminals before work but time enough to select and buy this . . . heart-warming gift.'

'Ugh.' Grace looked at Evie and pointed her thumb at Kitt. 'Kids these days, no gratitude.'

'Thank you, Grace,' said Kitt, though Evie could tell from her expression that she was already thinking about how she was going to get rid of the monstrosity. 'If we could move onto more pressing issues though . . .' She lowered her voice to make sure what she was about to say couldn't be heard by the smattering of students trying to work in the vicinity, despite the dancing Christmas tree. 'No sign of the books so far then?'

'Not yet,' said Grace, taking Kitt's cue and lowering her voice. 'To be honest, the police will already be looking into this and with their resources are much more likely to find a hit than we are. Especially as the culprits might use back channels as opposed to official auctions.'

'I know, but we've got to try. It may all be for nothing but at least we'll have tried to help Banks. If the information goes direct to Ricci, Halloran won't get a sniff of it. He's sent me some pretty dry texts to suggest Ricci is watching his every move.'

Evie slumped down in the chair in front of the student enquiry desk. She had checked her phone on the way to the library too, but she hadn't heard anything from Charley. She had begun to wonder if she would hear from her at all or whether she was just being polite when she said she'd keep her informed. It's not like they had known each other a long time or anything. She wasn't obliged to keep her word. Especially given she had no idea that they were looking into this case on her behalf. Evie didn't relish the thought of keeping a secret from her but she did rather enjoy thinking about how happy Charley would be if this all came off and they were able to find who had stolen those books, and who had set her up.

'You thought Olivia's behaviour was a bit strange, didn't you, Evie?' said Kitt, breaking her train of thought.

'Um, yeah ... she was a bit on edge at times. But she did help us in the end. Telling us all that stuff about their financial situation and . . .' Evie looked over her shoulders to see who was around. One or two people were meandering amongst the book stacks quite close to them so she would have to continue to keep it down. 'About the suspected affair.'

'What finances? What affair?' asked Grace, forgetting to lower her voice in her excitement. 'And who's Olivia?'

'Shhhhh,' Kitt hissed, and kept her voice low as she spoke. 'Olivia's the shop assistant at Bootham Bar Books. She says there's all sorts of trouble brewing for the shop owners just at the minute, and she's not the only one.'

'Sounds like a lot of drama,' said Grace.

'That we agree on,' said Kitt. 'I've known them for a long time and they did seem a little bit on edge this afternoon. All three of them did, actually, Olivia included. There's definitely something amiss there.'

'Not surprising if half the town thinks their business is going under any minute,' said Evie. 'You know, the more I think about it, the more likely it seems that they might have got desperate and staged the whole thing like Derek said.'

'What's that now?' asked Grace. 'I really hate the fact that I always miss out on this stuff.'

'You don't *always* miss out,' said Kitt. 'This is only the second time we've ever looked into something like this. But sometimes it can't be helped. We have to try and stay under the radar and going round town in a gang asking questions probably isn't going to achieve that.'

'I know,' said Grace. 'I guess being filled in – no detail spared – is the next best thing.'

Kitt rolled her eyes but obliged her assistant anyway.

'God,' said Grace, once Kitt had relayed what they found out from Derek and Olivia. 'Do you think any of it's true?'

Kitt shook her head. 'If you ask me this whole thing sounds very out of character for him, and Shereen.'

'You never know what goes on though, do you?' said Evie thinking back to some of her recent experiences. 'People can often seem perfectly friendly, but you never really know what's going underneath it all. Especially in relationships. Donald and Shereen did seem like nice people but they might just be putting on a show for everyone.'

'Yes, you're right,' said Kitt. 'I suppose I just like to think of myself as a good judge of other people, and Donald never struck me as the kind of person who would stoop to that level.'

'We all like to think of ourselves as good judges of character,' said Evie.

'But when people are desperate, they do desperate things,' said Grace. 'Though one thing I don't understand is why, if they needed money, they wouldn't just sell the books at auction anyway. Surely that's easier than an insurance scam?'

'Easier maybe, but at auction you have to find a bidder willing to pay top price for the books to really make your money,' said Kitt. 'And that can take time, maybe time they don't have.'

Grace nodded, conceding Kitt's point. 'And I suppose if they were doing it for the insurance money then they might not even go to an auction house to sell the books. They might just want to make them disappear. Get rid of the evidence.'

'I hadn't thought of that,' said Kitt. 'Although, if you were going to do it, wouldn't it make sense to go for broke and get the insurance money *and* sell the books?'

'Depends on how much money you needed and how likely you thought it was that you'd get caught,' said Grace. 'If the insurance money is enough you'd be wiser to destroy those books.'

'Oh . . .' Kitt sank into her office chair. 'I feel rather faint at that thought. Imagine, first editions like that being thrown into the river or burned in a bonfire. Books deserve a better fate than that.'

What was undoubtedly about to become a mini-monologue on the sanctity of the written word was interrupted by the buzzing of Kitt's mobile. She fished it out of her pocket and scrolled down to a text message. Her shoulders drooped as she read.

'What is it?' asked Evie.

'Halloran,' said Kitt. 'The financial check on Amira Buruk – Alim's mother – turned up nothing. There's no hard evidence she orchestrated the robbery – or the beating of her son.'

Grace's eyes widened. 'The beating of her son? Surely nobody would do that to their own flesh and blood?'

'If you had met her you wouldn't think it was such an

outlandish idea,' said Evie. 'They might not have found any-thing in her finances but I'm telling you she's involved somehow.'

'Until we can prove it, there's nothing we can do. And Halloran has told us to steer clear of her anyway. Though she's never been officially charged with anything she has a reputation among the officers as a dangerous entity.'

'No financial proof and no hits at auction houses,' said Grace. 'What do we do now?'

'We keep looking,' said Evie. 'There has to be something we can find that will help Charley out.'

'I think we've already found out quite a lot,' said Kitt. 'The possibility of insurance fraud and affairs – I'll relay it all to Halloran tonight and see what he says. But for now I think the best thing we can do is go home and sleep on it.'

THIRTEEN

It had just turned afternoon when Evie awoke the next day. She'd had a fitful night's sleep and once she'd finally managed to drift off for good she had slept right through to midday. Eight straight hours was the minimum amount of sleep she could function on these days and, given the sight of her face, she reasoned she could use all the beauty sleep she could get.

On waking, her first instinct was to reach across to her phone which stood on the bedside table next to her current read: an early edition of *To Catch a Thief* that Kitt had lent from her own personal library. Evie smiled as her hand brushed past the book, remembering the personalized plate she'd discovered in the inside cover complete with an inscription that read: *From the Library of Kitt Hartley*. She supposed it was no surprise that a professional librarian kept their private collection of books in order.

Evie switched her phone on. The light from the screen

blared in the dimness of the bedroom but the message box was empty.

Still no word from Charley.

She could have sent Charley a text message, of course. In fact, that was what she would normally do, if it was anyone else. She never thought twice about texting people on the whole, especially if they were having a tough time. But somehow this wasn't the case when it came to Charley. Perhaps it was the fact that she probably had enough going on just now, without having to manage a series of questions and concerns from a person she knew very little.

Sighing and throwing her head back on the pillow, Evie thought back to the people she and Kitt had spoken to yesterday. She had hoped she might wake up this morning well-rested and full of epiphanies about the case that would save the day. But the whole thing was just a jumble.

This burglary seemed to be a case that only became more complicated the more you looked into it and this in turn probably meant that she, Grace and even Kitt were somewhat out of their depths here. Evie was struggling to put her finger on why she had been so keen to involve herself with this investigation when the police were already dealing with it, or why she cared so much for Charley's career after just a few meetings, but the truth, whatever it meant, was that she did care. Moreover, an emptiness was starting to brew in the pit of Evie's stomach. Evie would have liked to put it down to missing breakfast but she knew the real cause: the fact Charley hadn't got in touch again was getting to her, and she had to do something to take her mind off it.

Nothing else in Evie's life required quite as much concentration as keeping Jacob, the 1968 Morris Minor parked in her garage, in working order. Consequently, as soon as she could bring herself to turn out of bed, she checked the silicone sheets the doctor had prescribed for her scars were still in place after a night's sleep, pulled on a T-shirt under a pair of dungarees, and then added the thickest jumper she could find to the ensemble. Once convinced she had sufficient layers to brave the cold, she swiped a banana from the fruit basket downstairs in lieu of brunch, and shivered her way out to the garage to see how the old machine was coping in the winter conditions.

It was one of those crisp December days that might almost feel like spring if it weren't for the nip in the air. She'd have to get as much done as possible before the sun began to set; after that it would be too cold to work out here and the cosiness of the sofa and Sunday night TV would be calling to her.

Evie pulled up the garage door and smiled at the baby-blue car. Her smile faded, however, when she noticed some rust that had crept in around the headlights. 'Oh, Jacob,' she said. 'You're getting cataracts. We'll have to sort those.'

The car didn't respond.

Job one on a cold winter afternoon was getting the small portable heater in the garage working, closely followed by flicking on a transistor radio which was ever-tuned into a radio station that exclusively played 1960s music. Once those tasks were sorted and the volume had been adjusted to a pleasing level, Evie grabbed some sandpaper sitting in the toolbox – or medical kit as she called it – which she used to patch up Jacob week-to-week, and began working on the rust. After a short while she saw shiny metal break through the brown and that was her cue to apply the primer. Pushing the brush into Jacob's every nook, Evie felt a smile form on her lips. Looking after her car was even more pleasurable now than it used to be. It wasn't just her newfound singlehood. Although, she couldn't deny she missed having someone to take care of, even if her last, and now deceased, boyfriend hadn't been so good at taking care of her in return. But more than that, she was able to feel at ease in her own skin. Jacob didn't notice her scars, let alone comment on them, and that made him the best kind of company as far as Evie was concerned.

By the time she had painted and buffed up the area around the rust and completed several other maintenance tasks such as hoovering out the interior, checking over the engine to make sure he still started up all right, and taking a pit stop for some tea and a sandwich, dusk was closing in on the short, winter day.

Evie had just made a start on clearing away the rags and tools when a voice came out of nowhere.

'I didn't have you down as a mechanic.'

Evie started: it was Charley's voice. She turned to face her and then realized she must have oil and grime all over the place. She did her best to clean herself off with the back of her sleeve and pulled her curls forward a bit in the hopes of disguising the state she was in.

She glanced up at Charley to take a better look at her. She was wearing a pair of blue jeans and a leather jacket. The sharp lines of the garment somehow emphasized the softness of her face whilst also giving her the air of a woman who was ready for anything.

'I think mechanic is a bit strong,' said Evie. 'With these old things it's mostly a matter of following a set of very simple instruction manuals.'

Charley smiled. 'Sorry to drop round unannounced. I tried texting but didn't get a response so at the risk of coming across as a bit of a stalker, I thought I would swing round on the off chance you were in.'

'I don't feel stalked,' said Evie, thinking how typical it was that she had been waiting on a text from Charley for the last couple of days and the moment she put her phone down for a couple of hours, she had got in touch – a watched phone never beeps. 'And I speak as someone who has a little bit of experience in the whole "being stalked" area.'

Charley put a hand to her face. 'Oh God, sorry. I forget I shouldn't joke about things like that. It's hard not to develop a bit of a dark sense of humour, you know? My line of work.'

'It's fine, really,' said Evie. 'How are you?' I've been

thinking about you. I mean – you know, wondering how you've been getting on.'

'Aye, sorry I haven't been in touch.' Charley looked at the concrete floor of the garage for a moment and then back up at Evie. 'I've been in talks with my rep, in meetings with my superiors and in between, well, I've got a membership to that 24-hour gym on Fossgate and let's just say I find their punchbags . . . therapeutic.'

'I can imagine,' Evie said. 'You've made progress on the five stages of grief then? Denial to anger?'

'I'm not sure I even visited denial. I think anger was my first port of call and if I get to choose, I'll skip straight to acceptance,' said Charley.

Evie forced a smile. Acceptance of all that had happened to her lately, especially the life-changing injuries she'd sustained, felt so out of reach right then. If Charley could jump straight to it, maybe she would be good enough to teach Evie how.

'Anyway, enough about my unhealthy processing of work-place difficulties. I wanted to get in touch and let you know the forensics came back on the window in my garage.'

Evie's heart leaped. 'And . . .?' she said, though she could tell by the sparkle in Charley's eyes that it was good news.

'They found DNA not belonging to me on the glass and on the frame. The same traces were found on the tool box where the hammer was kept.'

'Get in!' said Evie. 'So now they have proof someone else entered your garage?'

'Yes, whoever's trying to set me up clearly isn't a professional. They've been pretty sloppy about it . . .'

'Oh that's such a relief,' Evie said, bounding up to Charley and squeezing both her hands. Then, looking down at them she added: 'Oh . . . I've made you all dirty.'

As she reached for a clean rag, Evie tried not to blush. If Kitt had said that to Halloran she would have made sure she never heard the end of it. The silence between them grew thicker. Evie's skin was tingling and she felt an unfamiliar shyness creeping in. She didn't feel she could just laugh off that comment with an attached innuendo. Probably best to move on.

'It is a bit of a relief, but there's still a lot of evidence stacked against me so I won't know until tomorrow if my suspension has been revoked.'

'Oh,' Evie said, handing Charley the rag to wipe her hands on. 'You might not want to worry so much about that.'

'How do you mean?'

'I – well, we – me and Kitt – have been asking around, here and there.'

'I know,' Charley said with a small smile. 'I spoke to Halloran over the phone at lunchtime.'

'So he told you . . .'

'Possible insurance fraud, a possible affair, it definitely helps my case for innocence that this isn't all clear cut.'

'A lot of it is just rumour, that's the thing,' said Evie.

'The rumours might not be true, but often, in investigative

work, following the rumours leads you to the ultimate truth. A lot of the time, they start because someone sees something or hears something that doesn't add up. So although the rumour itself isn't true, it suggests there is something off about that person or situation.'

Evie looked into Charley's eyes. 'So, us looking into it, that might have helped you?'

'There's certainly hope, and right now I'll actually take any excuse to celebrate. So I thought . . .' Charley produced a handsomely sized bottle of gin from the bag she was carrying, 'you might stop me being one of those sad people who drinks alone at home on a Sunday night.'

Evie smiled. 'Monday morning hangover ahoy!'

Charlie chuckled while Evie wondered why such stupid things came out of her mouth in front of her. How difficult was it to say something normal like: 'Good call, I'll get the glasses'?

'I'll order us in some food as well,' said Charley. 'There's a top Indian takeaway not far from here.'

Evie shook her head. 'You don't have to do that. I could cook something.'

'I'd rather you just relaxed with me. Looks like you've had a day of hard graft,' said Charley, with a nod towards the car.

'I wouldn't quite go that far,' said Evie, trying to use her sleeve to wipe away another smear of engine oil off her face, 'but if you insist on making my life easier, I'm not going to put up a fight about it.'

'Good girl,' Charley said through a smile.

Evie's breath caught in her throat at that comment. Charley had said it in quite an easy, casual tone but something about those words went straight to her core. Confused by this reaction, she decided to try to act breezy until she could figure out why Charley's words had had such an effect on her. Granted, the amateur dramatics she'd tried on the Buruks at the hospital hadn't panned out so well but given there were a lot of weird thoughts and feelings circulating inside just now, what else could she really do? 'I'll need to get showered and changed first though,' she said, gesturing down to her grubby dungarees.

Charley looked Evie up and down for a moment. 'Whatever makes you feel comfortable,' she said.

FOURTEEN

Evie spent much longer upstairs getting changed than she meant to. Her top priority was removing the silicone sheets from her scars and applying some of the make-up she'd bought to cover them. After that, however, things became more complicated. For some reason, she could not decide what to wear. It shouldn't have been a difficult decision given that she and Charley weren't planning anything more extravagant than sitting in front of the TV with a takeaway. If she had been doing the same thing with Kitt, she would have thrown on a pair of leggings and a hoodie but, perhaps because she didn't know Charley that well, she didn't feel comfortable wearing something that casual in her company.

Things went a bit too far in the other direction, though, when Evie tried on a vintage evening dress in blue velvet before catching her reflection in the full-length mirror and tearing the garment off as quickly as she could. Charley herself was only in a tank top and jeans. There was no way she could go downstairs dressed as if they were off to a black tie event.

In the end, Evie settled for a yellow tea dress which came just over the knee and a thick lilac cardigan to go over the top.

When she at last made it downstairs, Charley was already examining the range of trinkets on a chalk-painted wooden dresser standing in the corner. Though the officer had had cause to search Evie's house a few weeks back, she was good enough not to bring that up and behave as though this was the first time she had seen the various ornaments on display. Evie always forgot what a good conversation starter the general make-up of her house was. Most collectors of vintage items settled on one particular era. Or at the very least, one era in each room. Evie, however, had never managed to be this organized and as a result every room in the house was like wandering into an Aladdin's Cave of sorts. It still made her smile to walk into the kitchen and see retro Babycham glasses sitting next to a Victorian tea-set. Any company she had never failed to comment on the strange assortment of wonders. The living room housed everything from a 1930s gramophone to the chaise longue Charley stretched herself out on the moment Evie made it clear it would be polite enough to do so.

Evie hoped the pair would talk some more about the burglary case to see if there was a way forward, but it was quickly apparent Banks would rather be talking about lighter topics. Thus, once they had exhausted the stories of just about every piece of furniture in the room, the pair somehow got onto childhood stories and it wasn't long after that that Evie found herself in a fit of hysterics, clutching her stomach. She couldn't remember the last time she had laughed this hard. Weeks and weeks, it seemed. Her cheekbones and her ribs ached, pleading for mercy.

'Wh-wh-what did your dad do?' asked Evie, in response to Charley's story about the time she'd cracked an egg on her dad's bald head while he was sitting in the living room watching the darts one Saturday afternoon.

Charley wiped small tears from her own eyes and tried to contain her own laughter enough to speak again. 'Oh, he went nuts. I got a real hiding for it. But in his defence, I think that's the sort of behaviour you've got to clamp down on. You can't have your bairns cracking eggs on the heads of bald strangers just for laughs. You can get into real trouble for stuff like that, especially in Glasgow.'

Evie started giggling again. 'I – I just wish I could have seen his face.'

'It was dark as thunder, I can tell you that. I thought it might be my last act on this planet.'

'But you survived,' Evie said, before reaching over to the mahogany coffee table sitting at the side of the sofa, tearing off another piece of the naan bread, and shoving it into her mouth. The gin made her worry less about the calories. Evie knew from previous occasions that there was a definite correlation between a person's alcohol consumption and their disregard for calorie intake but whenever this thought had occurred to her she had always been too intoxicated to set it out in her head as a measurable formula.

'Yes, I did survive,' said Banks. 'If there's one thing I've learned doing what I do, it's that it's amazing what people can survive.'

Evie's giggles fizzled out and she felt the smile drop off her face.

'Everything all right over there?' asked Charley, from her lolling position on the chaise longue, which was cushioned in green velvet.

Evie nodded and tried to smile even though she felt the sudden and ridiculous urge to cry. How could she swing between emotions so violently? Was it the gin having its way with her? She dare not look at Charley for fear she would see how close she was to tears.

'Oh, Evie . . .' The hard notes in Charley's accent had softened. It seemed Evie hadn't even had to look at Charley for her to know that something was wrong. When Evie thought about it, that made sense. She was a detective. She was highly unlikely to miss the small details.

Charley manoeuvred herself into a sitting position and looked harder at Evie. 'What's going on? Is it . . . are you still hurting over Owen?'

'No . . .' said Evie, feeling a sudden chill, despite the central heating, and wrapping her arms around herself to compensate. 'I mean, I still feel bad about what happened to him but I could feel a lot worse if I were a better person.'

Banks shook her head. 'That's just blether. You're one of the nicest people I know.'

'And yet, all I've thought about since Owen's death is myself, how it's affecting me,' said Evie.

'I don't believe that's true. And even if it was, being accused of a person's murder will do that for you; self-preservation kicks in. It's not something you should be beating yourself up over.' Charley paused and took another gulp of her gin. 'If you're not feeling so badly about Owen, I'm glad. But I would like to know what is causing you worry . . .'

Evie shook her head. 'It's difficult to talk about.'

'So are a lot of things. You don't think I tell everyone about cracking an egg on my dad's head now, do you?'

In spite of herself, Evie smiled again at that image but then let out a sigh.

'You don't have to tell me, of course you don't,' said Charley. 'It's just that telling people about something that's bothering you is often the first step on the road to feeling better about it.'

'I know, you're right,' said Evie. 'It's just a bit embarrassing.'

'You don't have to be embarrassed with me.'

Evie looked over at Charley then, wondering if that were true. Evie felt more embarrassed around the officer than she did around anyone else she knew and she couldn't understand why. Determined to push through this strange, and unnecessary, shyness around someone who had been nothing but kind to her, Evie ran her fingertips over the scars on her temple and jaw. 'It's . . . it's these.'

As she touched her scars, the urge to cry grew even stronger. When she sank into that river, she had soaked up grief like a sponge. Now it was squeezing out of her.

Charley was quiet for a moment and then stood. She walked over to the sofa and sat on the arm. Leaning down, she brushed Evie's face with her hand, swiping off a few of her tears as she did so. 'These? I think these make you look rather dashing. Like you've had an adventure or two.'

Evie frowned. Never had she thought of her scars in that light. She thought about the men she'd fancied over the years, some of whom had had scars. Some had even had them on their faces. They weren't as severe as her scars but they were still more than noticeable. It hadn't stopped her dating them. So why did she believe other people wouldn't look past her scars as she had theirs?

'The scars, they're part of you now,' Charley said.

Charley was sitting close enough for Evie to breathe in her perfume. It had a dark, fruity flavour to it. 'I just can't see anything beautiful when I look in the mirror any more. When I look at myself all I see is the scars.'

With a sigh, Charley rose once again, took a couple of paces away from the sofa and turned her back to Evie.

'Lots of us have scars,' she said, crossing her arm over

her body and tugging up her black tank top to reveal the cinch point where her waist curved in and then jutted out at her hip. A long, white scar slashed across her tanned skin, cutting upwards towards the base of her shoulder blades.

Distracted from her tears, Evie stood and took a step closer to examine Charley's body. 'What happened?'

'Trained as a copper in Glasgow. A lot of knives in Glasgow. This one was like a machete. I was lucky not to bleed to death.'

'God. I – I'm glad you didn't,' said Evie swallowing hard and staring at the scar. She knew the pain of that kind of cut. How deep it went. How much it hurt. 'I mean, that would have been very inconsiderate of you. If you weren't around I'd have to drink this bottle of gin myself. And that wouldn't be pretty.'

Charley turned her head so that Evie could see her smile in profile. 'Don't sell yourself short.'

The strange tingling Evie had felt earlier out in the garage returned now. 'At least you can hide your scars if you want to – that's something to be thankful for.'

'This doesn't stop me wearing a bikini, you know?'

Evie took a deep breath, giving herself just a second to imagine Charley in a bikini. 'Not much bikini weather going on in York anyway, but it's good that you seize the opportunity when you can.'

Charley didn't laugh. 'Evie, your scars aren't ugly. They're like tattoos. Tattoos that mark your survival.' She began to lower her tank top but Evie reached out, putting her hand on top of Charley's to stop her. She wasn't finished looking at the way the silver river wound across the plain of Charley's waistline. She traced her fingertips along the scar that passed under her own jaw and then along the path Charley's scar marked out on her bared back.

A shiver pulsed through Charley's body.

'Oh . . . sorry,' Evie said, snatching her hand away.

'No.' There was a shake to Charley's voice. 'I liked that.'

Evie's breathing deepened. She had liked that too. Liked touching Charley. Liked feeling the warmth of her skin, there was something reassuring about how firm she was.

Evie's hand reached out a second time, her fingertips once again grazed that silver scar and she watched as Charley's back arched.

The smallest touch from Evie had made Charley bend with pleasure. Evie's stomach turned over at that thought. Something about that idea made her feel more powerful than she ever had before.

'I want to . . . kiss it,' she heard herself say.

For a moment, Evie wasn't sure if it was her talking or the gin. But when Charley, without a word, lifted her top over her head in a slow striptease Evie's eyes fixed on the muscular shape of Charley's upper torso. Inch by inch, it slid into view and it was then Evie knew that the words had belonged to her, completely.

'Then kiss it,' said Charley, her words still coming out with a noticeable quiver. 'Kiss . . . me.'

Evie took another step closer and stared at the back of Charley's black bra. Her eyes riveted on the clasp, her mind absorbed by the joyous thought of undoing it. She had never been this eager to take clothes off a man. It was an unspoken opinion of hers that men were designed in such a way that they looked better with their clothes on. It wasn't until now that she realized that might be a rather odd thought for a heterosexual woman to have, which was perhaps why she had never voiced it to anyone.

Leaning forward, Evie pressed her lips against the scar.

'Oh God,' Charley whispered. 'Is this really happening?'

This comment made Evie smile. She circled her tongue around the swerve of Charley's hip, kissing her there the way she wanted to kiss her on the mouth.

Looking up, she saw Charley's charcoal eyes smouldering down into hers. Charley's hands stroked blonde curls as Evie kissed upwards from her navel to the point between her breasts.

Gasping, Charley put a hand on either side of Evie's head and pulled her face close enough to kiss. Instead of leaning forward so that their lips could meet, however, she tilted Evie's head back and stared into her eyes.

'Are you sure you want this?' Charley asked.

The bigger implications of that question made Evie feel dizzy. She didn't want to think about them right now. The question was: did she want this, and right now she did. She ached to be tangled up in a tight knot with Charley long enough to forget everything and everybody else.

'Yes,' Evie said with a nod. 'I want this . . . I want you.'

She saw a small smile creep over Charley's lips.

'Arms up.'

'Am I . . . under arrest for kissing an officer?' Evie said, smiling herself now.

'Arms . . . up,' Charley repeated in a voice so soft, Evie couldn't help but comply. She raised her arms in the air, her heart thumping as she watched Charley lean down to catch hold of the hemline of her tea dress and begin to lift the skirt.

FIFTEEN

The lush, fruity fragrance of another body in her bed was the first thing Evie noticed when she awoke the next morning. The first clue that what had happened the night before hadn't been a dream. The first hint that she might have to work through the consequences of what had, at the time, seemed like a dizzyingly stellar idea.

The next thing she was aware of was a buzzing sound. She groaned and reached over to her phone on the bedside table even though some part of her already knew that the rhythm of the vibration was different to that of her own phone. Sure enough, there was no sound or movement from her mobile.

Evie could feel Charley's body starting to stir. That soft, warm body that had been such a comfort and a delight the night before. Taking a deep breath, she turned over to look at her.

In the rose quartz light sifting through the curtains, Evie was able to make out that Charley's hair was tangled after a wild night of little sleep. Her eyes were half-closed. More than anything, she wanted to lean over and kiss her awake but she managed to check herself. To shuffle backwards so that there was a little distance between her body and Charley's before she spoke.

'I think that's your phone,' Evie said, just as the buzzing stopped.

Charley put a hand up to cover her eyes but a small smile formed on her lips. 'Good morning to you too.'

'Sorry, I thought it might be important police business. I have to get into work, myself.'

Charley's smile disappeared, something about those words had jolted her from her half-daze and she reached her hand up to Evie's cheek. 'Are you OK?'

'I'm fine.'

'Your boyfriends may have bought that but I'm not them. I'm a woman. I know what "I'm fine" really means.'

'I'm fine, really,' Evie insisted, shaking her head and shaking off Charley's hand too. 'Just need to use the facilities.'

Evie sat up to manoeuvre herself out of bed and realized, just as the bedsheets slipped downwards, that she wasn't wearing any pyjamas. She wasn't, in fact, wearing anything at all.

She squealed, and grabbed the sheet to cover herself up as quick as her hands would move. Ensuring one hand was gripped tight around the bedding, she covered her face with the other and let out a nervous giggle. 'Oh my God, I'm sorry. I didn't mean to flash you.'

'You're not going to hear any complaints from me,' Charley said with an amused note in her voice.

Goosebumps rose on Evie's skin at that comment but still she pulled the covers up to her neck and said: 'Could . . . could you not look?'

Charley lowered her eyes and nodded. 'Whatever makes you feel comfortable.'

Evie could hear the disappointment in Charley's voice but she didn't have the head space to process that right now. This was totally new to her and she wasn't sure she liked it. Or perhaps she was sure she liked it, but she wasn't sure she wanted to.

Charley turned her back to Evie and picked her phone up off the bedside table. The moment Charley's eyes were averted, Evie made a dash for her dressing gown and then the bathroom.

Evie locked the door and leant her back against it. She caught her reflection in the small mirror fitted over the sink and peered more closely at herself.

She looked a fright. Her hair was stuck out at angles she didn't know were physically possible, and in her drunkenness she hadn't thought to remove the make-up she'd slapped on the night before so her mascara had formed a dark, menacing line under each eye. She looked like she was moonlighting as a villain in a Star Wars film. Her foundation, meanwhile, had almost completely evaporated so her scars were on full show.

Evie ran some water and splashed it over her face. Grabbing the soap bar, she did what she could to get rid of the dark lines under her eyes and then concentrated on trying to arrange her hair as neatly she could over her scars.

Now that it was possible to look at her own reflection without cringing, it was also possible to work out a plan on handling the situation she'd got herself into.

'Just . . . be honest,' Evie said to her reflection. 'Not too honest but just the right amount of honest.' She wasn't sure what the right amount of honest was in this scenario but she couldn't let Charley think that this was the start of something.

Yes, last night had been great. Better than great, actually. Probably the most fulfilling sexual experience Evie had ever had but that was probably fuelled part by curiosity and part by how vulnerable she had been feeling about her appearance. Of course it felt extra-intense to receive sexual attention when she had thought she would never receive any again. But this was a blip. Just one of those things. Not something she planned on repeating.

Taking a deep breath, Evie opened the bathroom door and returned to the bedroom. She was surprised to see Charley was already dressed.

Evie tried not to focus on how beautiful she found her in that moment. Right now, she needed to focus on letting

Charley down easy, and above all else not saying or doing something that would make her feel as though she had been used.

'That was work,' Charley said. 'I just called them back. I've been reinstated.'

'That's great news,' Evie said, for a moment forgetting herself and rushing towards Charley. She stopped herself after a few paces and smiled. 'I'm so pleased this nightmare is over for you.'

'Not quite,' said Charley. 'I've been put on desk duty until the matter has been fully investigated. The DNA at the garage has put enough doubt on Alim's testimony that they can't rightfully keep the suspension in place, especially given my impeccable record.'

'Oh,' said Evie. 'So, you're still in a little bit of hot water.'

'You could put it that way. But if I keep my head down and get on with whatever mind-numbing admin they push my way, I might win some favour with Ricci.'

'She creeps me out,' said Evie. A little shudder ran through her as she remembered how she had asked about her scars. She felt again what she felt in that moment: the blunt force of shame.

'She's not my favourite person either, but she's in charge now and I've got to do whatever I can to help my situation.'

Evie nodded. 'About last night ... I had ... such a wonderful time with you,' she said, making sure she held Charley's gaze. 'I'm sure you could probably tell.'

Charley half-smiled, but there was a watery look in her eyes. 'You seemed to be having a good time.'

'I was,' said Evie. 'It's just, I've never done anything like that before. I'm . . . I'm sure that showed too.'

'Not particularly,' said Charley, taking a step closer. 'But perhaps what happened last night just felt natural to you.'

Evie felt her cheeks reddening. Being with Charley had been easy. She hadn't felt self-conscious or unsure, and there hadn't been a need to fake anything. Still, she couldn't just leap into this, or anything like this. It was just too . . . strange and unexpected.

'I think maybe you're just a good teacher,' Evie said.

'Who can recognize natural talent when she sees it,' said Charley, the smile on her lips broadening.

'I'm sure,' said Evie. 'But I don't really know what happened last night. This just isn't me. It's not what I . . . do.'

'Are you sure?' Charley asked, taking yet another step closer to Evie so the pair were now standing just a pace apart.

'Yes,' said Evie. 'I don't think it should happen again. It was lovely but it was just for last night.'

Charley's eyes lowered to the carpet and she sighed. 'Can I say something now?'

'Yes, I will allow it,' Evie said, trying to lighten the mood.

'Unlike you, last night wasn't my first time with a woman. And I can tell you, it doesn't always feel like that for me. It . . .' Charley seemed on the brink of saying something but paused mid-sentence. 'It's rare for two people to have this kind of chemistry, that's all I'm saying.'

Slowly, Evie crossed her arms. 'I hear you. But, I'm sorry, I just can't. It doesn't feel right to me.'

Charley didn't say anything else. She nodded and then gave Evie what could only be described as the kind of smile a stranger might give if they bumped into another in the street. Slowly, she walked past Evie and out the bedroom door.

Evie listened to Charley's footsteps descending the stairs and waited for the inevitable slam of the front door. The second she heard that thud, she slumped down on the end of the bed while slow, silent tears slipped down her cheeks.

What was wrong with her? What the hell had she been thinking? Why had she done this with Charley in the first place?

Evie could think of quite a few different answers to these questions but she didn't like any of them. Consequently, she reached over to her phone resting on her bedside table and began to type a text message to Kitt.

SIXTEEN

'Did you know lesbian couples have the best sex?' said Evie, before Kitt had even sat down with her cup of Lady Grey in the second-floor office of the library.

Kitt gave her friend a lengthy stare, before taking a seat in one of the shabby, floral armchairs. 'While I appreciate your attempts to keep the conversation between us lively after all these years of friendship, it is customary to ease into a topic like that. Perhaps start with some idle chit-chat about the weather, and then broach the topic of lesbian sex.'

Evie smirked. 'Sorry, I read an article about it on the *Guardian* website on my lunch break today and I can't get it out of my head.' Of course, it wasn't like she'd happened across this article by accident. She had typed 'the truth about lesbian sex' into Google.

Kitt narrowed her eyes and placed her teacup on the table in front of them, next to a stack of books that someone had abandoned without note or explanation. 'You're fooling nobody, you know?'

'What?' Evie said, her body stiffening. 'What do you mean?

'I mean, you're talking to a librarian turned detective here,' Kitt said, pointing her thumb at herself.

Kitt had never referred to herself in this manner before. Perhaps she had been enjoying their latest investigation more than she was letting on.

'Nothing gets past me,' Kitt continued. 'Just ask Grace. And if you think starting a conversation about girl-on-girl-action is subtle, you need to look up the word subtle.'

Evie didn't dare move. She felt any gesture might give away more than she would like, though it seemed her mouth had done that for her already. 'What are you suggesting?'

'Oh, nothing too much really,' Kitt said, stirring her tea even though it didn't need stirring. 'Just that you've shown more than a passing interest in a certain female officer of our acquaintance.'

Evie felt the blood rushing to her cheeks and knew Kitt couldn't have failed to notice.

'Text messages, meetings at the Christmas Fayre, launching your own investigation to overturn her suspension, masquerading as me down at the hospital in a bid to get answers, getting all shiny-eyed whenever her name gets mentioned –'

'All right,' said Evie, unable to listen to any more of the damning evidence. 'I did it. I slept with Charley.'

There was a pause and Kitt slowly raised her eyebrows.

'Well, I was just going to tease you about having taken a shine to her. But this is much more exciting. When did this happen?'

'Last night,' Evie said in the smallest voice she ever remembered using.

'And, was the *Guardian* right in its assessment?' Kitt asked.

'You're enjoying this . . .'

'Too right I am. Just as you enjoyed teasing the life out of me before me and Halloran made things official.'

'This is different.'

'Why?'

'Because . . . making it official with Halloran didn't involve a major lifestyle choice.'

Kitt offered a playful smile that Evie had never seen before the librarian had crossed paths with Halloran. 'That remains to be seen.'

Then it was Evie's turn to narrow her eyes. She was about to ask what that was supposed to mean but Kitt gave a dismissive wave, indicating she wouldn't be drawn.

'Aren't you at least a bit shocked?'

'Not really.'

Looking at her friend, Evie could see this was true. Her face was completely level and she took another sip of her tea as though Evie had told her she had found some cut-price lamb at the supermarket rather than having confessed that she had slept with a woman for the first time. 'Well, I am,' Evie said.

'Was it really so out of the blue?' asked Kitt. 'I've never really heard you talk positively about the sex you've had with men.'

'That's not true, there was . . .' Evie paused. 'Well . . . what about . . .' Again she found herself lost for words. 'Well, it was always over so quick it was difficult to form a proper opinion.' She covered her face with her hands. 'Oh God, am I the only one who couldn't see this coming?'

'No . . . but your concerning obsession with innuendo was a clue that perhaps you were missing out on something.'

Evie's head jerked back an inch. 'Do you really think that finding the right partner is going to curb the innuendo?'

'No. But the hope lives on.' Kitt looked hard and long at her friend. 'You seem pretty rattled. Are you afraid of something?'

'Yes!' said Evie. 'Not least what it says about me that I got to the age of thirty-three and never even entertained the possibility that I might be gay.'

'Never?'

'Well . . . there was the odd . . . thought. In the privacy of my own bedroom. But everyone has thoughts like that sometimes, don't they?'

'Almost everyone has thoughts about sexuality, though the content often differs.'

Evie sighed.

'Just give yourself some time,' said Kitt. 'Sometimes it's not about thinking, but feeling. Rather than piling pressure on yourself, you might be better off just enjoying the gift of a pleasurable sexual experience.'

The second these words left her mouth the office door swung open and Halloran stepped through it.

The inspector smiled between Kitt and Evie, raised an eyebrow as he stepped in and closed the door behind him. 'Sounds like an interesting conversation?'

Evie's stomach tightened – for a second she thought that Kitt might actually tell Halloran and that if she did it might get back to Charley that she had been gossiping about what happened between them. But she should have known better. Kitt wasn't one for sharing secrets that weren't her place to share.

'Oh, just the usual womanly chit-chat. Manicures, yoga positions and the inconsistency of men,' Kitt said, bringing her teacup to her lips to try to hide a smile. Whenever Halloran was in the room however, the smile was visible in Kitt's eyes, if not on her lips.

'Books would have been a more believable lie,' said Halloran, crossing his arms and staring at his girlfriend.

'I thought we were meeting at the cottage in a couple of hours?' said Kitt.

'We were but something's come up with Banks's case. Things have got worse.'

'Worse how?' asked Evie, her thoughts dashing back to Charley and the way she had left things between them this morning. She had started the day by being brushed off by Evie, and had only a return to desk duty as a consolation. It wasn't fair for the work situation to get worse. Things were supposed to be looking up for her.

'Alim Buruk is dead.'

SEVENTEEN

'Dead?' said Kitt, at last finding her voice. 'But his injuries weren't that bad.'

Halloran shook his head. 'He's been murdered.'

At those words Evie felt her whole body start to shake. She had only just begun healing since the last time Halloran walked into a room and told her someone had been murdered. Things like this weren't supposed to happen in York. Saturday nights aside, it was quaint and quiet. She looked over at Kitt to see her friend taking some deep breaths. But Halloran wasn't finished.

'And in what is unlikely to be a coincidence Donald Oakes has been reported as missing.'

'What? Donald? When did he . . .' said Kitt, but then stopped herself. 'No, wait. I've got to try and handle this logically if I'm to . . .'

Halloran frowned. 'If you're to what?'

'Nothing,' Kitt said. 'If I'm to get it all straight in my head, that's all. Start with Alim. Murdered, how?'

'Somebody tampered with his IV in hospital. He died of a sodium overdose. Cardiac arrest.'

'Oh my God,' said Evie, running her fingers through her hair. 'He was only young. Twenty-five, if that. What a waste of a life.'

'I know,' said Halloran. 'Percival, Wilkinson and Ricci visited him just this morning. Percival and Ricci would usually leave that kind of work to us but they wanted to underline the complaint against Banks was being taken seriously and, in light of the DNA found in Banks's garage, wanted to go over his statement for themselves. See if he wanted to revise anything. They didn't get anything concrete but they felt they were making some progress with him. Getting close to coaxing him into revealing something important about the case.'

'And the next thing we know he's dead,' said Kitt.

'And Donald Oakes is reported missing.'

'Oh no,' said Kitt, shaking her head. 'You don't think . . .'

'I'm reserving judgement,' said Halloran, 'but the timing doesn't look good.'

'But was there anything at the scene that pointed to Donald's involvement?' said Kitt.

Halloran shook his head. 'Not as yet. We've been through the footage of the hospital entrance and couldn't place him there during the six-hour window we're looking at. But we are still waiting on forensics to come back.'

'So you can't place him there,' said Kitt. 'And if he did do it, wouldn't it be a bit silly of him to disappear? Doesn't it just make him look guilty? He would have been better off taking his chances that you wouldn't find out it was him than to run.'

'Planning a murder, and carrying it out are two very different things,' said Halloran. 'When a person realizes what they have actually done it can lead to all kinds of irrational behaviour. Which is usually how they get caught.'

'So you think Donald has gone full Lady Macbeth?' Kitt said.

'As I said, I'm reserving judgement.'

'What's Donald's motive for killing Alim? Burgling his bookshop? Why not just take whatever evidence he had to the police?' asked Evie.

'That's not the most likely scenario, given what you and Kitt have gleaned over the past few days.'

Evie frowned. 'How do you mean?'

'It's not the only possibility but there's a stronger chance that Donald orchestrated the robbery for the insurance, thought Alim was going to give him up and killed him before he could,' said Halloran.

'But Donald wouldn't kill anyone,' said Kitt. 'I can't believe that.'

Halloran sighed. 'None of us want to believe it of someone

we know, pet. But sometimes people do desperate things. I'm not suggesting he's evil.'

'All right, I need to think about this,' said Kitt. 'Who found Alim's body?'

'He died while his mother was visiting him,' said Halloran. 'She called for help but the medical staff couldn't save him.'

'His mother?' said Evie. 'She was there when it happened?'

'Yes,' said Halloran. 'But an IV slowly releases fluid into the body. It would take hours for the sodium overdose to take hold. The best we can do is narrow it down to between the last time his IV was changed to his time of death. That gives us a six-hour window. From nine this morning until about three this afternoon. His mother only arrived at the hospital fifteen minutes before he died. That wouldn't be long enough for the overdose to flood through his system. If she had tampered with his IV then he would have died much later.'

'Fifteen minutes,' said Evie, 'almost like she knew when he was likely to die and went to say her last goodbyes.'

'The timing is a bit suspicious even if she didn't poison her son for herself,' said Kitt. 'What if she got someone else to do it and she was visiting him so she could be with him in the end, knowing roughly when his time would be up?'

'We're talking about a mother killing her son,' said Halloran.

'Amira Buruk isn't your average mother though, at least not from my experience of her,' said Evie.

'And you said yourself, Mal, there's no real telling what she's capable of. "Dangerous entity", that's the wording you used. If she knew that Percival, Ricci and Wilkinson were getting close to the truth, if she thought her son was going to give in to pressure from the police, she might have taken drastic measures.'

'She hasn't been discounted as a suspect,' said Halloran. 'And we're trying to get a sense of who else visited Alim this morning. But right now Donald Oakes's disappearance is even more dubious than Amira Buruk's general disposition or anything else related.'

'Donald . . .' said Kitt, shaking her head. 'How long has he been missing?'

'His wife hasn't seen him since she left the bookshop yesterday. She left him to close up but he sent her a text message a couple of hours later to say he was going out for a pint with some friends. He never came home.'

'What about his friends, did they see him last night?' asked Kitt.

'His wife got in touch with all of his regular drinking buddies before she got in touch with us. None of them went out with him last night.'

'But if Donald's been missing since last night, how could he have killed Alim?' asked Evie.

'He hasn't been seen by his friends or family since last night,' said Halloran. 'It doesn't mean he's not in the area and if I knew I was going to commit a murder the next day,

I probably wouldn't want friends or family around me in the run-up to it either.'

'But doesn't he have to be missing twenty-four hours before he can be presumed a missing person? Perhaps there's some explanation?' Kitt asked.

'Under ordinary circumstances that'd be true. But with the death of Alim, and the fact we still haven't arrested the culprits of the robbery, we have to take it as a serious development in the case, and Banks . . .'

'What about her?' said Evie.

'Ricci hasn't said as much but given how quick she was to suspend Banks when this was just a burglary case, she might suspect foul play.'

'How do you mean?' asked Kitt.

'If we don't catch up with Oakes soon, Ricci might start looking at Banks again. Might suspect her of shutting down Oakes and Buruk for good. If that happens, I can only hope she's more forthcoming with Ricci than she was with me.'

'She's being evasive?' said Kitt.

'Banks wouldn't tell me where she was last night when Donald went missing.'

Slowly, Evie looked over at Kitt and when she did she found her friend's eyes were already on her.

'What? What is it?' asked Halloran. 'Do you know something about all this that I don't?'

It felt as though the temperature in the room was rising with every passing moment. 'Charley didn't tell you where she was last night because she was being discreet,' she said, lowering her eyes to the carpet. 'She was with me.'

'You saw Banks last night?' said Halloran.

'Yes, she was at my house.'

'All night?'

Evie paused. 'Yes.'

'I see.'

Evie raised her eyes to meet the inspector's stare. He gave a gentle nod then, confirming that he did see, entirely.

'Will it help if I make a statement?' asked Evie.

'We're not there yet,' said Halloran. 'But if Ricci goes so far as to accuse Banks of anything, it will be good for her to know she can rely on your alibi.'

'She can,' said Evie.

'Can't CCTV footage shed some light on what happened to both Alim and Donald?' asked Kitt. Evie wasn't sure if Kitt was deliberately moving the conversation away from the exact nature of Charley's visit, but either way she was relieved to not have to say any more about it just now.

'We've got people checking through the footage from the hospital entrance and the traffic cameras at Bootham Bar,' said Halloran.

'You have? Has Ricci let you both continue working on this case?' said Kitt.

Halloran nodded. 'When the DNA was found in Banks's garage, she made a personal appeal to Ricci. Convinced her somehow to allow us back on the case. She has an impeccable service record up until now, which might be why Ricci granted the request. Or it might be because the situation has escalated. Whatever the reason, we are now both allowed to investigate further.'

'That's good news, isn't it?' said Kitt.

'Possibly. We're always short on resources so it might be that Ricci didn't have much of a choice but to reinstate us. There is, however, another possibility.'

'What's that?' said Kitt.

'She might have let us back on the case purely to monitor us. There's a chance she's also got the anti-corruption unit on our backs.'

'Neither of you have anything to hide though,' said Kitt. 'So, if that's her game, she won't find anything untoward.'

'No, except perhaps my communications with you about the case,' said Halloran. 'I'll be looking at disciplinary action if anyone finds out the things I've told you. The people at the top won't care how helpful you've been. Or how discreet.'

'I know you put a lot on the line when you share things with us,' said Kitt, 'but please don't tell me you're here to say that we have to stay away from the case. Not when someone I've known for almost all the time I've lived in York is missing.'

'No, I'm not here to do that,' said Halloran. 'I tried that last time and it got me nowhere. I know even if I tell you to stay out of it, you're going to investigate it anyway because you feel a personal involvement, and frankly I've never known anyone as curious as you.'

'I'm choosing to take that as a compliment,' Kitt said, her nose crinkling.

Halloran continued. 'But I'm going to have to be really careful about what information I share with you and you are going to have to watch your step twice as much as you were before. If Ricci even gets a sniff of what you're doing, it could be the end of my career, and Banks's too.'

'I have no desire to get you into any trouble at work,' said Kitt. 'But Donald's disappearance is very concerning.'

'Hmm,' said Evie.

'What?' asked Kitt.

'Shereen is reported to have had a blazing row with her husband about an affair and then a couple of days later, her husband goes missing,' said Evie.

'You're not suggesting Shereen is behind Donald's disappearance?' said Kitt.

'Why not?'

'Besides the fact that I've known her for donkey's years, she would have to overpower Donald. He's not a big man but I'm not convinced she could lift him even if she did knock him out.'

'But she wouldn't be working alone. It's in someone else's interests to get Donald out of the picture,' said Evie.

'The person she's having the affair with,' said Kitt.

'He could have helped her get rid of Donald, and that way

she could keep all of the insurance money to herself and start a new life with her lover.'

'*The Mysterious Affair at Styles*,' said Kitt.

Evie frowned at Halloran but he just shook his head to indicate this meant nothing to him either. 'What's that, old chum?' said Evie.

'Classic Agatha Christie,' said Kitt. 'The murderers are two people having an affair. They kill the gentleman's wife so they can be together but try and pin it on lots of other people so the evidence doesn't point to them.'

'Maybe Shereen and whoever she's having an affair with are playing the same game?' said Evie.

'If that's the case, you're saying that Shereen is behind the disappearance of the books as well as the disappearance of her husband?'

'It makes sense,' said Evie. 'She put all those years into the business with Donald but it never really made them enough money. She meets someone new and wants to start a new life with them but divorce is costly and the business isn't worth carving up anyway.'

'But then she realizes there is something in her possession that is worth a bit of money,' said Kitt. 'The first edition books that have never sold.'

'She tries to convince Donald to put them into an auction but for some reason he resists,' said Evie.

'So instead she orchestrates a robbery for the insurance money without Donald's knowledge,' said Kitt.

'He finds some clue, some piece of evidence that suggests she's having an affair and perhaps that's not all he suspects. Shereen realizes he knows too much and might go to the police with what he knows.'

'So she begs her new lover to get rid of Donald so that they can enjoy the insurance money to themselves.'

'An interesting story,' said Halloran, with a vague smile. 'But investigations are reliant on evidence and without a body, there's no murder. At present, we've got to focus on the body we have got – Alim Buruk's.'

'So you're discounting Shereen for now?' said Kitt.

'We don't have any evidence of this alleged affair,' said Halloran. 'But alongside running down leads on any visitors Alim had, we can look into Shereen's phone records. If she was having an affair with someone it's very likely she sent them text messages or called them on a semi-regular basis.'

'In the meantime,' said Kitt, 'we should maybe find out what other rumours – if any – are circulating about Donald and Shereen.'

'How are you going to do that?' asked Halloran.

'Oh, I have my ways,' Kitt said.

EIGHTEEN

Evie yawned as the 59 bus pulled up to the stop on Piccadilly. It was nearing ten a.m., which was late enough in the day for the morning frost to have melted off the pavements but was still earlier than she liked to rise when she wasn't due into the salon until the afternoon.

Following the death of Alim and the disappearance of Donald, Kitt had swapped her morning shift at the library to an afternoon shift so that she and Evie could do a bit more digging around Shereen and Bootham Bar Books. Kitt's plan to gather intel, however, hadn't quite been what Evie was expecting.

'Do you really think we're going to crack the case by taking a ride on the 59?' said Evie, as she fished some change out of her bag to pay the driver.

'According to Ruby, there's nothing going on in town that you can't learn about on the 59 bus,' said Kitt, stepping on and paying her fare. 'Just please don't tell Ruby that we've resorted to this, otherwise she'll think there's real hope that I'll let her read my tarot cards one day.'

No sooner had these words left Kitt's mouth than a familiar "Ello, love,' carried down the central aisle of the vehicle.

Evie and Kitt turned to see Ruby sitting in one of the window seats about halfway up the bus. Evie couldn't help but smile but Kitt looked less than amused that they were going to have outside interference on their quest to find out more about Shereen. It would be impolite to sit away from Ruby when she was always so friendly but at the same time they didn't want her to find out more about the Bootham Bar Books case than she should.

The bus rumbled to a start and Kitt walked briskly to a seat just behind the old woman in the hopes of winning the usual race against the driver and trying to sit down before he set off.

'What brings you out in this direction?' Ruby asked Kitt.

'Oh, we just fancied a ride out,' said Kitt. 'It's a bit cold for walking around and chatting today so we thought we'd hop on the bus and take in our beloved city that way.'

Evie looked at Ruby, unsure whether anyone would buy that story. So far, Kitt had been able to come up with smarter or more convincing excuses than that when they had been investigating things they perhaps shouldn't be. Still, nobody's mind can be sharp all the time.

'Oh aye?' said Ruby, with a note of suspicion in her voice. 'Would have thought there were more scenic routes than the 59, like.'

'Nonsense. Who doesn't like . . .' Kitt rubbed the steamy bus window with the sleeve of her winter coat and squinted through the glass, 'the poetry of empty warehouses and the stark lines of that dilapidated pub.'

'Ooh, and look, there's that swanky new boxpark thing,' Evie chimed in.

'Yes, rather simplistic in design,' said Kitt, 'but it's not without aesthetic appeal.'

Ruby stared at Kitt.

'Oh all right,' said the librarian. 'We were looking for a bit of information.'

Ruby grinned. 'You've come to the right place. Information about what?'

'We heard a rumour that we're hoping isn't true.'

'What's that?'

'I won't be a person who spreads idle gossip,' said Kitt. 'But I will tell you who it concerns and if you know anything, perhaps you might tell us if you've heard anything yourself recently?'

'All right, I'll give it a go,' said Ruby.

'You know Bootham Bar Books?'

'Aye, I've been in once or twice.'

'Well, we've been hearing some unfortunate rumours about Shereen Oakes, who part owns the business with her husband. I've been a friend of Shereen's for years and am hoping that the rumours are all wrong.'

'Hmmm,' said Ruby. 'I've not heard a thing about her.'

'This was a fool's plan,' Kitt muttered under her breath to Evie.

'It was your plan,' Evie muttered back.

'Hang on, hang on,' said Ruby. 'I'm not the only one on the bus, you know. 'Ere, Margaret!' The old woman called to another lady sitting across from them on the other side of the aisle, wearing a brown floral headscarf and a green duffel coat.

'What are you doing?' Kitt hissed.

'Do you want the truth or not?' said Ruby.

Kitt looked across at Evie. Evie shrugged. It was too late to stop this now. They would just have to try to laugh it off as no big deal if it got out of hand.

'What's the matter?' said Margaret, as though Ruby had interrupted something much more important than her sitting alone on a bus, staring into space.

'Bootham Bar Books ... heard anything?'

Margaret shook her head. 'Not heard owt about it, should I have?'

'No, no, never mind,' said Ruby.

Evie watched as Kitt issued what could only be described as a sigh of relief but her reprieve was short as Ruby began calling up the bus behind her. A series of names, one after the other. Judy, Parveen, Lionel, Kenneth, Rita. With each one Kitt winced. Under any other circumstances, Evie would have found the situation highly entertaining. There was nothing much funnier than watching the somewhat strait-laced Kitt in an awkward situation. But given that it could backfire badly for Charley if their amateur investigation spun out of control, Evie wasn't finding it so funny just now.

She was just about to open her mouth and suggest to Ruby that she had probably asked around enough when a white-haired man sitting a few seats in front of them turned around to look at Ruby. 'Bootham Bar Books?' he said. 'There was a burglary there a few weeks back. Burglars took some expensive books.'

'Everybody knows that, Dennis. That's not news. What else is there?' said Ruby, a little rudely to Evie's mind, though Dennis didn't seem fazed by her tone.

'Not heard anything else about the burglary, but I was talking to June the other day and she says someone from that shop was seen in a bit of a compromising position a few weeks back.'

Evie and Kitt looked at each other. A compromising position . . . that was certainly a phrase you could use to describe a married woman having an affair.

Kitt cleared her throat, but kept her voice at a volume that only just allowed Dennis to hear what she was saying above the rumble of the bus engine. 'Did she mention who it was from the shop?'

'She didn't know her name. Just described her as "that young slip of a thing from Bootham Bar Books".'

Evie watched the frown form on Kitt's face and was pretty sure she had one to match. Shereen really couldn't be described in those terms. But there was someone else who could be . . .

'Olivia!' they cried in unison.

'What kind of compromising position was she in, exactly?' Kitt asked.

Dennis leant further over the back of his seat as he spoke. 'She was sat in the corner of one of the pubs on the Wetherby road out of town with a man who looked old enough to be her father, and then some.'

Kitt raised her eyebrow. 'Are you sure she wasn't just actually spending some time with her father?'

'From the way June told it, I wouldn't be carrying on with my daughter the way he was carrying on with her,' said Dennis.

'Did June say what the man looked like?' said Kitt.

'Well it wasn't June that saw her, it was her niece who's a barmaid in the pub. But when she was passing a couple of times, collecting glasses and such, she said she overheard them talking about the bookshop quite a bit. To the point she thought the chap might be her boss.'

'Olivia and Donald . . .' Evie said, shaking her head.

Kitt pressed her lips together, and said in a quiet voice to make it difficult for Dennis to hear: 'This is third-hand information, I don't think it's the kind of thing that can be counted on.'

'But you didn't think Shereen was the kind to be having an affair.'

'I don't, but . . .'

'So isn't it more likely, given what Olivia told us, that she is the one having an affair with Donald and is trying to throw us off the trail by pointing the finger at Shereen?'

'I don't know about more likely . . . but I admit we can't discount the possibility,' said Kitt.

'What do you want to know all this for, anyway?' said Dennis.

Casually as she could, Evie brought her hand up to her mouth so Dennis wouldn't see her smiling. He had just dished out all that information and was only now thinking to check why she and Kitt were snooping around.

'No reason in particular,' Kitt lied, and Evie noticed a faint blush rising to her cheeks as she did so. 'I was at the bookshop at the weekend and the staff there seemed a little bit unsettled. They're my friends and I just want to do right by them.'

'Fair enough,' said Dennis. 'But June's niece isn't the kind to make things up, just so you know.'

Kitt nodded. 'I'm sure she's very honest.'

'It's not so much that,' said Dennis. 'So much happens in that pub on the Wetherby road she doesn't need to make things up. Plenty of real-life drama going on.'

'I see,' said Kitt, before pulling her phone out of her pocket. She looked at the screen and sighed.

'What is it?'

'It's one of Grace's cryptic emoji text messages. I get them whenever Michelle is lurking around our part of the library and she can't speak on the phone. Tell me what on earth I'm supposed to make of this?'

Evie looked at the screen. There was a book emoji. Followed by a money bag emoji. Followed by a hammer emoji. Followed by an umbrella emoji. Followed by a smiley face emoji.

'I think she's trying to tell you she's found the books on sale somewhere,' said Evie.

'What?' Kitt said, looking again at the screen. 'Oh yes, it does look that way now that you mention it. But what do the umbrella and the smiley face symbolize?'

'Not sure about the umbrella, but I think the smiley face is just a sign that she's happy about the discovery,' said Evie.

Without a word then, Kitt pressed the nearest stop button.

'Where are you going?' asked Ruby.

'Change of plan,' said Kitt. 'Something more important than the alleged affairs of the staff at Bootham Bar Books has come up. But, I'm grateful, Ruby. For you asking around. And maybe if you hear anything else about the bookshop, you'll keep us updated?'

'I will that,' said Ruby. 'When I get home, I'll have a look at the runes as well. They're good for cutting through nonsense, those stones. I'll let you know what they say. I'm sure whatever they point to will be of use to you. As two concerned citizens just trying to do right by their friends, of course.'

Ruby's smile was slow and sly. Had she somehow worked out that the pair were on another investigation? She wouldn't have had to work too hard at figuring that out given how lame their cover story had been.

Kitt only gave Ruby a knowing half-smile in response.

The bus pulled up at the side of the road, and Kitt disembarked with Evie following just behind her.

'Where are we going?' she called after her best friend who had gone from zero to power walk in under a second.

'Back to the library, to find out what Grace knows and to plan our next move.'

'Wouldn't it be quicker to send her a text message?'

'I'd like the full story, not the abridged emoji version,' said Kitt.

'Well, we're not far from mine. Let's swing round there and go in Jacob.'

'Good idea, the sooner we get to the library the better. I've run out of Lady Grey tea back at the cottage and need to raid my stash at work.'

'Run out of Lady Grey? You *must* be preoccupied with this case.'

'Too true.'

NINETEEN

'Right, Grace,' Kitt said, raising her voice to a level that she could be heard over the sound of Jacob's motor. 'You're in the car. You're not being left out or left behind. Now will you please tell us what you've found out about the case.'

Grace was sitting in the back seat with her arms crossed. She hadn't said a word since they had set off from the library almost ten minutes ago. Before that, all she had been willing to tell Evie and Kitt was that they needed to head out of town on Wetherby road, which apparently was what the umbrella emoji was about. Grace was surprised the two hadn't made the connection between weather and Wetherby, but Evie suspected she may have been laying it on thick to wind Kitt up further.

'I'm sorry I had to go to these lengths,' said Grace, 'but I'm not going to be the one stuck behind a computer all the time. I want a piece of the real action.'

'You've made your feelings quite clear,' said Kitt. 'We

can only hope Michelle doesn't clock you've taken an early lunch break.'

'Is it really that big a deal?' said Evie.

'Everything's a big deal with Michelle,' said Grace, and then looking at her phone added, 'but it's not far out of town, just another fifteen minutes from here.'

'Where exactly are we going?' asked Kitt. 'If you think I'm blindly following you for another fifteen minutes you've got another thing coming.'

Evie met Grace's eye for a second in the rear-view mirror and they exchanged a look of mild amusement. It wasn't very difficult to get Kitt worked up, and they both had a lot of fun doing it.

'Grace,' Kitt pushed, turning in her seat to look at her assistant.

'North Riding Auction House,' said Grace.

'Are the books on sale there?' said Evie, slowing the car a little so that a motorbike could ease into the flow of traffic from a T-junction.

'No,' Grace replied. 'But the person in possession of the books is.'

'And who might that be?' asked Kitt.

Looking into the rear-view mirror once again, Evie saw a small smile cross Grace's lips as she drove around a small roundabout. 'A Mr Jarvis Holt,' she said. 'From what I can tell he makes his money in buying and selling, mostly property but he has his fingers in a few other pies too.'

'If he's not selling the books at auction, how do you know they're in his possession?' asked Kitt.

'I found a listing on an eBay account in Holt's name for a first edition copy of *The Big Sleep*.'

'What about the other books?' said Kitt.

'No, it was just that one. I think he's too clever to sell all of the books in one go. The book was hidden among lots of other vintage items on sale from teapots to typewriters.'

'If the other books weren't there, how do you know it's the copy stolen from Bootham Bar Books?' said Kitt.

'Because eBay makes business users display their contact information and this book was the only one listed in the York area. The title of the listing was also odd. Instead of writing the title of the book, which would be the obvious way of attracting attention to the listing, it was listed as "First edition of a Raymond Chandler classic." The photograph was of a first edition copy of *The Big Sleep* but the title wasn't mentioned anywhere in the listing.'

'That is a bit strange, I'll grant you,' Kitt mused. 'And you're sure Jarvis Holt is at this auction house, even though he's not selling the book there?'

Grace nodded. 'He made the mistake of posting to their Facebook page a couple of hours ago to say he would be going to the auction house this afternoon to bid on some choice items. He didn't bargain for Grace Edwards, Online Investigator Extraordinaire.'

Evie saw Grace's hands waving about in her mirrors, a

sure sign she was getting a bit overexcited. Not that it took much, and not that Evie begrudged Grace a bit of excitement. She lived in Leeds, which had a bit more going on, but it was fair to say that studying and working in the city of York was likely to make any young soul keen to pounce on whatever excitement came their way.

Evie glanced at Kitt while also keeping one eye on the road. She had expected her friend to pass some comment on Grace's behaviour, or at the very least her new self-proclaimed title, but instead the librarian had pulled out her mobile and started dialling. 'Who are you calling?'

'Halloran. You heard what he said yesterday, we have to let him know about every new development. He might want to talk to Jarvis Holt himself. Or maybe even take him in for questioning.'

Evie returned her full attention to the road as she approached a crossroads.

A moment later she heard Kitt sigh. 'Voicemail,' she said before leaving him a message that explained Grace's findings and where they were heading.

Once she had hung up the phone, Kitt asked, 'Why would Holt use a business account to sell the book when all of his details are listed on the eBay page?'

'My guess?' said Grace. 'He's trying to make it look legit. If he does it through his business he can pretend he bought the book in good faith and was just selling it on. If he had tried to sell it through an anonymous account, that would have looked beyond shady if the police had caught up with him.'

'Wait a minute,' said Kitt. 'We're on the Wetherby road.'

Evie smiled. 'You're usually a bit quicker at picking up the finer details than that.'

'No,' Kitt said. 'Remember what Dennis said? About where he saw Olivia?'

'In the pub on the Wetherby road, we passed it while you were on the phone with Halloran,' said Evie. 'So? You think there's a connection between Olivia and Holt?'

'Grace, is Holt's business based in Wetherby?' said Kitt.

'Yeah, that's what the eBay page said, why?'

'Olivia, the shop assistant at Bootham Books, is seen with a mysterious man old enough to be her father out on the Wetherby road, and the man who is selling the books online happens to be based in Wetherby.'

'Yeah,' said Evie. 'When you put it like that, it doesn't sound like much of a coincidence.'

'So, you think this guy used Olivia for insider information?' said Grace.

'Or . . .' said Kitt.

'Or she knew exactly what she was doing and it was a true inside job,' said Grace.

'She was acting a bit defensive when you asked her about the burglary,' said Evie.

Kitt nodded. 'I put it down to her wanting to cover up the argument about Shereen's affair, but given what we know

now I'm not sure we can trust anything that came out of Olivia's mouth that day.'

An emptiness stirred in the pit of Evie's stomach. 'You think that Holt is the thief and Olivia in on it?'

'Perhaps he's not just a thief,' said Kitt. 'Perhaps he's Alim's murderer too.'

At this, Evie pressed her foot harder on the accelerator. Jarvis Holt could be the key to unravelling this whole mystery. To unmasking the murderer who had killed Alim the moment he had become an inconvenience and to ensuring Charley's name was cleared once and for all. If she could help it, Evie wasn't going to let him get away.

TWENTY

'Shouldn't we wait for Halloran?' asked Evie as she, Grace and Kitt approached the entrance of North Riding Auction House on a quiet street on the outskirts of Wetherby. Though she had played a bit fast and loose with the out of town speed limit in the hope of catching Holt while they had the chance, Evie was suddenly very aware of the fact that they could be about to have a showdown with a murderer – her second in six weeks – and for that kind of thing she would be much more comfortable with police back-up.

'We can't hang around,' said Kitt. 'Who knows when he'll pick up that message? I'm hardly going to waste time waiting for him to get back to me if there's a chance of recovering a first edition copy of *The Big Sleep* from the hands of thieves.'

'This just feels like it's escalating fast all of a sudden,' said Evie, thinking back to her trip to the hospital and how much trouble she managed to cause with that one visit.

'Escalating is good,' said Grace. 'Escalating is better than slow or dull. Like most days.'

Evie pouted. She knew she couldn't have counted on back-up from those quarters. From what Kitt had told her about their last adventure, Grace was more than happy to leap into things and just hope for the best. Looks like she was outnumbered.

The auction house was comprised completely of brown stone save for its lead-paned, circular windows. The weather vane shaped like a fish on top of the ornate gable roof pointed south-west. There was something intimidating about it for such a small building and the closer Evie got to the tall wooden door the more sick she felt. The strong scent of pipe smoke lingering by the entrance didn't help. The sweetly sour smell always turned her stomach.

'Besides anything else,' said Kitt, apparently not quite finished convincing her friend of the urgency, 'both Grace and myself have got to be back at the library in about forty minutes unless we want to suffer the wrath of Michelle, and you've got massage appointments to keep this after-noon.'

'All right, I get it – time is of the essence,' Evie said with a sigh. 'But let's just go steady. We could just suss the guy out. We don't have to approach him.'

'Are you kidding?' said Grace. 'I didn't come out here to watch someone bid on a vintage teapot.'

'Sadly, that does sound like my idea of fun,' said Evie.

'Given his weakness for younger women, I've got a much better idea,' said Grace.

Kitt narrowed her eyes at her assistant. 'What?'

'You'll see, just follow my lead,' said Grace, pulling open the door to the auction house.

'Er, wait a minute, that's not how this works, is it?' said Kitt.

'It does this time . . .'

Kitt shook her head at Evie. 'Oh dear. Why couldn't I have recruited a shy and retiring assistant?'

They hurried after Grace and the second Evie was over the threshold she was hit by yet another less-than-homely aroma, a mix of strong wood polish and damp bank notes that she decided was the reek of the upper class.

The entrance to the auction house was fitted with a small reception desk, behind which a lady sat with a pair of gold-rimmed glasses perched on the very end of her nose. She was giving all of her attention to a list of some nature and ticking off items as she went.

Grace was already standing at the desk but the woman had yet to look up.

'Excuse me,' Kitt said, as she approached the desk.

The woman, without looking up from what she was doing, held a single finger in the air. Evie watched as Kitt's nose crinkled in agitation and Grace started pointing towards a set of heavy double doors nearby.

Evie shook her head. Getting into trouble might result

in them being pulled up in front of Ricci for another dress-ing-down – or worse.

Kitt cleared her throat, trying to get the lady's attention a second time. Still, she didn't look up from her work. Kitt's mouth tightened, and she turned to her two conspirators, put a finger to her lips and nodded in the direction of the doors. Grace started creeping towards the auction room and Kitt gave Evie a nudge, leaving her little choice but to follow on.

The trio approached the doors. The handle was almost within reach but just as Kitt reached out for it, a floorboard creaked underfoot. All three of them cringed at once. Evie looked back at the woman at the desk but she was still engrossed in her work. Evie's shoulders relaxed. They may as well have walked past with a brass band. Not even that, it seemed, would have roused the woman from whatever vital paperwork she was completing.

Without waiting another second to be caught out, they scurried into the main hall and whipped the door shut behind them. Inside, somewhere near a hundred punters were seated, some of them raising their paddles as the auc-tioneer called out ever-rising prices for a pottery ornament of a frog sitting on a lily pad reading a book. Evie had some weird and wonderful things in her vintage-inspired home but she decided there and then that this was one trinket she could do without and kept her arms straight at her side in case there was any confusion.

'Going once. Going twice. Sold for the sum of £12,000!'

The auctioneer slammed her hammer down and an assistant approached the lectern to take away the ornament and replace it with a crystal punchbowl.

Evie curled her lip. 'Twelve grand for that thing?'

'When you've got money to burn there probably comes a point where you don't much care what you spend it on. Let's focus on the bigger issues, shall we?' Kitt said with a knowing smile. 'Grace, can you see Holt?'

Grace pulled her phone out of her pocket and tapped the screen a couple of times. 'Difficult to identify him from the back of his head,' she said. 'But this is the guy you're looking for.'

Grace held up her phone while Evie and Kitt examined a screenshot taken off Facebook. At Evie's guess he was somewhere in his forties. He had blue, watery-looking eyes, and a full crop of ginger hair with a grey streak at the front.

'The fact that he's a redhead narrows it down,' said Kitt, stroking the end of her own red locks. 'Just ten per cent of the UK population have naturally red hair, you know.'

'I do now,' said Grace, scanning the crowds. 'All right, I can make out two guys with red hair. How about you?'

Evie and Kitt stared at the back of the crowd's heads just as Grace had a moment ago.

'Two,' said Kitt, and Evie nodded her agreement.

Grace put her phone back into her pocket. 'Right. I'll take a look at this guy on the left, you two check out the guy over there and just give me the nod if you think it's him.'

Kitt sighed. 'Fine, but please don't do anything rash, will you? I can handle answering to Halloran but Superintendent Ricci is another matter entirely.'

'Not to mention the impact any wrong moves might have on Charley's career,' Evie chipped in.

'I haven't forgotten the stakes,' said Grace. 'Let's regroup in a couple of minutes.'

The women nodded to each other before Grace walked off towards the left of the room and Kitt and Evie walked off to the right.

The man Evie and Kitt were approaching had shorter hair than the man in Grace's picture, but nobody looks exactly like their profile picture.

'Now, where shall we sit?' said Kitt. Evie could tell by the tone Kitt had no intention of taking a seat but was using her feigned search as an excuse to walk around a bit and get a good look at the red-haired man. This was made more difficult by the fact that his head was tilted downwards as he read from the auction catalogue.

'That's not him,' Kitt whispered as they edged a bit further round.

'Are you sure?' Evie said, craning her neck as though she was looking generally for a seat rather than at a particular person.

'He's too young,' said Kitt.

'You're right. Grace must have – Oh, my God. Grace . . .' Evie said. Her eyes widened as she looked across the other side of the room to see Kitt's assistant take a seat right next to the other red-haired gentleman, flashing him a smile.

Kitt and Evie exchanged a wide-eyed look and then quickly, yet still casually, walked around the back of the seating area to get closer to where Grace was sitting.

'There's a couple of seats a row behind them, let's just squeeze past these people,' Kitt muttered to Evie. 'Excuse me, sorry. Excuse me.'

Kitt and Evie squeezed past a sixty-something woman who was wearing a suffocating amount of designer perfume, a man wearing a flat cap even though he was indoors, and another man who tutted as the pair hurried past.

Evie and Kitt sat down as quickly as they could. Grace and Holt were just in front of them, a little off to their left, but they could still hear the conversation that had already got going.

'I can't quite believe you've never been to an auction before,' Holt said to Grace in a tone one might expect an adult to talk to a small child.

'I've never had a reason to come to an auction before,' Grace said, removing her coat to reveal the silky salmon-pink kurta she was wearing over her jeans. 'But maybe that's changed.'

Holt made no attempt to conceal the fact he was ogling Grace and Evie noticed Kitt's jaw tightening as he did so. Kitt was rather protective about the people she cared about, a fact Evie had always been grateful for. And if he wasn't careful, it looked like Holt might find out just how protective she could be.

Grace toyed with one of her dark curls. 'Do you have your eye on anything in particular today?'

Holt leant closer to Grace. 'You might say that. How about you?'

'Oh I don't know,' she said with a teasing little smile. 'I have what you might call particular passions.'

'I'd love to know more about them,' said Holt. Evie couldn't quite see his face from this vantage point but she imagined it was fixed in a leer. She could see Grace's expression, however, and she seemed unruffled by his obvious lechery. Perhaps because Holt was playing right into her hands.

'I don't know if I'm ready to reveal them to you just yet,' Grace said with a giggle.

'Oh but I wish you would.' Holt's arm crept around the back of Grace's chair. That move alone was enough to make Evie shudder but somehow the mustard chinos he was wearing made the whole scene even more sickening.

'I don't know if I'm ready for you to know just how much of a nerd I am.'

'Nothing about you screams "nerd" to me.'

Grace again toyed with her hair. 'Looks can be deceiving. Would you guess that I work in a library?'

'No. But that isn't in the least bit off-putting. I've always wondered what goes on underneath the calm exterior of those quiet librarian types.'

Evie noticed Kitt's fists clenching at this and tried not to laugh. Her friend couldn't really be described as the stereotypical librarian which was why perhaps the stereo-types riled her so much.

'Oh, there's more to us than meets the eye,' said Grace.

'What meets the eye is already enticing but do tell me more.'

'I can't speak for all librarians, naturally,' said Grace. 'But personally speaking I find intelligence an incredibly attractive quality in a person.'

'Oh really . . .' Holt reached up and toyed with the ends of Grace's hair. Somehow, she managed not to flinch. Beyond impressive, given the level of smarm on display.

'Yes, I'm almost helplessly drawn to bookish individuals. People who read fine works of literature. People who are well-versed in poetry. People who own rare editions just for the beauty of them, no matter just how much money they set them back.'

Holt paused. Not being able to see his facial expression was starting to make Evie wish they had better seats to the show but she imagined, given his silence, that he was making some calculation. 'You may be interested to hear then,' he said at last, 'that I have in my possession a rather beautiful first edition of *Jamaica Inn* by Daphne du Maurier. Perhaps you're a bit young to be familiar with that title.'

'She's a bit young for a lot of things,' Kitt said to Evie in a low voice. 'But I think we've found the brains behind the burglary.'

Evie nodded at her friend. One of the titles from the burglary on his eBay account and another one stashed away in his private collection: this was definitely their guy. But if he had been behind the burglary there was a good chance he also had something to do with Alim's death, and perhaps Donald's disappearance. Something clenched inside Evie's chest as she looked at the back of Holt's head and prayed for Grace to tread lightly here.

'I'm more than familiar with it, it's one of my favourites,' said Grace and then letting her face drop added, 'But I've never seen a first edition.'

'Perhaps we could arrange a viewing of sorts,' said Holt.

'What an exciting idea,' said Grace. 'Is *Jamaica Inn* the only first edition you own?'

'Actually, I've happened across a few of them lately,' said Holt.

'Let me guess the titles, sir,' said a deep voice off to the left. '*The Big Sleep*, *Endymion*, *Jamaica Inn* and *Goodbye to Berlin*.' Halloran had arrived and Evie breathed out a sigh of relief. As casually as she could, she looked around the hall to see if Charley was here backing him up, but there was no sign of her.

'What the –' Holt began, then sprang to his feet as Halloran held up his badge and started shuffling backwards along the row towards the central aisle. Gasps and tuts rose up from the people Holt was barging past.

'Stop where you are!' boomed Halloran.

Kitt rose to her feet and tried to grab hold of Holt's arm as he came near but he moved too quickly and in a moment he was out of the end of the row and walking briskly towards the door at the back of the room. Evie watched as Halloran quickly scanned the seating arrangements, then leaped onto a nearby empty chair and continued to jump empty seat to empty seat in a bid to cut Holt off before he made it out of the door. 'Stop! Police!' he shouted, as people in the room cried out in surprise.

Evie's mouth hung open as she watched Halloran leap from chair to chair like Indiana Jones. If she hadn't been so astonished she would have laughed at the sight of him, a grown man, jumping about a similarly open-mouthed audience of the well-to-do. The inspector spent most of his time being so serious and staid but there was no denying that he did have his moments, and this was one of them.

Holt had his hand on one of the double doors at the back of the room but just before he pushed and found his freedom, Halloran grabbed him by the back of his collar and pulled him back inside.

'Stand against the wall with your hands behind your head,' Halloran barked, as he pushed the man into position and conducted a quick body search. Everybody in the room was watching the display and yet more gasps rose from the room when Halloran pulled a gun from one of Holt's pockets.

Evie put a hand over her mouth and looked at Grace. All that time, she had been sat next to him, talking to him, and he had had that in his pocket.

'A strange thing to bring along to an antiques auction,' was all Halloran had to say on the matter as he ushered Holt out of the bidding hall.

TWENTY-ONE

'You can start by confirming your full name,' said Halloran as he indicated a chair in the back room of the auction house. Evie, Grace and Kitt had been permitted to watch on the condition that they didn't interrupt the inspector's initial questions. Without another police officer at the scene, Evie reasoned Halloran probably wanted witnesses to him cautioning the man and perhaps it wouldn't hurt either to have others bear witness to his answers. Regardless of what he had to say for himself, however, it didn't seem Holt had much hope of escaping a formal interrogation down at the station. Just outside the door, Evie could still hear the bustle of the wealthy leaving the premises and cut-glass accents spouting phrases such as 'In all my time, I've never seen such a ruckus.'

Holt sat in the chair and then looked up at Halloran. 'Mr Jarvis Holt,' he said. 'And now that you know who you're dealing with, I expect a prompt, quiet resolution to this matter.'

Evie and Kitt exchanged a frown. Kitt looked as though she was going to open her mouth to speak but then clearly remembered Halloran's instructions and for once decided to do as she had been instructed.

The inspector pulled a notebook out of his pocket and scribbled what Evie assumed was Holt's name on one of the pages. 'I have heard of you, Mr Holt. You manage quite a lot of property in the York area. But all hope of a swift and quiet resolution went out the moment I shouted the words "stop, police" and you decided to run away.'

Holt looked at Halloran's notebook and then down at his brown leather loafers which were polished to such a degree that Evie felt she could see her face in them from five paces away. 'Are you arresting me?'

'Not yet . . . but I fear that in the long run you might leave me no choice,' said Halloran. 'I overheard enough, and I'm fairly sure Ms Edwards over there would be willing to make a statement detailing the fact that you claimed to be in possession of a list of first edition books that were stolen from Bootham Bar Books a few weeks back.'

Grace jumped at being addressed as 'Ms Edwards'. She wasn't at a stage in her life where anyone would really think to do that.

'And that's before,' Halloran continued, standing a little taller, 'we even get into the matter of you carrying a handgun.'

Holt then did something that Evie didn't believe anyone would dare do in the face of an interrogation from DI

Halloran – he rolled his eyes. 'Oh please, I collect antique firearms. It's perfectly legal.'

'Oh, we'll be checking out everything you say,' said Halloran, his face darkening. 'If it was a collector's item, it should be kept in a display cabinet, not in your pocket. Is it loaded? Have you sourced ammunition for it?'

Holt hesitated but did at last respond. 'Yes. But I wasn't going to hurt anyone with it. I just needed it as a deterrent, for . . . protection.'

'Seems somewhat contradictory, Mr Holt, to load a weapon and then claim you had no intention of hurting anybody.'

Holt sat in silence and looked down at the yellow carpet.

'Who were you trying to protect yourself from?'

Holt's silence continued.

'Mr Holt, if you need protection from somebody, that is what the police are for. You shouldn't be taking matters into your own hands. As it is, this whole circumstance is deeply suspicious. You're in possession of stolen property and ran from a police officer. Just running away is grounds for me to arrest you.'

Holt glared at Halloran and pointed at Grace. 'She tricked me into saying I had those books. That's entrapment!'

'No, it isn't. It would only be entrapment if Ms Edwards tricked you into stealing the books with her. And, if she worked for the police, which she doesn't.'

Holt looked from Grace, to Kitt and then to Evie. 'If they don't work for the police, then what are they doing here?'

'They discovered a certain eBay listing of yours.'

'So?'

'So.' Halloran sighed. 'That listing was for a first edition copy of The Big Sleep, an item that was stolen from Bootham Bar Books.'

Mr Holt's face was perfectly still. 'I bought those books in good faith. There was nothing remotely suspicious about the person who sold them to me.'

Halloran stared at Holt for a moment and then folded his arms. 'Are you aware that those stolen books have an associated missing persons case and a charge of grievous bodily harm against, and murder of, Alim Buruk?'

Holt's face drained of colour.

'You know, any person who was innocent of any wrongdoing might look surprised at this point,' Halloran said. 'But you're not surprised, are you, Mr Holt?'

'I don't think I should say anything else without my lawyer.'

'We will contact your lawyer when you get to the station,' said Halloran.

'But – ' Holt tried, but Halloran had stopped listening. He had already pulled his phone out of his pocket and was on the line to the station.

'This isn't what you think, you know,' Holt said to Evie, Kitt and Grace. 'None of it.'

'What exactly do you mean by that?' asked Kitt.

'You'll find out soon enough,' said Holt, his eyes narrowing.

Evie looked at Grace and Kitt in turn, and they looked back at her. What was that supposed to mean?

'Stand up, Mr Holt,' Halloran said. 'You are under arrest under suspicion of conspiracy to burgle, and conspiracy to murder.'

Holt's eyes widened at this. 'This is ridiculous, an outrage.'

Halloran ignored Holt's protestations and continued to appraise him of his rights before cuffing him and leading him out of the room.

As Holt and Halloran disappeared into the corridor, Evie sensed a sinking feeling in her stomach. 'What do you think he meant when he said that we'd know soon enough that this wasn't what it seemed?'

'Who knows?' said Grace with a little shiver.

'A person like him might say anything to save face in that situation,' said Kitt. 'But if what he says is anywhere near true then there's a good chance this whole business is far from over.'

TWENTY-TWO

Raindrops dashed themselves against the windscreen at a faster rate than Jacob's little wipers could cope with as Evie drove at a cautious pace up the A63. Just over an hour ago she had been having a cup of tea at Kitt's cottage when a phone call had come through from Inspector Halloran. Donald Oakes's body had washed up near the Humber Bridge and although Halloran had warned Kitt not to come to the crime scene as Ricci was likely to put in an appearance, she had been unable to sit at the cottage and do nothing.

Evie had not said too much to Kitt on the journey. They had been friends long enough that it was possible to sit in comfortable silence if that's what the other needed.

'This . . . Donald's death, doesn't look good on Shereen, does it? I mean, if there was any truth to anything Olivia told us.'

'That's a big "if",' said Evie. 'She's not exactly what you would describe as a reliable source. If Olivia was having some kind of affair with Holt, she might be mixed up in this more than we know.'

'It's true, this Holt character seems deeply suspicious,' said Kitt. 'But isn't Olivia a bit young to be masterminding something on this scale?'

'She might just be another pawn, like Alim. Making Shereen look guilty might be just another step in Holt's get-rich-quick plan. But then ... there's a big difference between burgling a bookshop and murdering two people.'

'True,' said Kitt. 'But burglary and murder are sometimes linked. Like in *The Adventure of the Reigate Squire*.'

'Let me guess,' said Evie, 'a mystery book?'

'Sherlock Holmes,' Kitt said, with a hollow note in her voice.

Evie turned right off the A-road to get closer to the bridge. Somewhere close to there, they would find Halloran, and possibly Charley too.

'Maybe the reason this case is so messy is because it's just a burglary gone wrong,' said Kitt.

'Gone wrong in what way?'

'Well, maybe Donald was in on it and alongside Alim was promised a cut of any money Holt made on the books,' said Kitt. 'That way, Donald could claim his insurance money and take a cut of the value of the books sold at auction.'

'But how does that result in two dead bodies?' asked Evie.

'Maybe Holt decided he wanted to keep all the money for himself and got rid of the other two.'

'For the sake of fifty grand?' said Evie. 'I can maybe see that for a hundred grand but is fifty grand really worth killing two people to someone as rich as Holt?'

'I don't know,' said Kitt. 'From what Halloran has told me about some of the things he's seen, some people will kill for a lot less.'

'A comforting thought,' said Evie.

'Over there,' Kitt said, pointing off at a set of blue flashing lights flickering up ahead.

Evie indicated and pulled over to the verge. If they had come here in daylight hours some comfort would have been provided by the quaint spires and rooftops of the nearby town of Hessle, famous for its shipbuilding and known to most as the doorway to the Yorkshire Wolds Way, seventy-nine miles of rolling chalk hills between here and Filey. The vantage point provided by the peaks offered unparal-leled views across some of the most stunning scenery in the region, but not tonight. Tonight this stretch was shrouded in a mask of thick rain and mist, the only relief from which was the glow of the Humber Bridge, illuminated by a proces-sion of yellow lights while its tall concrete towers stretched seemingly ever upward into the dark December sky.

Evie turned off the ignition and turned to her friend. 'I still don't think this is a very good idea, us being here. Donald was a friend.'

Kitt nodded and released the seat belt. 'I know that. But I need to see for myself.'

Evie knew from past experience that there was no point in trying to argue with her friend about this. She watched her open the car door and pick a holdall she had brought with her out of the footwell. Kitt didn't usually carry this much luggage but when Evie had pressed her about what was in the bag, all she would say was that it was just a few things in case of emergency.

Evie undid her seat belt and exited the vehicle, taking a deep breath as she did so. She was at a disadvantage to Kitt, who confessed after their last escapade that she had seen a dead body before, but wouldn't be drawn into the context. Evie had, fortunately, never come into contact with a corpse so there was no real telling how she would react to whatever it was she was about to witness.

Evie followed Kitt as she walked towards some yellow tape. Beyond the police line, Evie could make out a small huddle of police officers in the darkness, Halloran and Charley among them. Evie didn't recognize the other officers present. They were more than likely not from York Police Station but from whichever station happened to be nearest this stretch of river. Hull, perhaps?

Halloran and Charley were listening carefully to a tall, skinny officer who on account of his pointed nose and narrow, beady eyes, reminded Evie of a weasel. After a few moments, Halloran glanced over in the direction of the cordon and noticed Kitt. His face at once morphed into a frown, whether of confusion or of annoyance Evie couldn't quite say. Charley followed his stare and looked at Evie for just a moment too long.

Less than a minute later Halloran managed to excuse himself and walked towards Kitt. Charley followed close behind him but stared straight ahead as she walked, without any acknowledgement of Evie.

She had forgotten how no-nonsense Charley looked in her work suit with her dark hair twisted back into a bun. There was something really enticing about the many things Charley was. Playful and serious as the situation called for it. Intelligent and kind. Strong, but tender. Not to mention beautiful in her own unique way. Evie had never given much thought to how sexy the Scottish accent was until she had listened to Banks whisper a few choice phrases the other night.

'I told you not to come out here, didn't I, pet? There's nothing you can do,' said Halloran.

'I heard what you said. But I wanted to be sure. Are you sure? It's Donald?'

'You know we can identify him,' said Halloran. 'From the interviews we conducted about the burglary.'

'I don't know why I came. I . . . can I see him?'

'Kitt,' said Charley. 'If he was a friend, that's probably not a good idea. Might be better just to remember him as he was.'

'I understand why you're saying that, and thank you,' said Kitt. 'But, I need to see him.'

Evie looked from Kitt to Charley, who at last caught her eye, but almost at once looked away. Was she trying to act casual to protect the privacy of what they'd shared? Or being cruel and ignoring her? Evie tried to push that last thought out of her mind. She was in a professional setting and her behaviour was probably a reflection of that and nothing more. Probably.

Halloran studied Kitt's face for a moment. 'All right, but you can't stay long and you mustn't touch a thing,' he said, lifting the tape to allow Kitt to slip over. Evie tried to follow but Halloran lowered the tape.

'What about me?' Evie wasn't particularly convinced she wanted to see a dead body. But she also didn't want to stand alone in the dark and cold on the other side of the cordon to everyone else.

'Just Kitt,' said the inspector.

On hearing this Kitt stopped walking and turned back to Halloran.

'You can't make Evie wait on her own, Mal, she's driven me all the way here.'

Halloran sighed and then waved Evie under. 'Come on then. You two are insistent on costing me my job, it seems.'

'Just try and make this quick,' said Charley, as Evie ducked under the tape. Together they approached the body. A small group of Humberside officers stood nearby, chatting and recording some details in their notebooks.

'These two are with me,' Halloran said to the officer who

looked like a weasel. A pair of beady eyes fixed themselves first on Kitt and then on Evie.

'Not exactly protocol, is it? We've got a crime scene to protect 'ere,' said the weasel.

'I'm perfectly capable of supervising two grown adults around a crime scene,' said Halloran.

The weasel looked Halloran up and down. 'If you say so, sir.'

'You've got a torch or two with you?' Halloran asked.

'Yeah, the tide is rising and with every inch evidence might be lost so we've got to get down there sooner rather than later.'

'We'll join you shortly, and do anything we can to help,' said Halloran.

The officer nodded and walked off.

To the right of where they were standing, an orange stretcher lay in the grass. It was covered with a white water-proof sheet. Evie glanced at Kitt to see she was also looking at the stretcher.

'Is that him?' asked Kitt.

'That's him,' Charley said in a gentle voice.

Kitt stood a little straighter, and then began walking towards the stretcher.

Evie followed on and could hear the officers' boots crunching over wet shingle just behind them. As they approached the patch of shore where Donald was lying, Evie noticed Kitt's steps start to slow. Halloran reached forward and put a hand on her shoulder. She patted it before taking the last few steps towards the body.

Halloran stepped round the body then knelt next to it and gripped the sheet. He looked up one last time at Kitt and when she gave him a nod, he slowly revealed what lay beneath.

Evie hadn't known Donald the way Kitt had. But she had met him, talked to him just a few days ago, and thus when Halloran unveiled his corpse her gut reaction was to look beyond the body, into the shrubbery, before she glimpsed anything she couldn't handle. But thinking about all the times Kitt had been strong for Evie over the time the pair had known each other, Evie realized it was now her turn to be the strong one. She stepped forward and joined her friend by Donald's side, even though the sight of his pale face in the darkness was enough to make her shiver. His grey hair was slicked back against his head by the rain and river water and the brown trousers he had been wearing were torn around the cuffs from the body's time in the water. Poor Donald's shoes were missing and his socks were soaked right through.

Evie took in a deep breath and let it out as slowly as she could. If Halloran hadn't pulled her out of the river a few weeks back, this could have been her. Washed up on the banks of the Humber. Her face vacant, unfeeling. All this time, she had been fixated on her scars when in truth things could have been much, much worse for her.

'Oh, Donald,' Kitt said, setting down her holdall and crouching by his side. Kitt looked at the body for a minute and then out towards the water. 'Did he drown?'

'We can't know for sure,' said Halloran with a sigh. 'We're still waiting for the pathologist to arrive but there is a large gash on the back of his head. Whether he was dead when he went into the river or was unconscious, I can't say yet.'

Kitt looked again at Donald's face. Evie couldn't be sure what she was thinking, but it looked almost as though she expected him to wake up. After a few moments of silence, she spoke just to him, so quietly Evie could barely hear the words. 'I don't know who's done this to you, but I am going to find out.'

TWENTY-THREE

Five minutes later, on the other side of the cordon, Evie and Kitt were still trying to recover after the shock of seeing Donald's body. A man both of them had spoken to mere days ago.

'What can I do to help track down Donald's killer?' Kitt said at last. 'I don't care how small or menial the task, I just need to do something.'

'The most likely suspect is sitting in a cell back at the nick,' said Charley.

'Who? Holt?'

Halloran nodded. 'We were able to get a search warrant for his house and found the stolen books just sitting there in his study.'

'All of them? Secret Seven included?' asked Kitt.

'No, the whereabouts of the less valuable items stolen remain a mystery but they're not really the top priority at this second,' said Halloran.

'But making sure we've got every scrap of information out of Holt is,' said Charley.

'So . . . you were able to arrest Holt?' Evie asked Halloran, unable to look at Charley directly.

'Aye,' Charley answered with some force. 'After finding those books in his possession we were able to officially charge him. His lawyer is one of the snidest in the local area though, which frankly we could do without right now.'

Kitt frowned. 'So, you didn't get anything out of him?'

'Oh, I wouldn't say that,' said Halloran. 'When me and Banks started the interrogation his story was that he bought the books off a local dealer. It sounded plausible enough given that there was a withdrawal on his account for £60,000 in cash. He could have used some of that to buy the books.'

Charley folded her arms. 'But, two of our officers, DS Redmond and DCS Percival were watching from behind the mirror and, like us, they thought something was off. When we interviewed the book dealer, he claimed he had bought the books as part of a much bigger job lot – which he paid a few hundred pounds for – and hadn't realized the first editions were in there until the customer had long gone.'

'So someone steals these books that are worth a mint and then offloads them at the first opportunity as a job lot? For a small fraction of their true value?' said Evie.

'And are we supposed to believe this dealer hadn't heard about the burglary at Bootham Bar Books? If he's part of the book trade in the area there's no way he could've missed that headline,' said Kitt. 'All logic dictates he should have handed over those first editions to the police as soon as he saw them.'

'We asked him the same questions. We barely had to apply any pressure and he rolled. Explained that Holt had paid him to say he sold those books on to him,' said Charley.

Just then somebody behind the group cleared their throat. Evie's heart jumped as she was sure when she turned she would see Superintendent Ricci standing there glowering at them. Instead, however, she turned to find a black woman wearing a blue protective suit that looked similar to the scrubs doctors wore on TV.

'Ah, Candice, you're here,' said Halloran.

'And all dolled up in your favourite outfit, DI Halloran.' Candice gestured at the less-than-flattering forensic garment. 'He says this colour brings out the amber in my eyes.'

Kitt, who had been looking quite pensive, smiled softly and raised an eyebrow at Halloran.

'Always nice to be reminded that working with the dead hasn't dented your sense of humour, Candice.'

Candice chuckled. 'I shouldn't embarrass you like this really, especially in front of civilians, but then, you shouldn't really have civilians here in the first place. Anyway, winding you up is just so much fun.'

Despite the macabre situation, Charley, Evie and Kitt joined in Candice's chuckling.

'All right, all right, if we can maintain some level of

professionalism, the body will need to be moved soon because of the rising tide.'

'You're all business, you,' Candice said, ducking under the yellow tape.

Halloran looked at Kitt. 'She's joking, you know.'

'Yes, I clocked that much,' Kitt replied. 'I'm much more interested in the identity of the bookseller Holt is paying off than some imaginary flirtation with the pathologist.'

'Oh, right. A Mr Derek Prince,' said Halloran.

'Derek – owner of Tower Street Books?' said Kitt.

'Oh my God,' said Evie, her mouth dropping open at this revelation.

'What's the matter?' said Charley, looking between Evie and Kitt. 'Spill.'

'Derek was the person who told us about the rumour that Donald and Shereen had orchestrated the burglary for their insurance fraud,' Kitt explained.

'Alongside Olivia,' said Evie. 'I wonder if Holt paid her off too?'

'You're not a million miles away with that theory,' said Charley. For the first time since they had arrived at the crime scene, she cracked a smile.

'Why? What did Holt have to say when Derek gave him up?' asked Kitt.

'We had to apply a bit of pressure. Remind him that there was a murder charge associated with those books and that was when he broke and told us,' said Charley.

'The whole thing at Bootham Bar Books was an inside job,' said Halloran.

'Olivia?' said Kitt.

'Bingo,' said Halloran.

'But why?' asked Evie. 'Was Olivia promised some of the money?'

'Nope,' said Charley. 'Holt and Olivia were having a full-blown affair. Someone found out about it and was extorting Holt. He's married, you know?'

'I didn't know,' said Kitt. 'But I might have guessed.'

'Holt is wealthy but he doesn't have large sums of cash sitting in the bank because it's all invested, most of it in property,' said Halloran.

'So Olivia suggested he steal the first editions from the bookshop, sell them and pay the blackmailers that way?' said Evie.

'And the large cash withdrawal from his bank account wasn't to buy books,' said Kitt, 'it was presumably to go towards the blackmail money.'

'Holt was instructed to pay the sum of £100,000 in two cash lump sums. He paid the first fifty grand and the burglary was going to help him with the second.'

'But you said he withdrew £60,000,' said Kitt. 'What happened to the other ten grand?'

'He used it to pay Alim Buruk to rob Bootham Bar Books,' said Halloran.

'But he didn't kill Alim?' said Evie.

'That's the story he's telling,' said Charley.

'Does he have any idea who the blackmailer is?' asked Kitt.

Halloran shook his head. 'The blackmailer hasn't been seen or heard. He used old-school snail mail. Postmarked Helmsley.'

'Well, surely that narrows it down?' said Kitt. 'Helmsley is tiny. Can't be more than a couple of thousand people living there . . .'

'In the town itself,' said Halloran. 'But there are quite a few other little places in the area, not to mention the farms in the outlying land.'

Kitt sighed. 'Well, is there anyone connected with the case that comes from there?'

'Not that we know of yet,' said Charley.

'And Holt is really denying any involvement in Alim's murder?' Kitt pushed.

'Holt eventually confessed to orchestrating the burglary and to staging Buruk's beating, paid a woman of roughly Banks's size to do his dirty work, of course, in the hope that it would make her evidence unreliable in court,' said Halloran.

'Will you be able to question this woman?' asked Kitt.

'We are trying to find her but she was a professional,' said Banks. 'Expert enough to disappear when it suits her, so we're not holding our breaths on that one.'

'In hiring her, Holt was hoping it would be more difficult

to track the burglary and assault back to him. But he was adamant he would never kill anyone and that this whole situation was just a blackmail gone wrong.'

Everyone was quiet for a moment, and in that time Candice returned from her examination.

'Right,' she said, pulling off her plastic gloves. 'It won't be news, given the depth of the wound, that the most likely cause of death is blunt force trauma to the back of the head. It's possible he was just about alive before he went into the river and drowned.'

'Either way, not an end you would wish on someone,' Kitt said, her voice hollow.

'No argument here,' said Candice. 'There aren't any scratches or bruises on his body. I can't see anything obvious under his fingernails so it doesn't look like there was a struggle.'

'What does that mean?' asked Evie.

'It means he wasn't expecting to be attacked,' said Charley.

'So, either the attacker was very sneaky, or he trusted the person he was with,' said Halloran.

'One imagines he trusted his wife,' said Evie.

'And Olivia,' said Kitt.

'Do you really think Olivia would be strong enough to cause that much damage to Donald?' said Evie. 'She's tiny.'

'An injury like that doesn't happen with your bare hands,' said Charley. 'Whoever did it was using a weapon.'

'I assume these are all potential suspects. There's one

obvious thing that might help you narrow it down,' said Candice. 'A mark on his hand, it looked like faded ink. I could definitely make out an "a" in lower case. But if there's anything else there it's too faded to read. I'd need to get the body back to the lab to take a closer look.'

'The letter a . . .' Halloran mused.

'It might be nothing,' said Candice. 'Might just be a reminder he wrote on his hand himself.'

'Even that kind of detail can tell us something about the victim's last movements. It's still worth a look,' said Halloran. 'Thank you for bringing it to our attention.'

'Do you believe Holt?' said Kitt. 'That he didn't have anything to do with these deaths?'

'I do, and he has an alibi for the hours during which we think Alim's IV was tampered with,' said Halloran. 'But now that we have a second dead body on our hands connected with this case I wonder what else Holt did or paid someone else to do in the hope the trail would never lead back to him.'

'He might have paid someone off,' said Evie. 'But I've been in that hospital room and spoken to Alim myself.'

'Is there a reason you are reminding me you took the law into your own hands?' said Halloran.

'I know you think I was an absolute ninnyhammer for visiting Alim like that.'

'A what?' said Candice.

'But, I did it with all the best intentions,' Evie said, glancing at Charley. 'And I can tell you that if a person went into that room they would be noticed by someone. It's a small room with several other patients in there. If someone Alim didn't recognize showed up, they'd likely overhear the conversation and know something was wrong. But they might go unnoticed if they seemed like a natural person to visit Alim.'

'Like a friend, or a relative,' said Halloran. 'Someone who wouldn't seem out of place, but who wasn't his mother. I – Oh God.' Halloran's face drained of colour. 'Ricci's here,' he almost hissed.

Evie's eyes widened but Kitt didn't flinch. Instead, she turned towards Ricci as she approached and smiled as though the two were friends. Though if that were true it was news to Evie.

'DI Halloran, DS Banks, are you running a crime scene or a circus?'

'A crime scene, ma'am,' Halloran replied.

'Then would you mind telling me what these civilians are doing here?' Ricci was wearing a long, dark, waterproof coat over her brown suit. At the collar, Evie could just make out a crimson silk scarf, much like the turquoise scarf she was wearing last time they had crossed paths with her.

'I just came to drop off this,' said Kitt, holding up the holdall.

'What's in there?' Ricci asked.

Kitt unzipped the bag, and produced a small square Tupperware box. 'Halloran texted me to let me know he wouldn't get home until late and so had to cancel a dinner we had planned. I couldn't stand the thought of him going without. Especially not after I'd taken so much trouble to find the recipe for this delicious beef and vegetable stew with crusted rosemary dumplings. I read about it in an issue of *Good Food* a few months back and couldn't for the life of me remember where I'd put the clipping. I tried to find it online but none of the recipes were quite right so after a hunt through every drawer in the kitchen I finally unearthed it. After all that I'm sure you can understand I didn't want it to go to waste so I brought some of the meal I'd cooked out here for him. In fact, I put it into several packages so there's plenty for everyone.' Kitt pushed the box into Ricci's hand and offered her an over-sized smile.

Evie looked down at her Converse. It was the only safe place to look. If she made eye contact with anyone right now she would likely start laughing about what she'd just witnessed. Kitt Hartley playing the ditsy girlfriend. That's something she thought she'd never see.

Ricci sighed, eyeing the Tupperware. 'I suppose I could overlook this infringement of protocol under the circumstances, if you leave the scene this second.'

'That's so kind of you, I shan't forget this,' said Kitt as she handed the bag over to Halloran, who had a somewhat dazed look on his face after Kitt's unexpected display. 'There's some cake in there for you all too. Fresh ginger, I made it the other day. I hope it helps see you through.'

With that, Kitt gave Ricci a final nod of gratitude and marched off towards Jacob.

Evie followed as quickly as she could. It was best they got out of there before Ricci asked any more questions.

'You didn't have dinner plans with Halloran,' Evie said when they were safely out of earshot. 'Me and you were just going to have a night in at the cottage.'

'Yes,' said Kitt, 'but if there's something I've learned in my brief time as a sleuth it's that an alibi always comes in handy. Speaking of which, we've got some investigating to do around which of Alim's acquaintances does and doesn't have an alibi for the time he was murdered.'

TWENTY-FOUR

Evie sucked her banana milkshake up through a straw and then looked at her watch again. Kitt had sent her a text message mid-morning asking her to meet for lunch at Shake It! – one of the city's three milkshake bars. It was situated in Coffee Yard, York's longest snickelway that led off Grape Lane, where Evie worked at Daisy Chain Beauty. Kitt had said to meet at one o'clock and it was now seven minutes past. Even though Kitt had much further to walk from the library than Evie had to walk from the salon, it wasn't like her to be late. But then, it wasn't like Kitt to suggest meeting up in a milkshake bar either. As a rule she favoured tea rooms where she was much more likely to be able to get a cup of Lady Grey. Evie had sent Kitt a return text message asking why she wanted to meet here but hadn't received a response. Given the revelations of the night before, and how set Kitt was on solving this case, there was only one likely conclusion to be drawn:

somehow, this place was connected with the crimes surrounding Bootham Bar Books.

Kitt had instructed Evie, again without any explanation, to find a seat at the counter if possible, which she had done. Perched on her tall stool, she started looking around for any clue that might help her understand what all this was about.

Because of the slim shape of the snickelways that wound through the centre of town, the establishment was also long and thin. The walls were painted in aquamarine and stencilled with milkshakes in shades of pink and yellow. The seats were upholstered in red and white leather in typical American diner style and small friendship groups comprised of people much younger than Evie clustered around the tables and huddled in the booths. All in all, it seemed a perfectly innocent scene.

Evie was just about to look at her watch again when the door swung open and Kitt bustled in, followed closely by Grace. Even from her seat at the counter, Evie could tell that they were mid-argument about something; Kitt had the tight look about her that she always got when she was trying to keep her cool.

The librarian broke off her conversation for a moment to look around for her friend and, on catching Evie's eye, marched straight to the counter. In her maroon trilby and double-breasted winter coat, she looked a great deal more formal than the other patrons, who were mostly lolling about in jeans and jumpers. Grace looked a bit more like she belonged.

'Sorry we're late, there was a complication . . .' said Kitt, eyeing her assistant.

'It's only nine minutes past,' said Grace. 'We'd have got here sooner if we'd come the way I suggested.'

'It's six and two threes,' Kitt said. 'We'd have been nine minutes late whichever way we came.'

'Well, I didn't want to be left out, like I was last night.'

Kitt glanced at Evie. 'And now you know why we're late. Grace insisted in coming along so we had to find someone to cover the enquiry desk. No easy thing during the lunching hours.'

'But we managed,' said Grace, sitting up to the counter on a stool.

Placing her trilby on the counter, Kitt did the same.

'So, I take it we're not here because you've developed a taste for milkshakes?' said Evie.

'For the record, I don't exclusively drink Lady Grey. But a milkshake wouldn't be my drink of choice for the middle of December, no.'

Evie giggled. She and Kitt differed here. For Evie, ice cream and ice-cream-related goods were fair game any time of the year. She would eat an ice-cream sundae on a freezing January morning if the mood took her.

Grace lowered her voice and then nodded to the waiter

and waitress standing behind the counter. 'We're here because Alim Buruk's girlfriend is on the staff.'

'What?' Evie said, louder than she meant to. She readjusted her volume and hissed, 'Alim had a girlfriend?'

Kitt nodded. 'Follow my lead.'

And with that, the librarian took a newspaper out of her handbag, opened it and began to read.

Evie frowned over at Grace who offered Evie a wink in return. Clearly she had had the luxury of being briefed on the walk to the milkshake bar.

'Excuse me,' Grace called over to the waitress. 'Do you mind if we order? We're on our lunch break and short of time.'

The waitress, who had long black hair and a cherubic face, didn't say anything but came over with her notepad and pen in hand. She was wearing a knee-length dress that was the same aquamarine as the walls. She had a white apron tied around her waist and her name tag read 'Cammie'. Evie couldn't see her feet because the counter was in her way, but in her imagination she was wearing roller skates like the diner waitresses she remembered from old American TV shows. It was obvious from the way the waitress was moving that she couldn't possibly be wearing skates but Evie wasn't about to let reality get in the way of a fun fantasy. After the drama of the last twenty-four hours, fun fantasies were a welcome relief.

'What are you having?' Cammie asked Grace.

'A chocolate milkshake for me please, and some fries.'

Cammie again didn't say anything but noted down the order in her notebook.

'What are you having, Kitt?' asked Grace, and then when Kitt didn't respond she pushed again, 'Kitt?'

'What? Oh sorry, I was totally distracted by the newspaper. Donald Oakes from the bookshop was found dead near the Humber Bridge last night. Had you heard?'

'No, I hadn't,' Grace lied. 'That's terrible.'

'I know. He was such a lovely man. But the tragedy doesn't end there. Apparently his death might be linked with somebody else's. A poor young man who was murdered in hospital a couple of days ago.'

'Well, what are the police doing about it?' asked Grace in what Evie recognized as mock outrage. Truth be told, they were both going a bit OTT with this charade and Evie had to bite her lip to keep from smirking.

'Not enough,' Cammie said at last, putting a hand on her hip. 'That's what.'

'Do you ... know something about these deaths?' Kitt asked, her eyes wide and innocent.

Cammie shook her head. 'I knew the lad who died, Alim.'

'Excuse me,' said Kitt. 'I didn't think. York's a small place. I should have been more careful about what I was saying.'

The girl shrugged one shoulder and looked down at the counter.

'I really am sorry,' Kitt said, leaning forward in her seat. 'Were you close?'

'We were sort of . . . seeing each other. You know, on and off.'

'I'm so sorry for your loss,' Evie said, and then realizing she might be useful in coaxing more than a shrug or a monosyllabic response. 'I had a boyfriend die a couple of months ago. I know the sadness and guilt that goes with that.'

'Guilt?' said Cammie, and then jabbing her thumb into her chest added, 'I don't feel guilty. Just livid.'

'About the police not doing enough to find Alim's killer?' asked Grace.

'Aye,' said Cammie. 'I know who his killer is. I told the police and they did nothing about it.'

'That seems strange,' said Kitt. 'Why didn't they act on your information?'

'Probably because I sound soft in the head when I say it. Doesn't make it any less true though.'

'I don't see how pointing the police in the direction of a prime suspect in a murder case could make you seem soft,' said Kitt.

Cammie looked Kitt up and down before speaking. 'Because I named Alim's mother as his killer and the police won't touch her.'

'His mother?' Evie said, remembering her own encounter with Amira Buruk and how she had threatened her just for talking to her son.

'I know, everyone thinks nobody would do something

like that to their own son. Alim's mum is the exception and anyone who's met her would know exactly what I mean.'

Evie pressed her lips together. She wanted to agree with Cammie. Though the idea of being responsible for your own child's death seemed unthinkable, having met Amira Buruk in person, there wasn't much she wouldn't put past her.

'Have you tried going back to the police?' asked Grace. 'Sometimes applying a bit of pressure can help. Surely they want to solve this case as quick as they can?'

Cammie sighed. 'I tried a couple of times. Wouldn't usually be so keen to spend that much time in a police station but I thought I had to try, for Alim. They reckon they don't have any proof of her involvement. I reckon they're just scared of her.'

'Maybe it's hard for them to think about a woman killing her own child,' said Evie. 'It is difficult to understand what might drive a person to do something like that.'

'It's just proof that Alim's mum doesn't care about anyone except herself. Never has done, never will.'

'So, killing her son somehow benefited her?' Kitt said.

Cammie looked over at her colleague who was making a milkshake a little further down the counter and lowered her voice. 'It's been in the news that Alim was involved in a robbery just before he died. It was his mum who put him up to it. But the police caught up with Alim and all hell broke loose. His mum was convinced Alim was going to say something about her involvement.'

'Surely she didn't believe her own son would testify against her?' said Grace.

'No, she knew he would be too afraid to do something like that but, well, Alim could be really sweet when he wanted to be but he wasn't a criminal mastermind. She thought he was going to give her away by accident. The last time I talked to him, he said that's all she kept going on about. How careful he had to be about what he said to anyone and to keep his mouth shut while she sorted out the mess he'd made.'

'God,' said Evie, holding a hand to her chest as she remembered how Alim had reacted to his mother walking through the hospital door. 'I don't mean to be funny, but I sort of hope you've got it wrong. I can't imagine living a life where I was that scared of my mother.'

Cammie nodded. 'I'm not going to pretend Alim was an angel, because he wasn't. But he didn't deserve to die like that. He was soft at heart really.'

'Was he good to you?' Grace asked with a smile.

'Most of the time,' Cammie said. 'I probably shouldn't say this but I don't suppose it matters much now. When he did that robbery for his mother, he stole a couple of things for me. I didn't want to tell the police about them because I thought they'd take them away as evidence and they are the last things he ever gave me.'

'Were they expensive rare books like the other things that were taken from the bookshop?' asked Kitt.

'No, nothing expensive. But thoughtful. A soft toy and a copy of my favourite childhood book.'

So that explained the giant Peter Rabbit and the Secret Seven book that had also gone missing.

'When was the last time you saw Alim?' asked Kitt.

'The night after the robbery, when he gave me the things he took. We'd been 'aving an argument and he gave me those presents to sort of make up.' As Cammie spoke, Evie noticed tears forming in the young girl's eyes.

'I'm really sorry to have brought this up,' said Kitt.

'It's all right,' said Cammie with a sniff. 'It's sort of nice to have someone to talk to about it. I'll – I'll get you your milkshake . . . did you want to add anything to the order?'

'Let's see now, I think I still have time for a little something,' Kitt said glancing at the menu. 'I'll try the Christmas Caramallow Milkshake with added candy cane syrup, festive fudge chunks, extra-thick snow cream and a gingerbread wafer.'

'Would you like to add an extra sauce?' Cammie asked.

'Oh no,' said Kitt. 'I don't want to go overboard.'

Evie smirked at Grace to find Kitt's assistant was also trying to stifle a smile.

'Oh and Cammie,' Kitt said, pulling a card out from her handbag. 'Here. If you ever want someone to talk to, you can call me and I'll be happy to listen.'

Cammie looked at the card with a certain degree of suspicion but accepted it anyway and put it in the pocket of her apron. 'Thanks,' she managed, before trotting off to the milkshake machine to whip up their order.

TWENTY-FIVE

Evie tried to get comfortable in one of the floral armchairs in the second-floor office of the library. No matter which way she turned, however, she just couldn't sit in a position that felt right.

'Everything OK over there?' said Kitt, eyeing her best friend while she set their tea down on the table.

'Groovy,' Evie replied.

'Interesting choice of words considering you look like you're doing a little jig.'

At this Evie tried with all her might to sit still – no small feat given everything that was going on just now. After all the information gathered over the past day or so, Halloran had called an emergency off-the-books meeting and he would be arriving any minute, presumably with Charley in tow. Evie had thought it rather out of character for Halloran to suggest a meeting like this – previously he had just passed information on through Kitt – but perhaps he had finally come to the same conclusion she had: that this case was getting more complicated by the minute and the more information they could collate by working together, the better.

'I'm nervous,' Evie admitted. 'I haven't spoken to Charley properly since . . . you know.'

'You saw her last night and she seemed all right,' Kitt said, stirring her tea.

Evie shrugged. 'I'm not convinced, she seemed a bit offish at times. We didn't part on exactly pristine terms.'

'I'm sorry, I didn't realize,' said Kitt. 'Why not?'

Evie did what she could to keep her tone casual. 'I said what happened had to be a one-off.'

'And Banks was hoping for more than that?'

'From what she said, yes, I think so.'

'Well, it's never ideal news to find out a person you care for doesn't want the same things as you,' said Kitt. 'But if that's what you wanted I'm sure Banks can understand that, she's a grown woman.'

'Yeah,' said Evie, toying with one of her blonde curls. 'Thing is, I think she could see that it wasn't what I wanted. Or at least that I wasn't sure if it was what I really wanted.'

'So . . . you do want to see her again? As more than friends I mean,' Kitt said with a frown.

'Too soon to say.'

The office door swung open then and Grace stepped through it closely followed by Halloran. This Evie had been expecting. What she wasn't expecting was for two more men to walk through the door, one much older than the other, who she didn't recognize. Charley followed on afterwards. Evie was momentarily distracted from the two strangers by her attempts to gauge Charley's general demeanour. Was Charley as nervous as she was? She didn't look it.

Remembering that staring was the height of bad manners, Evie offered Halloran, Banks and the men she didn't recognize a polite smile but then looked down at her cup of tea and took a sip, trying to refocus her thoughts. She needed to keep her mind on the business of solving this book mystery. She had urged Kitt to get involved before her night with Charley and though it might be easier to just stop helping out and keep her distance, Evie knew that wasn't the right thing to do. She'd made a commitment to help solve this case and she had to see it through.

'You sure the coast is clear?' Kitt said to Grace, who had been tasked with making sure that Michelle had left the building before any representatives from North Yorkshire Police arrived on the scene.

Grace nodded. 'Michelle left about half an hour ago, just after half seven. We're safe from her gorgon glare, for today at least.'

'I'm sorry there aren't quite enough seats, I didn't realize we would be receiving so many of you,' said Kitt. 'Any of you fancy a cuppa? Kettle's just boiled.'

The visitors shook their heads and murmured their

refusals but Grace went over and helped herself to a cup. Meanwhile, Halloran turned to the office door to make sure it was closed before looking back at the assembly of faces.

'Now, I think you're well aware of our policy on involving civilians in police work but something has just come to light that's thrown us into unusual circumstances,' he said. 'This is Detective Chief Superintendent Noah Percival.' Halloran indicated the older man. Though Evie had never met Percival, she had heard Halloran and Charley mention his name once or twice. He was, she understood, their ultimate superior at the station, or at least he would be until his retirement when Ricci was due to take over. His presence meant that whatever the new twist on the case was, it must be deeply serious. The superintendent, who had mid-length grey hair and a beard to match, nodded his head. Like Halloran, Percival was tall and broad and, looking between them, Evie fancied that Halloran would look a lot like Percival did in about thirty years from now. Given Halloran's dedication, he would probably have worked his way up the police ladder to such an important position too.

'And this,' Halloran added, 'is Detective Sergeant Miles Redmond.'

''Ow do,' said Redmond. By the cut of him, Evie guessed DS Redmond to be somewhere in his early thirties. He had a thick crop of blond hair but the frown lines across his forehead suggested he had a few years behind him.

Evie noticed Banks had been watching her looking at

Redmond and she averted her eyes back to her teacup. Though Redmond was easy enough on the eye, she didn't want Banks to get the wrong idea.

'Thank you all for meeting us here under such mysterious circumstances,' Percival said. 'I apologize for the cloak and dagger routine and for meeting here rather than down at the station but I think when you hear what I have to say it will soon become clear why things had to be done this way.' He paused and cleared his throat. 'There have been some further developments on the Bootham Bar Books case. I think DI Halloran has probably made it known to you that the police are not in the habit of sharing information with civilians but, as it stands, you have proven more trustworthy than some of our own officers.'

Evie exchanged a look with Kitt. Given the slight widening of the librarian's eyes, it seemed she knew little more about what this was all about than herself and Grace.

'I need to know,' Percival continued, 'that the details I'm going to share with you will under no circumstances be passed on to any other party, including the press. If you don't think you can keep that promise, now is the time to leave.'

Evie, Kitt and Grace all remained seated and stared expectantly at the chief superintendent. Though Evie knew she wasn't the best at keeping secrets as she often got overexcited or saw an opportunity for a joke and let something slip in the process, she was certain that when it came to something this important she would find a way to keep her peace.

'What I'm about to say, I don't say lightly and it may be that I am completely wrong about the situation. That's what I'd like to believe, but the truth is I have my suspicions that we can't trust one or more of the officers who are working at York Police Station just now.'

'You have evidence to suggest an officer is somehow mixed up in this case?' said Kitt.

'I'm afraid so,' Percival said, with a slow shake of his head. 'My suspicions were first aroused when Redmond, here, discovered yesterday that one of Alim Buruk's credit cards had been used to make a purchase in Helmsley.'

Grace frowned. 'Did he buy something suspicious? Something linked with the robbery?'

'We'll get to that,' said Redmond. 'But that weren't what roused suspicion. The card were used after Buruk died in t' hospital.'

Evie shuddered. Was it not bad enough that someone had murdered Alim without tampering with his life after the fact? She could hardly believe there were people in the world who acted with such cruelty and indifference. But her eyes had been opened in the last couple of months, and this particular situation was growing darker and darker.

'You think the killer stole Alim's credit card?' said Kitt.

'We don't know exactly,' said Halloran. 'But the two incidents are linked. We knew from looking at Buruk's financial records in more detail after his death that the card was missing from his personal effects. We thought Buruk, or perhaps Mrs Buruk, had stashed it somewhere because it was linked to their criminal activity. Now it seems the disappearance of his credit card is linked with his death.'

'So you're not sure if his card was stolen by a police officer?' asked Grace.

Percival paused. 'I'm sorry. It's difficult for me to talk about this. One of my own . . .'

'Makes yer sick,' said Redmond.

'It does that, lad,' said Percival. 'It does that. I believe some of you have met Superintendent Ricci, who is due to take over from me when I retire next week?'

Kitt and Evie nodded and Grace, who had not met Ricci, looked outraged at this omission.

'Ricci lives in Helmsley,' Percival said, each word with weight.

Evie, Kitt and Grace looked between each other.

'Is that enough to arouse suspicion?' asked Evie.

'Not on its own, but when me, Wilkinson and Ricci visited Buruk, we excused ourselves for a few minutes to talk to one of the nurses, find out if Buruk had said anything in passing that might help us with the case. When we came back, the curtain was drawn around Alim's bed and Ricci was with Buruk on the other side of it, alone.'

'Did you ask her why she had drawn the curtain?' asked Kitt.

'I didn't have to,' said Percival. 'She volunteered the fact that she had drawn the curtain to see if a bit of privacy helped Buruk feel more willing to cooperate and offer up some information.'

'That . . . seems plausible enough,' said Kitt.

'I agree, and at the time I didn't question it any further but I couldn't help but notice that there was something odd about the way she was acting.' Percival narrowed his eyes, remembering. 'She seemed . . . on edge. After thirty years in the force, I've become an expert in spotting a person who's lying to me. She was hiding something, there's no doubt about that.'

'So you think Ricci tampered with Alim's IV, and stole his credit card?' asked Kitt.

'I think she's too bloody clever to steal his credit card,' said Percival. 'But I think there's a chance that she took that opportunity to tamper with his IV because it would be very difficult to prove exactly who did that. Added to that, she's a police officer. Nobody would suspect her of doing anything untoward and she could have abused that trust for her own ends if she wanted to.'

'But if she'd go to those lengths, what makes you think she wouldn't take his credit card too?' asked Kitt.

'First, we think she's too clever to do all the dirty work herself. Second, stolen credit cards have a habit of turning up in people's places of residence and work. They are unto themselves pieces of evidence that have to be disposed of.

Third, she needed a patsy. She had to make sure Buruk was dead and couldn't tell any tales on her so she handled that bit herself, relying on her good standing to save her. But she likely found someone else to take the credit card so she had someone to pin this on if it went south.'

'An accomplice,' said Grace.

'She's sharp, this one. Wrong 'uns better watch out.' said Redmond, who coupled his remark with a snorty little laugh. Grace offered Redmond an over-polite smile in response.

'And you think the patsy stole the credit card and made the purchase?' said Evie.

'We think it's likely,' said Percival.

'Do you think her accomplice is a police officer?' asked Kitt.

Percival shook his head. 'I think she'd choose someone with a record, someone she could convince us was behind it all, or manipulate into taking the rap. And if any of this is true, there'll be a media circus. It'll ruin the reputation of York Police Station for months to come. A reputation I've worked hard to build.'

'What was the credit card used to buy?' asked Grace. 'Anything incriminating?'

Redmond nodded. 'You might say that.'

'That's another reason why we don't think Ricci would be stupid enough to use the credit card herself,' said Charley.

''Cording tut' shopkeeper, it was used to buy ropes, shovels, and thick plastic bags.'

'Oh, that's not good,' said Evie.

'The kind of shopping list you have if you want to bury something,' said Grace.

'Like a body,' said Banks.

'Whose body?' said Kitt. 'Buruk was just left in his hospital bed, wasn't he?'

'Donald Oakes,' Halloran said, his voice gentle.

'Donald?' Kitt said. 'But his body washed up in the Humber.'

'Maybe that wasn't the original plan?' said Halloran. 'Maybe something went wrong. So they changed their plan. Ditched the body in the river.'

'And . . . you think because Ricci was the only person to be alone with Buruk at this stage, she is the one behind all this?' Kitt said slowly, visibly trying to digest the idea.

Percival nodded. 'I don't want to think it. I wish to God we'd found something else on Holt. He's shady enough. I mean, carrying on with that young girl, orchestrating a robbery – not to mention Buruk's beating to frame Banks here. When he walked through the doors of the nick, I thought it was case closed.'

'But you can't find anything that links him to the murders?' said Kitt.

'We believe Donald Oakes was murdered between six and eight the evening before last,' said Charley. 'And Holt has an alibi for those times.'

'What about the shopkeepers who sold the goods to

whoever it was using Alim's credit card? Did you get a description?'

Redmond cleared his throat. 'The lady who owned t' shop said that she remembered that customer very well. It was a gent in his fifties with long brown hair, a long beard and moustache. He were wearing a baseball cap, she couldn't remember the logo on it but it was dark blue in colour. She said he were also wearing sunglasses even though it was dark outside by the time he got tut' shop.'

'So we can't rule out Jake or Elwood,' Evie said, without thinking. A Mexican wave of disapproving looks rippled around the room at her flippancy but stopped when it hit Charley, who had a small but unmissable smile on her lips.

'Anyway,' she continued, enjoying the warmth building inside at the sight of Charley's smile, 'that doesn't sound a lot how I remember Superintendent Ricci looking.'

'Long hair, sunglasses, a cap and a moustache?' said Kitt. 'Sounds more like a silly disguise to me.'

'I suppose it could have been a disguise of some sort,' said Percival. 'But disguised or not I think it's likely that this individual, as yet unidentified, could be her accomplice. Certainly, during the canvassing we did at the hospital, none of the patients, medical professionals or administrative staff said they had seen anyone matching that description near Alim's room. Or even that area of the hospital.'

'In fact,' said Halloran, 'according to the statements we've

226

gathered, Alim didn't receive any visitors between Ricci and his mother.'

'According to Alim's girlfriend, we shouldn't be ruling out his mother,' said Grace.

'Are you talking about Cammie?' asked Charley.

'That's the one,' said Kitt.

'She has mentioned her suspicion of his mother, and we have looked into it but we've got nothing on her. She's slippery. The best we can do is keep an eye on her bank and phone records in case she makes a mistake.'

'It is also possible that someone visited Alim and nobody noticed,' said Halloran.

'I doubt it,' said Evie. 'The man in the bed next to Alim's was a bit too nosy for someone to get in and out without him seeing them.'

Percival's lips tightened. 'My blood ran cold when I realized that Ricci was the only person besides his mother to be alone with the victim during the time frame in which he could have been poisoned. On top of that, she doesn't have an alibi for the night Donald was killed.'

'You asked her for her alibi?' said Kitt. 'So she knows you suspect her?'

Percival shook his head. 'No, no, no. I had to be smarter than that about it. I asked her what she had been up to on her night off – which coincides with the night Mr Oakes was killed.'

'What did she say?' asked Grace.

'She said she had spent the night at home, alone.'

'The circumstantial evidence does seem to be racking up here,' said Kitt.

'I agree. Added to that is the fact that she was openly hostile towards Banks on a number of occasions. Nothing too aggressive, mostly making it clear to Banks who was in charge – but it seemed like overkill because Banks is not one to challenge our ranks.'

'Little goodie two-shoes, that's me,' Charley said with a slight glimmer in her eye.

Halloran snorted. 'I'm not sure if I would quite go that far, Banks. Your behaviour at the staff Christmas party last year was not necessarily that becoming.'

Charley rolled her eyes. 'Ach, live by the book three hundred and sixty-four days of the year and they'll hang you for the one day you drink too much mulled wine. Such injustice.'

Percival shook his head. 'But Ricci's behaviour towards Banks was unusually brusque, to say the least. And I'm afraid there is one more damning clue to Ricci's involvement. Possibly the most damning of them all.'

'That sounds sinister,' said Kitt.

'It's the mark Candice found on Donald's hand,' said Halloran.

'Yes, a lower case letter "a",' said Kitt. 'I've been wracking my brains about what that could relate to. I've done so many Google searches on it that it looks as though I might have been temporarily possessed by a *Sesame Street* character.'

Evie giggled at that idea. She started squinting at her friend, trying to work out which *Sesame Street* character she most resembled. Was she Bert to Evie's Ernie? Or perhaps, given her love for teaching others new things, she was more Count von Count?

'Well, when we got the body back to the lab we discovered it wasn't just an "a". Donald actually had "32a" written across his hand.'

'"32a"?' said Kitt. 'What could that relate to?'

'An address,' said Charley. 'Superintendent Ricci lives at 32a Hambleton Avenue, in Helmsley.'

TWENTY-SIX

A silence fell over the group as everyone digested this information.

'God,' said Grace at last. 'I just can't believe this is happening.'

'I do have one question,' said Kitt.

'I thought you might,' said Halloran.

Kitt raised her eyebrows at the inspector before speaking. 'Why would Donald have Ricci's door number written on his hand? How did he get it?'

'Donald must have found out t' address were somehow related to the burglary of his bookshop,' said Redmond.

'And when the person living at that address found out he was onto them, they . . . killed him?' said Evie.

'And the only real motive Ricci could have for killing Donald, and presumably Alim, is if she was behind Holt's blackmail,' said Kitt. 'Is that the current theory?'

'It's one of many,' said Percival. 'Ever since Redmond

reported to me that Ricci's house number was written on Donald's hand I've wondered if there is something at that address that either leads back to the blackmail, or these murders, or both. Of course, if we officially search the property the jig is up. Ricci knows we suspect her. But I've been trying to think of some way of getting invited round or even getting some of you invited round to her house for a closer look. Everything I've come up with so far seems much too obvious, though.'

'Didn't Holt provide a list of likely blackmailers?' said Kitt. 'Maybe one of them has a connection to Ricci.'

'Mr Holt,' said Percival, 'who I believe you had a hand in apprehending – '

'It was Grace's detective work that led us to Holt,' Kitt said, smiling at her assistant, who sat up a little straighter at the compliment.

'We are grateful to you,' said Percival. 'But Mr Holt wasn't able to shed any light whatsoever on the identity of this blackmailer. Even though he told us that he has already handed over half of the promised money to them.'

'But if he's met his blackmailer to hand over the money, he must know who they are,' said Evie.

'Unfortunately not,' said Percival. 'The blackmailer instructed him to drop the money off in a particular place at a particular time and told him if he hung around to find out the identity of who was extorting him, he would be killed.'

'I say,' said Evie. Percival and Redmond frowned at Evie's

expression but the rest of the room looked at her with a mixture of entertainment and weariness.

'Er, yes, quite,' said Percival. 'In fact, Holt did provide us with a list of people who might want to blackmail him, but it didn't narrow down the suspect list.'

'He's got a lot of enemies?' said Grace.

Percival nodded. 'He's been running a series of what he called investment opportunities over the past six months. Some properties, some start-up companies, almost all of them imploded and the investors lost their money. That's without us even starting with people who might be annoyed about the affair he's having should they find out. His wife, his three daughters, they're all being looked into as well. The only thing Holt could tell us about his blackmailer was that they asked for the money to be left behind a gravestone in a church in Rosedale Abbey.'

'Quaint little place,' said Kitt 'But does Ricci have any connection to Rosedale Abbey?'

'Not that we know of yet,' said Percival. 'But it's not a long drive between there and Helmsley and for all we know her accomplice might live near there.'

Again, the whole room descended into silence. There was so much to take in.

'Say there is something to the Helmsley link and Ricci is involved, shouldn't we just turn this information over to the Independent Office of Police Conduct and leave it with them?' said Kitt.

'My first thought was to notify the IOPC and tell them that I'd be willing to help an anti-corruption unit monitor Ricci,' said Percival. 'But then I remembered that they were the first people Ricci called when she suspected Banks of assaulting Buruk. And in retrospect the promptness with which she involved them made me wonder . . .'

'Wonder what?' said Grace.

'If they were people we could trust.'

'You mean, you suspect there might be corrupt officers working with Ricci inside anti-corruption?' said Kitt, frowning at the idea.

'Well, I don't know. But I hesitated on taking the chance. She has risen up the ranks very quickly. Faster than almost any other officer I've ever met, which is why I thought she would be an incredible candidate to take over from me when I retire. Every t was crossed. Every i was dotted. But given what we've uncovered, it may be that she has got to the top by not entirely playing by the rules. That she's had some help.'

'What I don't understand is Ricci's motive,' said Kitt. 'Why is she doing this? Does she need the money?'

Percival shook her head. 'I wondered that. She's supposed to declare it if she gets into debt because it makes her more vulnerable to corruption. But when we checked, her financials came back clean and healthy.'

'So, why?' said Kitt. 'She's got everything going for her, it doesn't make sense.'

'She has got everything going for her, hasn't she?' said

Percival. 'Unusual for someone of her age to have climbed so far up the ladder. I think this might all be some elaborate way of making sure she climbs even higher.'

'How?' asked Grace.

'I don't know what her long game is,' said Percival. 'But Ricci has solved high profile cases in all of her other roles in the force. All of them, though, have been in bigger cities and towns. Maybe she didn't think somewhere as sleepy as York would deliver something high profile enough for her to manage during her first few months in the post and decided to create a drama all of her own.'

'But how will this case make her look good?' asked Evie.

'I'm not sure if it's about making her look good or me look bad,' said Percival. 'There's been a lot of press about this case and no matter what we've tried to get to the bottom of it we've found ourselves going round in circles. Course, if someone on the inside is orchestrating the whole thing, that might be a good reason why.'

'But she couldn't have known Holt would orchestrate a robbery to pay his debt,' said Grace.

'No, I don't think she could have planned for all the variables but I think she might have set the ball rolling with the blackmail to see what would happen. She may have looked into Holt's financial records to ensure he didn't have enough cash to pay what she was asking. Mr Holt is a dubious character to say the least and not likely to run to the police to solve his problems. It seems to me she chose her victim carefully.'

'So he orchestrates this robbery, and frames Banks for the beating to cover his back, creating a compelling case ripe for media attention,' said Kitt. 'But isn't that enough? Why risk killing anyone?'

'Well, York police did bring down a serial killer recently with some civilian assistance. That happened under my watch,' said Percival.

'And you think Ricci is trying to match that?' said Evie.

'It's a theory. Maybe she's waiting for me to step down and then as her first triumph in post she will pin it on someone, miraculously solving the case, like she has in all the other places she's served in,' said Percival.

'Seems like a lot of trouble to go to just to advance your career prospects,' Kitt said.

'I agree,' said Percival. 'If you're going to put this much effort in, you might as well just put the bloody work in to get to the top. But there are some pretty cushy wage packets once you climb the ranks. Though I've served my time, I can't claim to have been badly paid. And she's in the same place in her forties as I am in my sixties. You just think about all the money that is due to come her way.'

'Especially if she's making some extra pocket money on the side from the likes of Holt. We came so close, Mr Holt and I. After the fleeting moments we spent together at the auction house I'll always think of him as the one that got away,' Grace said, attaching a dramatic sigh for effect.

'What?' said Percival.

'Nothing,' said Kitt. 'You'll have to forgive my assistant. She's very excitable for no reason I've ever got to the bottom of.'

'Because of Ricci's suspected involvement,' said Halloran, taking control of the conversation once more, 'it's more vital than ever that she doesn't know that you're helping us with this case.'

'Though she remains the chief suspect,' said Percival, 'we can't rule out other lines of enquiry. Not least, Ricci will want updates on how Halloran, Banks and Redmond are progressing with the case. More than that, though, it makes sense to look at it from every possible angle and Ricci isn't the only one without an alibi for Donald's murder.'

'Shereen Oakes also claims to have been at home alone that evening,' said Redmond.

'I know that we thought Shereen had motive,' said Kitt, 'but that was largely based on information dished out to us by both Olivia and Derek. Neither of whom are reliable sources given they both played a part in helping Holt pull off the burglary in the first place.'

'It's not just the insinuation about the affair that makes us suspect her though,' said Charley. 'Donald had an insurance policy out on his life.'

'But if Shereen killed Donald she must be mixed up in the robbery somehow too, and we know Holt is behind that,' Evie said slowly and without meeting Charley's eye.

'Maybe she is. In the spirit of looking at other lines of

enquiry, is there a chance that Shereen could be Holt's blackmailer?' said Halloran.

'Isn't that most likely to be someone connected to Holt?' said Evie.

'But Shereen is connected to Holt,' said Halloran.

'Through Olivia,' said Kitt. 'Shereen could have found out about the affair Olivia was having and used it as an opportunity to blackmail him.'

'There's a possibility that Shereen somehow managed to plant ideas in Olivia's head about the first editions, manipulating the theft of the books so she would look like the victim rather than the orchestrator,' said Halloran.

'But what about the number written on Donald's hand?' said Grace. 'Doesn't that pretty much confirm it's Ricci?'

'No, not necessarily,' said Kitt. 'Say it is Shereen, and I'm not saying I believe it, but she would already have gone to so much trouble to hide what's really going on, she could easily have followed Ricci to see where she lives.'

'She was very down on her when we talked to them in the shop,' said Evie. 'Ricci had asked her and Donald a few questions about Alim and she was particularly defensive.'

'So she might have followed Ricci, or had her followed by an accomplice – the man who bought the supplies from the shop in Helmsley for instance.'

'And then planted the house number on the victim's hand to make it look like she was involved,' said Halloran.

'Perhaps we shouldn't rule out some big coincidence though,' said Grace. 'Like maybe that mark is not an address but Donald was going to buy Shereen some lingerie for Christmas or something?'

'No,' said Kitt. 'There's no way on this earth Shereen wears an A cup.'

Redmond let out his snorty little laugh at this and Percival was quick to jump in and change the subject. 'Whoever's behind it has already tried to frame one of my officers and there's a good chance that they might try and frame another. By God, I hope you're right about Shereen. It will mean Ricci isn't involved after all. Nor Wilkinson.'

'Wilkinson?' said Evie, realizing for the first time that the young PC wasn't amongst those assembled in the second-floor office. 'You don't think he's involved?'

'He's been working very closely with Ricci over the past week,' said Percival. 'We couldn't take the risk of bringing him in and, to be honest, from now on, you cannot assume anyone's innocence. If one of our own is involved, anyone could be.' Percival paused and looked long and hard between Kitt, Evie and Grace. 'It's going to mean letting go, at least temporarily, of any inclination to give people outside this circle the benefit of the doubt.'

Evie watched as Kitt pursed her lips. She knew her friend didn't want to believe that Shereen had anything to do with her husband's death but she had also made Donald a promise that she would find out who had done this to him, and this justice, it seemed, was what mattered to her most.

'All right,' said Kitt. 'What do you need us to do?'

TWENTY-SEVEN

Evie smiled as she noticed Kitt standing beneath the arch of Bootham Bar. She had a sandwich in one hand and a copy of *The Maltese Falcon* in the other. She was paying a lot more attention to reading the book than eating the sandwich.

'Getting the most out of your lunch break, I see,' said Evie when she was within earshot.

'Right now, I've no choice but to multitask if I'm to do the proper research to solve this case and maintain my curves,' said Kitt.

'And reading a mystery novel counts as research, does it?' Evie flashed Kitt an impish smile.

'I was just trying to think of a case halfway as complicated as the one we're trying to unravel to see if I could get any tips. Anyway, today is the last day I have to worry about fitting sleuth activities in around my responsibilities at the library.'

'Stone the crows! You're not . . . quitting the library, are you?'

'Don't be absurd,' said Kitt. 'I've arranged to take a week of annual leave, that's all.'

'Wow, at this short notice I bet that was a popular request with Michelle.'

'I've not taken my full leave allowance in the last five years so she'll just have to get over it. Besides, a friend of mine has just been murdered. I don't think even she can blame me for wanting some time off.'

'I agree,' said Evie, patting Kitt's arm.

'Certainly, helping students locate books and journals when I could have been tracking down the person responsible for Donald's condition wasn't doing me any good,' said Kitt.

'I can imagine.'

'Of course Grace is pretty put out because she won't be able to take time off and you've seen how keen she is to be in on the act at every turn. I've tried to reassure her I'll include her as much as possible in the investigation but you know how excitable she gets.'

'Yes,' said Evie. 'On a related note, what are you doing this evening?'

'Nothing much, I've cleared all decks for this case.' Kitt said. 'Why?'

'Ruby paid a visit to the salon about an hour ago.'

'Oh? She must have come straight from the library because she was in the Women's Studies section not long before that trying to convince me to go round to her house to have my tarot cards read. Again. I gave her short shrift, of course. What did she want at the salon?'

'Well, she came to convince me of the same thing. To go round to her house and have the tarot cards read. Only whereas you turned her away, I caved.'

'Oh, Evie, you shouldn't encourage her.'

'I know, but she was just so insistent and it's quite hard to say no to her after a while because – well, it's apparent she hasn't got anyone waiting for her at home.'

'We have so many better things to be doing right now.'

'She doesn't know that. She might have read about the bodies in the newspaper but doesn't know how sinister the case has got. Police corruption and all that. Besides, I think she's a bit lonely.'

'And I do all I can to make her feel welcome at the library but right now I really need to focus on the investigation . . . Wait a second. I thought you said this was somehow related to Grace?'

'Well, I'm inviting her too.'

'So it will be you, Grace and Ruby, in a room together meddling with tarot cards?'

'I suppose you could put it that way.'

'Oh dear, then I will need to come along. I can't imagine the mischief you three could get up to unsupervised.'

'Thought that might be a deal-breaker,' said Evie. 'I suppose we should go and visit Shereen before our lunch breaks are up.'

'Yes, I suppose we had,' said Kitt, starting off up High Petergate.

'Is the plotline to *The Maltese Falcon* somehow related to this case?' asked Evie.

'Not unless a black statue made by the sixteenth-century Knights of Malta was also stolen from the bookshop and has yet to be noticed as missing,' said Kitt.

'Seems unlikely,' said Evie. 'I just feel it's been a while since you've put forward a fictional parallel for the case we're dealing with. I was expecting you to solve the case in a jiffy based on a plotline surrounding a blackmail gone awry.'

'There are far too many to choose from to even hope of doing something like that.'

'Oh I see,' said Evie, but Kitt wasn't finished.

'Even just taking the works of Agatha Christie you've got *The Secret of Chimneys*, *One Two, Buckle My Shoe*, *Hallowe'en Party*, *Three Act Tragedy* . . . The list goes on and that's without even getting into the TV adaptations that often take liberties and throw a blackmailing or two in for good measure.'

'All right, I take your point. People in detective novels often try to cash in the easy way.'

'On the contrary, the blackmail is almost never about money.'

'Really? Why blackmail people if you don't want the money?'

'To conceal an even darker motive for murder or to incriminate someone else, to distract from some other felony related to the case like bigamy, an earlier murder or an accidental death the parties were somehow answerable for. In the few cases where blackmail is about the money it's usually about desperation rather than a desire for a luxury lifestyle.'

Evie looked sidelong at her friend. 'I thought you read the Agatha Christie books some years ago now? You seem to remember them in striking detail.'

'I may have reread one or two of her best after playing the detective myself lately.'

'One or two?'

'Or twelve.'

Evie shook her head.

'But you have made me think, Evie. We probably shouldn't be looking at the obvious motives for blackmail here, i.e. the money. It makes me think that Chief Superintendent Percival was onto something when he suggested Ricci might be orchestrating these crimes to escalate her career.'

'It's a frightening thought,' said Evie.

'And perhaps a little bit far-fetched?'

'I've had to redefine the term far-fetched recently,' said Evie.

'Fair point,' said Kitt.

The pair stopped outside Bootham Bar Books.

'I'll discuss it further with Halloran when I talk to him this afternoon,' said Kitt. 'Maybe he can look at some of the past cases Ricci has been credited for closing and see if there's anything suspicious about them. That would at least help us see if there really is a pattern there.'

'Anything we can do to wind this nightmare up sooner rather than later is fine by me,' said Evie.

Kitt nodded and turned her attentions to the door of the shop.

'I can't believe she's opened again so soon after Donald's body was found washed up like that.'

'That in itself is a little bit suspicious,' said Evie. 'Though I know you don't really want to hear that.'

'What I want to hear isn't relevant right now,' said Kitt. 'Amateur sleuths don't have the luxury of having things turn out how they want, or seeing the best in people. It's like Percival said, we can't trust anyone.' And with that, she took a deep breath and pushed open the door.

TWENTY-EIGHT

'Oh, hello, love,' said Shereen as Kitt stepped over the threshold and Evie closed the door behind them.

Kitt walked up to the counter where Shereen was standing and put her arms around her. 'I'm so sorry. I really don't quite know what to say, except I'm sorry.'

'Just seeing your face is a comfort,' said Shereen, but she appeared to be having trouble focusing, and though she was looking in Kitt's direction she didn't appear to really see her. It seemed her mind was elsewhere. Whether she was focused on mourning the loss of her husband or covering up her guilt in his disappearance was the question.

As the pair embraced, Evie tried to recall the tips Percival had given them about this particular visit to Bootham Bar Books. He had been clear that the last thing he wanted to do was endanger the lives of civilians, and that he and the other officers would be the ones to dig deeper on Amira Buruk to see if she had anything to do with her son's death.

He did believe, however, that they could be of help when it came to Shereen, with little risk. He had explained that it was much more likely that Shereen might let something slip to a friend than she would to a police officer. Perhaps something almost unconscious that Shereen wouldn't even realize was a clue to her involvement. Their instructions were to stay vigilant throughout the entire visit. To look around for anything that might connect with the case or anything that seemed odd. Percival was also very keen for Kitt to make an assessment of Shereen's general behaviour. Whilst taking her recent bereavement into account, Percival wanted to know if Shereen was acting any different from usual, and if so how.

'I didn't know if you'd be open but thought I'd swing by just in case,' said Kitt.

'I tried sitting at home yesterday. I didn't know what to do with myself. I couldn't manage another day like that. I'll take some time off after the funeral but until then, I just can't face sitting in that house all alone again. Knowing he isn't coming home.'

'Completely understandable.'

'I'm so sorry, Shereen,' said Evie while Shereen nodded and half-smiled in response. She wondered about bringing up the death of her ex-boyfriend as a way of making a connection, the way she had with Cammie, but somehow it didn't seem right. She had dated Owen for two years, which was a significant chunk of time, but Kitt said Shereen and

Donald had been together for twenty-five, so there really didn't seem any comparison.

'Is there anything we can do to help?' said Kitt, looking around the shop, her eyes settling on a small, half-height bookcase pushed up against the wall near the counter. Kitt seemed to be giving the bookcase a great deal of attention and Evie sighed inwardly. They were supposed to be focused on Shereen and Kitt was busy eyeing up the next addition to her reading pile. Evie resisted the urge to roll her eyes.

'If you're really keen, you can help to find me a new shop assistant,' said Shereen.

'Oh, you've let Olivia go then?' Kitt said, tilting her head.

'I could barely bring myself to speak to her. But I did it. I phoned her up and told her not to bother coming back.' Shereen's voice became loud and shrill as she spoke and her face reddened. 'If it wasn't for her Donald would still be . . . still be . . . here.'

Tears slid down Shereen's cheeks as she apologized and grabbed a tissue from a box sitting behind the counter. 'I expect your inspector has told you all about what she did.'

Though Shereen's voice was bitter, Kitt didn't seem ruffled by it. 'Actually, the police aren't able to share information with civilians, not even their significant others.'

Evie's brain seized on Kitt's choice of wording. If they were in any other situation she would have at once begun teasing her friend about the fact she saw herself as Halloran's 'significant other'. As it was, even Evie could see this wasn't the time and the place, and besides, though she didn't think it was possible, something more tantalizing than teasing Kitt had caught her attention. A hammer was sitting on the cash desk next to the till. Candice had said that the likely cause of Donald's untimely death was blunt force trauma. A hammer would do that.

'The highlights are that Olivia was having an affair with a married man and when someone blackmailed him over it she suggested he steal our most valuable items of stock to pay the money,' said Shereen, her breath ragged as she spoke.

Evie watched Kitt's eyes widen as though she was hearing this information for the very first time. 'That's unbelievable!' she said.

Evie caught Kitt's eye and gave the hammer a long, pointed look before glancing back up at her friend.

Kitt subtly shook her head and gave a dismissive wave. So much for staying objective.

'What a betrayal,' Kitt said to Shereen, as though Evie hadn't even directed her to the hammer. 'But how did that lead to Donald's death?'

'I don't know. But the police say it can't be coincidence that this place was burgled and then just a couple of weeks later Donald is killed. And I don't know anything about these kinds of things really but I'd have to agree with them. It must be the same person behind Donald's death and that kid in the hospital.'

'And nobody knows who that is? Who blackmailed Olivia's . . . boyfriend?' Evie tried not to look at the hammer as she spoke and in averting her eyes to another part of the desk, noticed a stack of papers. Was that an insurance document sitting on top of the pile? The insurance claims form for the burglary perhaps? Or for Donald's life insurance . . .

'The police tell me they're pursuing several leads,' said Shereen, drawing Evie's attentions away from the paperwork. 'Which sounds very much like they've no idea who it is.'

Kitt pursed her lips.

'Oh, I'm sorry, love. I keep forgetting about your inspector. I should watch what I'm saying.'

'No need to apologize,' said Kitt. 'Or censor yourself for that matter, given what you've been through. I've felt frustration with the police force myself once or twice in the past few months. It's different when the case is personal. You feel like nothing anyone does is enough.'

'Exactly,' said Shereen. 'But I've been sat here today, thinking. And I've just come to realize that no matter what they do, they can't bring my Don back. Nothing can.'

'But we can get justice for him,' said Kitt. 'I know it might feel as though the police could do more but I promise you, from what I know of them, they are very committed to their work and will be doing everything in their power to find out who was behind your husband's murder.' Kitt patted Shereen's hand and Evie noticed as she did so that the woman was finding it difficult to hold Kitt's gaze.

'Well, I hope so,' Shereen said, looking down at the counter. 'I should've known when he sent that text message to say he was going out with his friends. He never does that on a week night. He's always too tired.'

'I don't think there's anything inherently suspicious about going out for a drink after work, you can't blame yourself,' said Kitt.

'But I knew,' Shereen said. 'I knew there was something wrong. The wording of the text, it sounded more formal than the words Donald usually used. I knew there was something wrong but I didn't do anything. I should've called him . . . I should've – '

'Shereen,' Kitt said, cutting her off. 'The only person to blame for your husband's death is the person who killed him.'

Shereen nodded but didn't say anything else. She was too busy grabbing more tissues to dab her eyes and cheeks with.

Again, Kitt looked over at the small bookcase pushed up against the wall at the side of the counter, a little more vaguely than she had the last time.

Perhaps Kitt wasn't eyeing up the books on the bookcase. Perhaps something about the bookcase itself was bothering her and she had been focused on the case all the time she was talking to Shereen. While Shereen finished drying her eyes, Evie meandered over to the bookcase for a closer look. There didn't seem to be anything special about it. What was Kitt looking at? She picked up a book off the top shelf, looked the back cover with feigned interest and went to return it to its place. As she did so, however, she noticed something on the wall, behind where the book had been standing.

She swung around, her breath short. 'Kitt . . . I think you better come and look at this.'

Kitt frowned and strode over and Evie couldn't help but notice the unreadable look on Shereen's face as she did so.

'Look,' Evie said, pointing at what was unmistakably a tiny speck of blood splashed against the yellow wall.

'Shereen, this bookcase isn't usually over here. I noticed it as soon as I walked in. Did you move it here?' asked Kitt.

'No,' she said. 'I assumed Donald moved it before . . . before . . . you know. And without a shop assistant I've not had a chance to move it back. It's not a very good place for it. I don't know what he was thinking. But he did have a little rearrange of things now and then.'

Without another word Kitt manoeuvred herself to the far end of the bookcase and signalled Evie to grab the other end. Kitt shunted her end of the case outward with what seemed like minimal effort.

'Oh, you don't have to –' Shereen began, but was cut off.

Evie managed to shuffle her side a few inches forward and Kitt exclaimed, 'Oh my God!'

'What? What is it? Have you hurt yourself?' said Shereen. 'There's some sharp edges on them damn things, I've had cuts and splinters, the lot.'

Kitt shook her head. 'Behind this bookcase. There's blood spatter.'

Evie frowned and leant over the top of the bookcase to take a look at the wall behind. Sure enough, as Kitt said, there were red splashes of blood all up the wall.

'Blood?' Shereen said in a small voice. 'It's not my Don's blood, is it?'

'I can't say for certain,' said Kitt. 'But if you were asking me to guess, I think Donald died here, in the bookshop before he was . . . taken down to the river. We need to call the police. This is now a crime scene.'

TWENTY-NINE

As Evie, Grace and Kitt approached Ruby's cottage, Kitt let out another sigh.

Grace had been in high spirits on the drive to the outlying village of Orpington. Even after several hours she was still caught up in the revelation that Evie and Kitt had discovered blood at Bootham Bar Books earlier that afternoon. In sharp contrast, Kitt had been almost monosyllabic and Evie didn't have to ask her friend why. She knew, given the breakthrough, that Kitt wanted to debate theories with Halloran about how far the fact that Donald had likely been killed in his own bookshop further incriminated Shereen Oakes. Being torn away to listen to Ruby read tarot cards wasn't at the top of Kitt's to-do list and she had put an admirable amount of effort into trying to wriggle out of it. In the end Evie had convinced her that, left to their own devices, she, Grace and Ruby might actually end up summoning some kind of malevolent spirit, or worse, and it was safer for mankind if she joined them.

Evie also knew there were probably better things they could be doing than indulging an old lady's 'psychic' tendencies, but admitted to herself that she was a little bit curious about what might come up in the card reading. Not just about the case, but about other areas of her life.

Ruby had given Evie her address when she agreed to come around that evening but even if she hadn't, the trio agreed that they would have been able to guess which residence in the small line of cottages belonged to the old woman.

Smoke snaked its way out of the fat-necked chimney and somewhere the faint jingling of wind chimes struck a melody into the sharp December breeze. In the yellow glow of the street lamps, Evie could see every other house on the street boasted trim hedgerows and manicured lawns but Ruby's garden looked more like a jungle. Ivy climbed the fence and the walls, the ground seemed mossy rather than grassy and long bamboo leaves spiked out in every direction, obscuring the path to the house. Ruby had arranged various weird and wonderful garden ornaments in unexpected places, or at least that was the way it felt in the dark. A large toadstool here. A weeping fairy there.

'Agh!' Kitt called out.

'What? What is it?' Evie asked, a little bit on edge in Ruby's jungle-like garden. If York was home to any abnormally large spiders they would more than likely live here.

'Stubbed my toe on that bloody weeping fairy ornament,' said Kitt, sucking air through her teeth and limping towards the threshold where an intimidating bull-headed figure carved of stone awaited. She was about to knock when the door swung open and Ruby appeared, clad in a long black satin gown.

'I sensed you were near.'

'You saw us from the window,' Kitt said, a little more curtly than Evie thought was polite. She shot Kitt a look dark enough to shame her into offering their host a frail smile.

'It's nice to see you, Ruby,' said Kitt, her tone softer than it had been before. 'Shall we come in?'

'Yes, enter, enter,' said Ruby who seemed unruffled by Kitt's earlier rudeness. The pair had known each other for years through the library so perhaps she was used to Kitt's scepticism.

Evie took a deep breath as she stepped inside and Kitt and Grace followed her. Ruby shut the door to keep out the bleak chill, while Evie stared around the room in quiet astonishment. It was one of the most curious places she had ever seen and given what her own living room looked like she didn't reach that conclusion lightly. The walls looked as though they had been whitewashed hundreds of years ago and not redecorated since. They had turned a strange mustard colour and the paint was crumbling away in the corners. Large orbs of crystal sat by the window, there was a shelf filled with odd-shaped bottles and jars, and bird feathers were piled up on a small desk in the corner. Evie, being Evie, wanted to touch each and every one of them to get a better sense of what they were and what they might be used for. Despite how near it was to Christmas there was not a shred of tinsel to be seen but there were some wicker stars hanging by the window and a garland of ivy draped over the mantelpiece with acorns, pine cones and holly sprigs strategically spaced along its boughs. A plump ginger cat sprawled out in front of a blazing fire. Despite the strangeness of her surroundings Evie felt herself drawn in to the warmth after the empty cold of the December night.

'Sit down, sit down,' Ruby said, gesturing to the sofa and a couple of armchairs. 'I've poured us some of my home-made dandelion wine.'

'Great,' said Kitt, her tone dripping with irony. Evie didn't particularly welcome the prospect of accepting anything digestible off the woman either, in light of what strange liquids were bottled in her living room. And hadn't Kitt once mentioned that Ruby home-brewed drinks in her bath tub? That didn't sound very sanitary.

The three of them sat and Evie's eyes were at once riveted on the deck of cards sitting on the coffee table. They had been placed on a length of dark purple fabric and were stacked face down so it was not yet possible to see all of the beautiful images Evie knew were drawn on the other side.

'With time ticking on a bit, laying out a Celtic cross might be a bit involved. It's probably best just to do a three-card spread,' said Kitt.

Everyone in the room looked at her.

'Where did that come from?' asked Evie.

'Ee, I 'ad no idea you practised the cards, love,' Ruby said with a knowing grin that Evie was sure would rile Kitt right up. She wasn't wrong.

'I have read some books about their history and philosophy,' Kitt sniffed, sitting up a little straighter in her armchair. 'Doesn't mean I believe a word of it.'

'Well, we can start with a three card spread and take it from there, but it's not going to be an in-depth reading if we stick with that alone.'

Evie smiled to herself; brevity was exactly what Kitt was hoping for.

'Now, who is the enquirer?'

'What do you mean?' said Evie.

'Who is asking the question?' Ruby said. 'Who wants to take a journey through the ancient wisdom? Who wants –'

'Yes, thank you, Ruby,' Kitt interrupted. 'We get the picture. I think as Evie was the person to arrange this meeting that it makes sense for her to ask the question.'

Grace, who had opened her mouth but not managed to speak before Kitt, let her posture slump in disappointment. 'Evie can go first,' she said, 'but I think it's only fair we all get a turn.'

'What do I do, then?' said Evie. 'I've never done this before.'

Ruby stared at Evie, her eyes piercing. 'First thing to do is you think of a question.' Evie looked over at Kitt and Grace, then back at the cards. She felt herself swallow hard. What question could she ask that would help with the case? And maybe help her sort out the tangle of thoughts she had been trying to unravel ever since she had spent the night with Charley? It seemed impossible to think of a question that would straddle those two issues, and it wasn't like she could ask about the other night specifically without both Ruby and Grace finding out what had happened between her and DS Banks.

Tempting as it was to ask something self-motivated, Evie decided she could probably work out what on earth was happening on a personal level after the culprit behind the terrible events surrounding Bootham Bar Books had been apprehended. The right thing to do now was to focus on the case.

'Who is behind the crimes committed in the Bootham Bar Books case?' Evie said, and then looked at Ruby. 'Will that work?'

'That'll do,' said Ruby. 'Now, pick up the cards and shuffle them. You'll need to stay focused while you do. Keep that question, and that question alone, in your mind and in your heart as you shuffle.'

Frowning, Evie picked up the pack of cards and followed Ruby's instructions. Focusing on one thing had never really been her speciality. But she did her best and then completed the remaining steps as instructed by Ruby, separating the cards into three piles before shuffling them back into one pile with all the cards facing down.

One by one Ruby turned over three cards. They had the most ornate pictures on them and the colouring was intense. Bright yellows and dark charcoal shades.

Grace let out a little gasp as she looked at the cards. 'The Devil?' she said, looking at the first card that Ruby had laid out. 'That can't be good.'

Ruby smiled. 'The cards themselves are not bad or good. They're just suggestions on how to manage life's lessons.'

'So what does it mean then, the Devil?' Evie asked. Kitt was sitting in silence, unwilling to engage even though Evie would have bet her entire collection of vintage tablecloths that she knew exactly what the card meant.

'This first card represents the recent past,' said Ruby, 'and the Devil represents temptation. Someone had the opportunity to take a quick, easy path to success. One that would hurt others. And they took it.'

A short cut to success? Ruby had to be talking about Ricci. Chief Superintendent Percival said she had risen to the top of the ladder faster than anyone he had ever known; it was one of the things that had put her under suspicion.

'What about that card in the middle?' asked Grace. 'The Lovers.'

Evie studied the card. It had a man and a woman standing next to each other, naked. That was what the world believed love was supposed to look like, or had for a very long time.

Despite all the progress that had happened in the last twenty years or so, quite a few people still thought of two men or two women together as something out of the ordinary. Her parents were definitely among those people. And probably her aunts and uncles. The problem was, to Evie, being with Charley hadn't felt out of the ordinary at all. At least, not in a negative way. To her, it had felt more natural than she ever could have expected. Still, it was too late now. She had told Charley that nothing else could happen and that was the end of it. Hopefully, she would look back on it in a few months and laugh. It would just be one of those strange blips. A story future boyfriends would no doubt beg her to tell.

'The Lovers,' said Ruby, wrenching Evie out of her thoughts, 'in this context, suggests whoever's behind the crimes at Bootham Bar Books has some big choice to make between lovers, or relationship paths. It could very well be this choice that's driven them to commit the crimes. The Lovers card is never about a simple choice. It's a decision that has long-lasting consequences.'

Evie and Grace frowned at each other again. After what Dennis had told them on the bus the other day, Ruby probably didn't have to be psychic to read their minds right now. That said, as far as they knew she wasn't aware of Shereen's alleged affair and Kitt had been clear that they must not give away anything about the investigation that Ruby couldn't have read in the local news. Thus the pair stayed silent.

There were a couple of people involved with this case who might have that kind of decision to make, but as far as any of them knew neither of them were Ricci. Holt was playing the victim, but what if this was all some elaborate ruse for a purpose they couldn't yet figure out? However, the most likely person this card linked to was Shereen. The wife of the man now dead. The person who was rumoured to have been involved in staging the burglary for the insurance money. Shereen's profile didn't fit what Ruby had said about the Devil card but maybe somehow Ricci and Shereen had been responsible for different parts of this mess? Maybe that was why it was so difficult to pin it on one person, because more than one person had played a part.

'The last card, sitting in the future position, is the ten of swords – ' Ruby began.

'Yes, but I hardly think you need to be an expert in tarot reading to work this one out,' Kitt interjected, at last breaking her silence.

'Be my guest,' Ruby said with a wide grin, gesturing at the card.

'Fine,' Kitt sighed, holding the card up so everyone had a fair look at it. She was doing all she could to make out that she didn't want to oblige but after years of friendship it was obvious to Evie that Kitt couldn't wait to communicate her expertise. Kitt lived to educate. As a rule, if she protested greatly about the sharing of knowledge, it was likely all for show. 'This card depicts a man lying face down on the ground with ten swords stabbed through his back. I'm going to go out on a limb and suggest this card is about betrayal?'

Despite Kitt's arid tone, Ruby nodded with enthusiasm. 'It's not just that though, love,' she said. 'It's the intensity of the betrayal. It suggests this person might be very close to the people of Bootham Bar Books. Somebody in their midst who they think they can trust above all others, but they're mistaken.'

Evie chewed on her bottom lip, thinking. Could this be a reference to Olivia? She had betrayed Shereen once before, could she be doing it again? If so, it would lend weight to the theory that Holt was somehow behind all this. But how, and more to the point why? Why would anyone stage their own blackmail over an affair they didn't want anyone to know about?

Perhaps the card referred to Ricci, the person overseeing the burglary case. The person Donald and Shereen should have been able to trust, but couldn't. Or maybe it related to Shereen herself. A person at the centre of this case who seemed like the victim but had had the opportunity to manipulate almost every element of the unfolding drama.

Shereen, Ricci and Holt. One of them was the Devil in all this and by the light of Ruby's fireplace Evie wished for a little Christmas magic. For some small miracle that would help them unmask the killer and stop them before anyone else fell victim to their plot.

THIRTY

After a somewhat surreal experience Evie had been looking forward to an hour of TV before bedtime. She was just about to drift off into a doze on the sofa when the doorbell rang. She looked at the clock that hung above the TV. Half past ten. Who calls round at this time? Granted she had shown up on Kitt's doorstep much later than this on the odd occasion but if something drastic had happened with the case between now and leaving Ruby's house, Kitt would more than likely have rung rather than called round.

Evie jumped off the sofa and turned off the TV before catching her reflection in the small mirror that hung on the back of the living room door and shrieking as she caught sight of the silicone strips she had forgotten she was wearing. The doorbell rang a second time. In panic, she peeled off the strips and shoved them in the nearest available receptacle, which in this instance was a VE celebratory mug sitting on the dresser with Winston Churchill's face emblazoned across it.

'Sorry, Winnie, help a girl out, won't you?' Evie said as she made sure the strips were out of sight. She then rearranged her curls over her scars as best she could and went through to the passage to answer the door.

On opening it she saw the back of a man's head walking down the path. 'DS Redmond?' Evie called, wrapping her arms around herself as the winter chill bit at her.

Redmond turned and flashed Evie a smile. 'Oh, you are in.'

'Yeah, sorry. I wasn't expecting company . . . as you can tell,' she said indicating her clothes.

Redmond chuckled. 'Not to worry. Just knocking off duty and on my way home I thought I'd come round and ask you out.'

Evie's eyes widened. 'Out?'

'Well, it wasn't my idea, like. I've been ordered to ask you out.'

'Ordered? By who?'

'Percival. Don't know how he's done it but he's managed to get us an invite round t' Ricci's house tomorrow night.'

'To her house?' Evie said, and then decided the next time Redmond said something she would put every ounce of energy into not repeating it like a feather-brained parrot. 'I know Percival said he was keen to find a way in there but is it really a good idea? There's a chance we'll rouse her suspicion and then the jig is up.'

'It is a risk,' said Redmond, 'but between you, me and t' gatepost, this case is really getting to Percival. His retirement party is on Saturday and he's desperate to see this tied up before he goes. He's past himself at the thought of leaving us under the possible control of a corrupt officer.'

'I can understand that,' said Evie. 'So he's stepped up the timetable.'

Redmond nodded. 'There's something else. Apparently, Percival was talking to Ricci the other day, just casual like, and she started talking about the fact that she's going to get a patio.'

'OK . . .' said Evie. 'Is that a police code I don't understand?'

'Y' know folk bury things they never want found under t' patio, don't you?' Redmond said.

'Now that you mention it, I do seem to remember that coming up in an episode of *Brookside* circa 1993, yes.'

'Well, according to Halloran your friend Kitt is keen on the idea that fiction and reality might not be that different. Sometimes she's right.'

Evie giggled. 'Not according to Halloran, he's pretty quick to shoot down her ideas.'

'DI Halloran takes his work serious, like, and I don't blame him for that,' said Redmond. 'But perhaps Ms Hartley might loosen 'im up a bit, eh?'

Not wishing to discuss her friend's love life with someone she had only met on one occasion, Evie just offered a polite nod. The temptation of course was to agree with him but, truth be told, after the long day she'd had she could have done without Redmond just dropping round because he felt like it. There was also something about the officer she couldn't quite warm to; though she couldn't explain what, she decided to bring this visit to a close as quickly as possible.

'So what reason did Percival give for having us traipsing round Ricci's house? How did he land an invite?'

'He said that it were most unhospitable of 'er not to have invited us round for a house-warming. Said it were station policy and as his retirement party is on Saturday, it'd better be sooner rather than later.'

'Is it department policy?' asked Evie.

'No, it's not, like, but she's only been with us a few weeks and 'as no idea.'

'Bit of a risk to lie about it like that,' said Evie. 'Here's hoping she doesn't ask around.'

'With a bit of luck Ricci'll be too busy trying to sort things out for t' party.'

'And she agreed to it, just like that?'

'No, she was reluctant. Which of course only made us all the more suspicious.'

'That could be just because she doesn't want the people she's managing trudging round her new house. Has she even unpacked yet?'

'Doubt it. And I hear what yer saying. Might just be a bad time for 'er. But given everything else we know it's more likely that she's worried someone might uncover something she doesn't want 'em to.'

'And I'm supposed to go with you? To this party? That's part of the plan?'

'Percival said it would be best if you came along, like. Kitt'll be coming with DI Halloran and she suggested she wanted you along too. To keep your eyes peeled for anything untoward, like the rest of us.'

'I don't know,' Evie said. 'The first time I met Ricci she wasn't exactly what you would call friendly. Wouldn't it seem a bit rude to just show up at her house after I've sort of had a run-in with her?'

'The DI's going to smooth it with 'er. 'E's going to pretend I've taken a bit of a shine to you ... given how sweet you seem I'm sure that won't be 'ard for her to believe.'

'That's ... kind of you to say,' said Evie, thinking of the many things she had done over the years that could hardly be described as sweet. Some of them just the other evening with this man's co-worker.

'So, you don't mind coming along with me? For t' sake of the case, like?'

Evie smiled. 'For the sake of the case I'm sure I can stand to be seen out with a dashing police officer for one evening.'

To her surprise, Redmond blushed at her comment and cleared his throat. 'Well, now that you've 'eard the crazy scheme, I'll let you relax for t' evening. And I'll pick you up on Saturday.'

'I've got my own car,' said Evie suddenly remembering that Charley was likely to be at this gathering and the two of them arriving together might be hurtful to her. 'I could meet you there.'

'Looks better if we show up together,' Redmond said. 'Sells t' idea of our date a bit better.'

'Good point,' said Evie, unable to think of a way out of it.

'So I'll pick you up at seven?'

'Yes,' said Evie with a smile. 'Seven.'

Redmond nodded and walked back along the path towards his car. Evie watched him get into his vehicle, trying to convince herself that Charley was a professional and would understand her showing up with Redmond would be part of the cover story. Slowly, she closed the door and wondered when she would be able to do the same when it came to her feelings for Charley.

THIRTY-ONE

Evie was pleasantly surprised that Redmond kept things businesslike on the way to Ricci's house in Helmsley. If they had taken the trip during daylight hours, they would have been able to spend the fifty-minute journey commenting on the quaint details of the villages that lay between points A and B. The glimpses of an ornate, early Georgian house built by local architect Thomas Atkinson at Sutton on the Forest, the views over the Howardian Hills and the decorative gate of Sproxton Hall which, Kitt had once explained to Evie, was a monument built in honour of Admiral Nelson.

As it was a dark and misty night, however, the pair had been forced to find other topics and, given their objective this evening, conversation naturally turned to the case. Between them, Evie and Redmond had turned over every aspect of it once again. Redmond was particularly interested to learn about the visits they had paid to the bookshops and what they had uncovered when they spoke to Holt, and he was also attentive when she described Halloran's Indiana Jones-esque, chair-hopping antics at the auction house. That is, he was particularly attentive to her words. He was laughing so hard at what she had to say she was a little concerned he might accidentally drive them into a ditch in a fit of hysterics.

Though the details of the case were grim, Evie preferred that to personal chit-chat. She chided herself for not cutting Redmond more slack. He was a police officer, after all, trying to do the right thing and solve the case. But for whatever reason she just couldn't feel at ease around him. There was something stiff about his manner. He paused before almost every sentence he uttered and whenever they stopped at traffic lights or at a junction, Evie could feel his eyes on her and she didn't much like the feeling. Perhaps the chap was just on edge because he was about to enter into a madcap undercover operation at his boss's house. Evie had to remember that Redmond and his colleagues had been through a great deal in the past week. Though to Evie's mind, nobody had been through more than Charley.

At last Redmond turned his silver Toyota into the driveway indicated by the satnav screen. An outside light beamed on as their car approached the white stone house. Like the other houses on this stretch, it wasn't exactly what you'd call a mansion but it wasn't small either. Evie guessed it must have at least four bedrooms by the size of it. Given the address of '32a' she expected it to be somehow smaller, perhaps even a terraced house. But it looked like a relatively new build so the odds were that it was built on a convenient spare plot of land between one house and another.

'Guess now we know what she did with all t' money she's earnt,' said Redmond. 'How much do houses like these cost out 'ere?'

Evie shook her head. 'I wouldn't even like to guess.' Her breath caught in her throat as she noticed the door number written in black lettering next to the door frame. '32a,' she said.

'Bit creepy, in't it?' said Redmond. 'Seeing that, knowing it was written on the hand of a murder victim.'

'Does Ricci know?' asked Evie. 'That her house number was found on Donald's hand?'

'No,' said Redmond. 'We kept it out of t' report and said it was just an "a" like we thought at first.'

'I guess we'd better go in,' said Evie, taking a deep breath.

'You don't have to, you know?' said Redmond. 'It's my job to go inside there, not yours. You're doing us a favour. I can drop you down't pub in town and pick you up in a couple of hours, just say t' word.'

'Thanks,' Evie said, smiling at Redmond's thoughtfulness and feeling guilty again for not taking more of a shine to him. 'But I can't let Kitt down, or Ch – or Banks or Halloran. I want to help, if I can.'

Redmond nodded but didn't say any more. He took off his seat belt and got out of the car, Evie following suit.

The pair walked towards the door, crunching over gravel. It was a bit difficult to walk over uneven surfaces in the vintage kitten heels Evie had selected for the evening but they were the shoes that went best with her black pencil skirt and a white blouse patterned with tiny red hearts.

Redmond knocked at the door. Evie's stomach muscles clenched. A moment later the door opened and Ricci's face appeared in the door frame, holding a glass of wine.

'Oh, it's the love birds,' she said with a smile. 'Come in.'

So, Halloran had done a good job of selling the idea that Redmond had taken a shine to Evie.

'That's a nice frock, ma'am,' Redmond said.

Ricci looked down at the blue satin dress she was wearing. The soft material made her features seem less sharp than they had the first time she and Evie crossed paths. 'It's a bit much for tonight, but I haven't even begun to unpack my wardrobe yet so you're all being treated to the outfit I wore at the dinner to celebrate my promotion to superintendent. It won't get another showing in a long time so make the most of it.'

Redmond issued that snorty little laugh of his and stepped through into the hallway. Evie followed. The faint beat of whatever music was playing in the living room could be heard through the walls. It sounded like some gentle fifties crooning, which lifted Evie's spirits right away. The rich velvet of Dean Martin's voice was just what she needed right now to keep it together.

'You'll have to forgive the sparse feel to the premises just now,' said Ricci. 'I haven't long moved in and everything's still in boxes upstairs.'

'Moving house is t' worst,' said Redmond.

'No argument from me there. You've got some catching up to do,' said Ricci as she took a left into the living room. A few people were standing in the centre of the room and, over by the fireplace, Evie spotted Kitt and Charley. 'Old Percival's already had too much. Halloran had to take him out in the garden to get some fresh air. I told them not to be long out there – it's bitter.'

Evie and Redmond looked at each other.

'That's no good,' said Redmond. 'Halloran's nowhere near quick-witted enough to fully exploit t' gaffer when 'e's rattled. 'E doesn't know any of the best stories about him or nothing. I'll go out tut' garden and check in.'

'You sure?' said Ricci, her mouth tightening. 'It's cold out there. Maybe there's enough people in the garden for now. The party is supposed to be in here, after all.'

Was there a reason Ricci didn't want people in the garden? Evie wondered. Surely she knew police officers have handled a lot tougher smites than a bit of a chill on a December night?

'I've still got me coat on. Won't be long,' said Redmond.

'All right,' said Ricci. 'If you must. It's back into the hall, turn left through the kitchen and you'll reach the back door.'

'Gotcha,' said Redmond.

'In the meantime, Evie, let me take your coat upstairs,' said Ricci.

'Oh, thank you,' said Evie, unbuttoning her coat and handing it over. Ricci offered her a brief smile and then followed Redmond out into the hall.

Evie turned back to the party then and walked towards Kitt and Charley.

Evie could only see Charley from behind but that was enough to take in the way the waistcoat she was wearing over a fitted white shirt and jeans cut close to her toned figure. The tension in her stomach subsided for a moment and was replaced with a little flutter. She smiled at the feeling as she approached her friend.

'I see you're your usual hour late,' Kitt said with a knowing smile. 'You're a few drinks behind too.'

'During the little chat I had with Redmond on the way here it came out that he preferred to be fashionably late to these things and I was at the mercy of him picking me up, so I'm not to blame this time,' said Evie, and as she did so she saw something flash across Charley's face. Pain?

'Well, you're here now,' said Kitt. 'Let me pour you a glass of wine.'

'Thanks, white please,' said Evie, before turning to Charley. 'How are you?'

'I'm fine,' Charley replied. Was Evie imagining it or did her tone sound a touch too casual?

'Just, fine?' said Evie.

'Just fine, can't expect better than that under the circumstances.'

Evie nodded, though she wasn't sure if Charley was referring to the fact they might be on the brink of unveiling her
boss to be a murderer or if it was more personal than that.

Kitt's phone buzzed and she swiped the screen while
handing Evie her glass of wine. A moment later her eyes
widened. 'Where's Ricci?'

'Upstairs, putting my coat away,' said Evie.

'The second she gets down we've got to engage her in
conversation somehow,' said Kitt.

Charley frowned. 'What's going on?'

Looking over her shoulders to make sure nobody was
paying much attention, Kitt turned her phone to Evie and
Charley. The text message on the screen read: *Disturbed earth
in the garden. Keep Ricci busy.*

'Oh my God,' said Evie, a little louder than she meant to.

'Everything all right?' said Ricci, from just a few feet
behind them.

'Yes,' said Evie. 'Just ... just ...' She stared helplessly at
her friend.

'I was just teasing Evie about the crush DS Redmond has
on her,' said Kitt.

'Oh yes,' said Ricci. 'Halloran mentioned he'd taken quite
a shine to you. Apparently he's found it quite difficult to talk
about anything else since you two crossed paths.'

'I'm going to get a glass of wine,' Charley said, her posture tighter than Evie had ever seen it. She must have known that Evie's relationship with Redmond was a cover, that was not the kind of thing Halloran would keep her in the dark about. So, why was she behaving as though Evie had done something to deliberately hurt her?

'I just poured Evie the last of that bottle,' Kitt said.

'Just across the hall in the dining room there's a little fridge set up for the white wines. The reds are in there too, on the table,' said Ricci.

'Thanks,' Charley said, before stalking off towards the door.

Evie watched after her but then noticed Ricci studying her face and averted her eyes. 'So, Superintendent Ricci –'

'Oh no, call me Sofia,' said Ricci.

'Oh . . . Sofia?' said Evie, with a slight frown.

Ricci put her glass of wine down on the mantelpiece and looked between Kitt and Evie. 'Look, now that you're both here, I want to tell you that I regret the fact that we got off on the wrong foot.'

'You do?' said Kitt.

'I know full well how I must have seemed to you both on that first meeting. It's difficult to explain. Let's just say, being a female officer – especially in a position of influence within the force – isn't easy. You spend all your time proving you're as tough as you need to be and with the intimidation of starting a new job, I overdid it that day in the library. I do stand by what I said in terms of police business but I shouldn't have said it the way I did.'

'Well,' said Kitt. 'It's very big of you to apologize and I want you to know that we would never intentionally meddle with a police investigation. You might have noticed I greatly admire police officers.'

'Well, one particular police officer anyway,' Evie teased.

Kitt narrowed her eyes at her friend. 'You're one to talk.'

Evie blushed. She knew Ricci would think she was blushing on account of Redmond, but in truth her thoughts were very much somewhere else.

Evie's clutch, which was sitting on the mantelpiece next to Ricci's glass of wine buzzed. 'You don't mind do you? It . . . it might be Redmond,' Evie said, opening the bag and pulling out her phone.

'Texting you from out the back?' said Ricci. 'Phones really do encourage the laziest habits.'

Evie smiled apologetically and then swiped her screen to get at the message which was, as she had thought, from Redmond.

Get Ricci into the garden now. Quick as you can.

THIRTY-TWO

If you'd asked her later, Evie couldn't have told you exactly what words she'd used to make it clear that she, Kitt and Ricci needed to go out into the garden. Something about the boys wanting to show them something. Or perhaps had a surprise for them? Whatever she said, it worked. Evie felt herself begin to tremble as she approached the back door and the garden where Halloran, Percival and Redmond were waiting with God knows what.

'Are you cold?' Ricci asked. 'I'm sure I've got a spare cardigan upstairs you can throw on. Or I could go and get your coat.'

'Oh no,' Evie said, trying to steady herself. 'I'll see how I go. I'm sure it will be fine and if I get too chilly I'll just come back inside.'

Redmond, Percival and Halloran were standing to the side of a freshly dug hole.

Ricci's eyes widened as she stared at the brown mound of earth. 'What have you done to my garden?' she asked.

'The state of your garden is the least of your worries right now, ma'am,' Halloran replied, holding up a clear plastic bag that contained a hammer. In the light cast by the strong bulb hanging over the doorway, Evie could see that there were splashes of red across the silver head. Was that Donald Oakes's blood?

Chief Superintendent Percival's face was a portrait of fury. 'I can barely speak,' he said. 'I had my reservations about promoting someone as young as you to such a senior position but your record was so impeccable, so impressive, I was won over. I vouched for you and this is how you repay us. Murder. Blackmail. Betrayal.'

'I've never seen that object before,' said Ricci, her tone hard and assured. 'I don't understand what's going on here.'

'Given what else we've found buried in your garden, I think you know exactly what is going on,' Percival said through gritted teeth.

'What?' Ricci said, taking a couple of steps towards Halloran.

'Buruk's credit card is here too. Alongside an empty syringe and a turquoise scarf I believe I've seen you wearing – spattered with blood.'

'That's ... that's impossible,' Ricci stuttered, and then out of nowhere her face hardened. 'You've planted them there, haven't you? Manipulated your way into my house and planted them because I suspended Banks. Or maybe you've just got a problem with taking orders from a female officer. Yes, that's it.'

'Before you hatch any other wild theories,' said Halloran, 'I think it's best that you get yourself a lawyer.'

'You can't be serious?' Ricci said, her face incredulous.

Redmond, who had been silent throughout the entire exchange, stepped forward holding a pair of handcuffs. 'Sofia Ricci, you are under arrest on suspicion of murdering Donald Oakes and Alim Buruk. You do not have to say anything but it may harm your defence if you fail to mention anything that you later rely on later in court.' Redmond paused. 'Will handcuffs be necessary?'

Ricci shook her head.

Evie rubbed her arms, suddenly feeling the cold. She glanced just over her shoulder then to see that Charley was standing on the back doorstep. Her eyes were dark, narrow slits and her fists were clenched tight. Each breath seemed to force its way out of her mouth, sending a big huff of steam up into the December air. A second later, she turned and shot back into the house.

'I better go and check Charley's all right,' Evie said to Kitt, and then quick as she could dashed inside, but Charley was nowhere to be seen.

'Charley?' she called, and then over and over again. 'Charley!'

Then Evie noticed the front door had been left open, swinging in the winter breeze and letting all the heat out. She walked outside to see Charley already in her car. Looking at her stern profile, Evie knew at once that she shouldn't be driving given the state she was in.

'Charley, wait!' Evie called as she ran out towards the car and started knocking on the window. Banks started, looked at her and then shook her head. The car inched forward.

'Charley, please,' said Evie, banging the flat of her palm against the window. 'Please let me in.'

The window wound down and Charley glared at Evie.

'What do you want?'

'I want to make sure you're OK, of course.'

'Well, I'm not. That's why I need to get out of here.'

'You can't drive, you've been drinking.'

'No I haven't. I had three sips of wine.'

'Then I'm coming with you.'

'I don't need you to.'

'I'm not saying you do. But I thought maybe you'd want me to.'

Charley swallowed hard and glared at Evie. 'You should go back inside, Evie. You should go back to your friends.'

'You're my friend.'

'We barely know each other.'

'Interesting choice of words,' Evie said with a smile.

Charley closed her eyes for a second and on opening them said, 'OK, we're friends. But nothing more. I've accepted that, all right? I just need to get out of here and blow off some steam.'

'But Charley –' Evie started, but it seemed Banks didn't want to hear any more. She wound up the window, revved the engine and shot off into the darkness.

THIRTY-THREE

Trying to ignore the faint smell of sweat hanging in the air, Evie navigated her way around cross trainers and chest presses towards a set of double doors at the back of Foss View Gymnasium. According to the young man at the reception desk this was the small studio where Evie would find the punchbags. It was after midnight now and there was nobody else here, which vaguely made Evie question the usefulness of a 24-hour gym. Who came here at midnight to work out?

When she pushed through the double doors, however, she had her answer and it was exactly the one she was hoping for.

Charley was giving some of her worst to one of the punchbags hanging from the low ceiling. As she punched she huffed and grunted and it took all of Evie's self-control to not let her mind wander onto other things. Onto some of the unforgettable sounds she heard from Charley the night they spent together.

Evie walked towards the officer and waited. After twenty seconds or so Charley paused in her assault and looked over to where Evie was standing.

She frowned. 'What are you doing here?'

'Just wanted to make sure you were OK.'

Charley's frown only deepened. She picked up a towel from a bench near the wall and dabbed her face and chest.

'How did you even find me?' she asked, still panting a little from the exertion.

Evie shrugged. 'This was the only 24-hour gym on Foss-gate. I took a chance this is where you'd be. Less than a week as a detective and I catch a break like this.'

'I didn't know you were a member too.'

'I'm not, I told the guy on the desk I wanted to trial the equipment to see if I wanted to join.'

'And he just let you in?'

'I don't think he was that bothered, to be honest,' said Evie. 'At this time of night, I doubt his boss is kicking about.'

'Well, you've seen I'm fine. So you can go now,' said Charley. Her tone wasn't mean, but it was distant. Which was as good as mean as far as Evie was concerned.

'Charley, we should be celebrating. We caught the bad guy . . . or gal.'

'Celebrating? Celebrating what? That my boss is a mur-derer who tried to have me framed for assault?' She let out an incredulous laugh and stalked out of a doorway that, according to the rudimentary signage printed on A4 paper, led to the changing rooms.

Evie sighed and followed her. Charley took a bag out of one of the lockers. There was nowhere convenient to rest her belongings so she stepped into one of the cubicles and set her bag down on a bench. Evie expected the door to close but it remained open.

She paused just outside. Charley started taking off her T-shirt. Underneath, she was wearing a little black crop top. Evie's eyes followed the toned lines of Charley's body down to the scar she had revealed to her almost a week ago now. Just looking at it made Evie want to kiss it again. She swallowed, trying to swallow that thought down with it. Charley opened the bag and pulled out a fresh tank top.

'When you put it like that, I suppose I can see how you might not be in the mood to celebrate,' said Evie. 'It might not feel like it, but this is a victory.'

'Can't you understand that right now I just need to be angry? That bitch almost cost me my whole career,' said Charley, her fists clenching at her sides. 'If you only knew the sacrifices I've made to get to where I am.'

'But we got her. We caught her, for you. It's over now.'

'Just because it's over, doesn't mean the pain just goes away,' said Charley.

'I know that better than anyone,' Evie half-shouted, tears rising in her eyes.

Charley jumped at Evie's unexpected outburst. Evie

gestured towards her face, towards her scars. The officer's whole body seemed to soften. In a moment, faster than Evie could even blink back her tears, Charley had closed the gap between them and wrapped her arms tight around Evie. Pecking her on the forehead, and then down along her cheek. 'I didn't mean that. I didn't think. I'm just so angry about Ricci.'

Evie was fairly sure that Charley wasn't being affectionate out of anything more than friendliness, but the second the officer's body was pressed against hers a heat rose inside anyway. She took a deep breath and smiled as Charley's intoxicating scent filled her lungs. She held onto it for a moment before breathing out.

'I know you wouldn't want to hurt me,' said Evie, wrapping her arms around Charley. 'I know I'm safe with you.' As those words left Evie's mouth, she realized just how true they were, and wondered if that was one of the reasons why she found herself so attracted to Charley. With the boyfriends she'd had in the past, she had never been able to fully relax – no matter how intimate the situation. She had always felt on edge, even though there was nothing particularly threatening or intimidating about them. It was some unspoken discomfort, some sense that she couldn't show her true self. But that wasn't how it was with Charley. Charley didn't see her vulnerabilities as weakness or expect her to be childish all the time just because she had a playful sense of humour. She just let Evie be whatever she wanted to be in the moment, and Evie wanted to do the same for her.

Slowly, Evie started to stroke Charley's hair. Charley's muscles tensed and she withdrew from the hug, frowning in what looked like confusion.

Evie continued to play with the chestnut strands framing Charley's face and looked steadily into those charcoal eyes. Evie leant forward.

'But . . . I thought – '

'Shh,' said Evie, before kissing the very corner of Charley's mouth, and then kissing her nose, and then returning once again to her lips. When their mouths met a second time, Evie felt Charley surrender to the kiss, making small desperate moans and pulling Evie's body tight against hers.

The pair parted and stared at each other, panting. Charley's head turned towards the mirror in the changing room and then back to Evie. Charley looked Evie's body and then smiled.

In spite of herself, Evie couldn't help but smirk at Charley's expression. 'Now what's going through that head of yours?'

Charley didn't answer; instead she placed both hands gently on Evie's shoulders and turned her to face the mirror. She moved to stand behind Evie and from this angle began unbuttoning Evie's winter coat.

'What are you – '

'Trust me,' Charley whispered in her ear, pausing at the

last button on her coat. 'I'm going to show you how beautiful you are.'

Evie wasn't sure exactly what this would entail but given the look on Charley's face reflected in the mirror, she definitely wanted to find out. She nodded and that was the only cue Charley needed to pop open the last button of Evie's coat and remove it. She placed it on the bench where her bag was still sitting and then, without skipping a beat, began unbuttoning her blouse. With every button popped, Evie felt a strange intensity building inside, the sense of being somehow lighter and heavier at the same time. Charley looked at Evie through the mirror and Evie looked right back at her as the blouse was taken off, revealing a red lace bra beneath.

'My God,' Charley whispered into Evie's ear as she admired the view of her standing in her bra, skirt and heels. A moment later, Charley's hands were on her zip and Evie's skirt dropped to the floor. Evie couldn't believe she was going along with this but was too curious to see where it might lead to even think of stopping it. She lowered her eyes and kicked the garment off to the side.

'Eyes on the mirror,' Charley said.

Slowly, Evie looked back at her reflection.

'You are beautiful,' Charley said. 'Beautiful.'

Evie stared at the woman looking back at her. In the full-length mirror, when she looked at her whole person, her scars were less of a focus. Right now they were offset by the contrast between her red underwear and the peachiness of her skin. The way her calves looked curvier in her black kitten heels. Whenever she had been naked in front of past boyfriends, Evie had always felt a coldness come over her. She was convinced they were sitting there thinking parts of her body were too saggy or that she was overall too pale. Right now, though, she didn't feel anything like that. The look in Charley's eyes was unmistakable. She saw beauty. In Evie. And, for what felt like the first time ever, Evie saw it too.

She smiled at herself, and then at Charley.

'You know, this was a cheap trick to see me in my underwear again?' Evie said, meeting the officer's eye.

'Well, can you blame me?' said Charley, walking around to face her. 'Who wouldn't want to drink in your body every chance they got?' Charley closed the cubicle door and leant a hand against it so that she was leaning over Evie the way she had seen boys lean over girls in the school corridor in countless American high school movies. 'Who wouldn't want to push you up against this door, and kiss every inch of you?'

At that suggestion, Evie's lungs failed her. Looking into Charley's eyes and trying to catch her breath she heard herself say: 'I wish you would.'

Charley tilted her head to the side then, as though this were some kind of trap. 'You do?'

Evie nodded. 'Look, Charley, this is new to me. I can't tell you I'm ready to go public or even if it will lead to anything. But you are on my mind a lot, I can tell you that and right now, today . . . I want you.'

At those words, Charley's breathing seemed to deepen.

'You have to decide whether that's enough for now,' said Evie.

Charley's eyes travelled all the way down Evie's body, and back up again. 'It's all I needed to hear.'

Without a moment's hesitation, she grabbed Evie with both hands and pushed her up against the changing room door. The jolt of it made Evie gasp, and then a short giggle was swallowed up in Charley's mouth. Evie had forgotten how deliciously soft Charley's lips were and nibbled on the bottom one. Charley moaned, a sound that only made Evie kiss more hungrily.

Charley wasted no time making good on her initial promise and began kissing along Evie's neck. She opened her eyes and her whole body arced as she saw their reflection in the mirror. The perfect view of the back of Charley's head as she kissed her way down, down, down the body that she had for so long believed didn't deserve any kisses at all.

THIRTY-FOUR

'Whatever it is,' said Kitt, 'you'd best be out with it before Grace gets here.'

'What do you mean?' said Evie, enjoying the warm smell of fresh popcorn as it mingled with the scent of the carrot and coriander soup being served up to the Saturday lunch-time crowd. Such were the delights of going for a coffee at the City Screen bar just off Coney Street, a stylish lounge bar with an attached cinema.

The building had a glorious glass frontage that offered panoramic views of the Ouse. Evie bagged one of the low tables nearest the window. From there, one could look out through the glass terrace doors and watch the river gush by. You could see down as far as Lendal Bridge without too much craning of the neck. It was the kind of view she had been avoiding since the incident in October but somehow looking out across that silver length of water today wasn't so much of an issue.

'I mean,' said Kitt, 'that you've had a funny smile on your face the whole time we've been sitting here. What's going on?'

Evie pursed her lips. Was she ready to say this out loud? She had already sort of said it out loud to Kitt once and she'd been perfectly all right about it so there was no reason to believe she would be surprised to learn about what had happened between her and Charley last night. Still, the words stuck in Evie's throat more than she would have expected.

'After you and Halloran dropped me off at the house last night, I went to see Charley.'

'And . . . ?' Kitt said, with a knowing look on her face.

'I tracked her down at the gym and we . . . you know, did stuff.' Evie could feel the grin spreading across her lips as she spoke.

'At the gym?' said Kitt. 'A public sex act, very daring.'

'Huh, I didn't think of it that way at the time,' said Evie. 'There was only us in the changing area so perhaps not quite as daring as it sounds.'

'So is this the start of something?' said Kitt.

'Yes,' said Evie. 'I don't know what, but the start of something.'

At that moment, Grace trotted over to where they were sitting.

'Sorry,' said Grace. 'I had to round off a couple of things at the library before getting here. We're a person down this week, you know.' Grace glanced at Kitt and Kitt rolled her eyes.

'Honestly, the way you go on, you make it sound as

though the place would fall apart without me,' Kitt said with a wry smile.

'It's not optimal,' said Grace. 'Let's just say I've had far too much to contend with this week to even look at tidying the journal shelves.'

'Yes, well, in the words of Scarlett O'Hara, I'll think about that tomorrow.'

'Who?' said Grace.

'From *Gone With* . . . Never mind,' said Kitt. 'This has been one of the most exhausting weeks of my life. I don't have the energy for it.'

'Never mind all right,' said Grace. 'It's one thing that I didn't get invited along to last night's little gathering.'

'You had no connection to Ricci, it was suspicious enough us going along as it was!'

'But to delay relaying every last detail about Ricci's arrest is just plain cruel.'

'We don't know every last detail about Ricci's arrest,' said Kitt. 'DS Redmond and Chief Superintendent Percival handled the matter while Halloran drove me and Evie back to York. The last I heard was a phone call from Halloran just after midnight. He went to the station after dropping me off just to see what was what and decided to stay and help with questioning Ricci, and from the sound of things quite a bit of paperwork.'

'Well, what about Redmond?' Grace said, turning on Evie. 'Did he tell you anything?'

'No,' said Evie. 'I haven't heard from him. He only took me to that thing because it was part of Percival's plan.'

'Yeah, a likely story. I'd keep it all business if my boss told me to take a Marilyn Monroe lookalike to a party too.'

Evie laughed. 'I don't think I'm quite a Marilyn. Besides anything else, I suspect Redmond has had his hands full at the station.'

Had Charley gone into the station this morning? Evie found herself wondering. When they parted ways at the gym last night, Charley promised she would call after she'd had some much needed rest. But Evie hadn't heard from her.

'Hello, you three,' said a deep voice.

Evie, Kitt and Grace all turned round to see DI Halloran and DS Banks. Charley at once flashed Evie a little smile which she couldn't help but return.

'How did you know we were here?' asked Kitt.

'We, er, have our ways,' said the inspector.

Kitt narrowed her eyes. 'Did you use police resources to triangulate the position of my phone?'

'I wouldn't do that, that would be an abuse of the system,' said Halloran, his face deadpan.

'But –'

'Kitt, look, we've got a problem,' said Halloran.

'What's going on?'

Halloran looked around the crowded bar. 'I can't go into every last detail here. It would be great if there were at least a handful of York residents who didn't know more than they should about this business by the time we catch whoever's responsible.'

'I don't understand,' said Grace. 'Haven't you got the culprit? Didn't you apprehend them last night?'

'I don't know,' said Halloran.

'Mal, you're not saying – ' Kitt started.

'We may not have the right person. We were going through some of Holt's older records to prepare our case against him for court and in doing so one of our officers made an alarming discovery.'

'About six months ago,' Charley said, 'a police officer invested and lost a great deal of money in one of Holt's property schemes.'

'Who was the officer?' asked Evie.

Charley lowered her voice. 'DS Miles Redmond.'

'What?' said Evie, her heart racing. She had sat next to Redmond last night. In his car. Had she been unwittingly making polite conversation with a murderer? A double murderer, in fact? Guess it wouldn't be the first time . . .

'Jinkies,' said Evie. 'Last night in the car, Redmond was asking about all the things we'd learned about the case. I thought he was just trying to help us solve it but now I'm wondering if he was trying to work out if we were onto him.'

'Have you broken the news to Percival?' asked Kitt.

Halloran shook his head. 'No, he only left the station at

three this morning. Bear in mind it's his retirement party in just a few hours. I can't tell him about this. There's too much evidence against Ricci, this might be nothing. Essentially what we need to do is rule Redmond out as a suspect.'

'So, you haven't already arrested him?' said Grace.

Charley shook her head. 'Just like we had to build a case against Ricci we'd have to do the same for Redmond. The fact that he might have done business with Holt six months ago is not enough to tie him to two murders.'

'Though the fact that he never mentioned it is a little suspicious,' mused Kitt. 'So, what are we going to do?'

'Well, you're right that it's strange he didn't mention it but he might have been embarrassed or worried he'd be taken of the case if he did. To be sure, I'm going to go back to Holt who is out on bail but has been given strict instructions to make himself available for questioning on demand. I'm going to take a statement on his interactions with Redmond, see what his reaction was when he lost the money.'

'Given my less than winning reaction to Ricci's arrest last night,' said Charley, 'it's been decided I'd be better placed looking through Holt's records to see if I can build more of a case. We really want to gather as much evidence as we can before Percival's retirement party later this afternoon. With a bit of luck, we can discount him as a suspect. If not, we'll be able to pick him up there – discreetly. Given the sharp deadline we were hoping you might be available to look through the records but you'll have to sign non-disclosure agreements, of course.'

Evie started an enthusiastic nod but her positivity was drowned out by Kitt and Grace.

'You're leaving us with the paperwork?' said Kitt.

'I can't believe I got my hopes up, I never get to do the interesting stuff,' said Grace.

'Well, it's sit with Banks and look through records or you can sit in the police car while I visit Holt, but those are the choices. You can't speak to Holt directly.'

'I've spoken to him before,' said Grace. 'We're practically old friends.'

'Time is of the essence,' said Halloran. 'We need to deal with this swiftly and professionally . . . so what's it going to be?'

THIRTY-FIVE

Sitting in the window seat at the Teddy Bear Tea Rooms on Stonegate, Evie smiled across at Charley as she watched her scanning yet another sheet of A4 paper. She highlighted the odd phrase here and there as she read. Though the streets below were full of Christmas shoppers, in the last hour they had only seen one family and another couple nip in for a quick pit stop, and both groups had now left the building. The kitchen staff could be heard chatting along the corridor from the main tea room but other than that the pair were completely alone, which enabled Evie to look at her new beau without any restrictions.

'What you looking at?' Charley asked without taking her eyes off the paper.

'How do you know I'm looking at you?'

'Industrial-strength peripheral vision, just one of my super powers,' Charley said, at last looking up from the stack of papers. She reached a hand over to Evie's cheek. 'Finding it difficult to concentrate?'

'Maybe, but we've got to behave. We've got company,' said Evie, her eyes drifting across to the large blue teddy bear seated on the third chair at their table.

Charley laughed. 'You're right, there are innocent minds present.'

'You didn't have to buy me a bear, you know.'

'I know, but I saw the way your face lit up when we walked in here. I couldn't help myself,' said Charley. 'Besides, we couldn't have left . . . Hamilton the Third on the shelf.'

'Oh, Kitt's going to go mad when she finds out that you've encouraged this.'

'I think, if pressed, Kitt would admit your playfulness is part of your appeal,' said Charley. 'But out of interest, I can understand naming a bear Hamilton, but why Hamilton the Third?'

'You're asking a thirty-three-year-old woman who likes teddy bears to explain her logic to you?' said Evie. 'And people think I'm dotty.'

Charley laughed again and this time Evie joined in.

'How do you think Kitt, Grace and Halloran are getting on?'

'I don't know.' Charley looked at her watch. 'They should be there by now so hopefully we'll hear from them soon.'

'Do you think Halloran really made Kitt and Grace wait in the car?'

'Of course,' said Charley with a frown.

'I'll bet you dinner at the Lamb and Lion that Kitt at least managed to talk her way into the conversation with Holt.'

'You're on. I hope you're good for it.'

'You underestimate how mad those two can drive you once they get going. You end up agreeing to anything for a quiet life,' said Evie.

'We'll see,' said Charley.

'Any luck with your documents?'

'Aye, a bit. I've found Redmond's account details popping up a couple of times in these papers so we've definitely got evidence of more than a brief relationship between him and Holt.'

'Sounds like you've had more luck than I have. These are just Holt's client profile documents as far as I can tell,' said Evie. 'I haven't found Redmond's yet, or anyone else connected with the case. I'm not even sure how accurate they are. Does Holt strike you as the kind of person who is a stickler for record-keeping?'

'I don't know, he might go that far. Trying to keep up the appearances and sucker people in to handing over their money? You'd be amazed at the lengths people will go to to cover up their criminality.'

'Not as amazed as I would have been two months ago,' said Evie, raising her eyebrows.

'I know,' said Charley. 'You've been through a lot but I'm going to do all I can to look after you now.'

'You've been through a lot too,' said Evie, putting her

hand on top of Charley's. 'And looking after you sounds like something I could get used to.'

The pair smiled at each other and then returned to the paperwork they were sifting through. Evie turned page after page of profile pictures and lists of investments. She couldn't decide if the people in the pictures looked dull to her because they generally had a lacklustre air to them or if it was down to the fact that the documents had been printed in patchy greyscale. Whatever the reason, she wanted to yawn just looking at some of them.

She took another sip of tea as she turned the page and it was then that her hand froze mid-air. Evie wasn't sure if she was about to spit out her beverage or choke on it but somehow she managed to swallow. Slowly, she reached across and tapped Charley's arm.

The officer looked up from her reading. 'What's wrong?'

'I found Holt's profile for Miles Redmond.'

'Anything useful on it?'

'Look.' Evie turned the paper around so Charley could see it. Or more specifically, so that Charley could see the photograph.

The officer's eyes widened. But then her brow lowered and the same shadow Evie had seen fall over it the night before was cast once more.

Without a word, Banks whipped her phone out of her jacket pocket and started dialling. 'Sir,' she said. 'I'm putting you on speaker phone so Evie can hear OK?'

Charley pressed a button on her keypad.

'What's going on?' Halloran's voice said down the line.

'Are you still with Holt?'

'Yes.'

'Do you have a photograph of Chief Superintendent Percival handy?'

'What is this, Banks? We don't have time to put together anything for the retirement party.'

Charley put a hand over her face in exasperation. 'No, sir, I need you to show a photograph of Chief Superintendent Percival to Holt and ask him if he recognizes him.'

'Why?'

'When he answers your question, sir, I suspect you'll understand why. Can you keep us on the line?'

'All right.'

There was some shuffling and a few moments later Charley and Evie heard Halloran speak again. 'Mr Holt, can you tell me if you recognize this man?'

There was a pause, and then Holt's voice came down the line. 'Yes, of course I can. That's a client of mine. Miles Redmond.'

'Oh my God,' two voices said in synchrony in the background. Evie would know them anywhere. It was Kitt and Grace.

'You owe me dinner,' Evie hissed.

Charley rolled her eyes to the ceiling.

'Banks?' came Halloran's voice. 'Does this mean what I think it means?'

'Sir, the account with Redmond's name next to it suffered a £100,000 loss on the investment made with Holt. Our murderer isn't Redmond sir, it's Chief Superintendent Percival. His photograph is on Holt's client records next to Redmond's name. I don't know how, but somehow he's behind all of this.'

'His retirement party will be starting around now,' said Halloran. 'I'll motor back from Helmsley as fast as I can but there's no doubt that you're going to be first on the scene. Banks, you're going to have to apprehend Percival.'

THIRTY-SIX

The second Halloran hung up the phone, Charley and Evie made a dash for the police motorbike Charley had parked in Parliament Square earlier that afternoon. The bike wasn't really designed for two but by placing Hamilton the Third in a deathly-looking head lock so he hung by her side, the pair of them were just able to squeeze on for the ten-minute journey. Charley insisted on giving Evie the helmet, making good on her promise to look after her. Evie relished the opportunity to wrap her arms tight around Banks's waist and held on tight to Hamilton the Third, whose blue fur ruffled in the breeze as they sped onwards through the city in the thickening dusk.

Chief Superintendent Percival's retirement party was being held on the top floor of the Ryedale Hotel, a swish new-build that overlooked the river. Given that they had driven there on a motorbike rather than in a car, there was nowhere to stash Hamilton the Third and thus Evie was forced to walk through the polished marble entrance hall, decorated with tall, gold vases filled with white lilies, clutching a large blue teddy bear.

It was only natural then, that people were staring at her. This was the first time since the incident by the river that she had attributed the less than kindly looks she received to something other than the scars on her face. That truth made her breathe a little easier.

Now that she really thought about it, she hadn't fixated on her scars at all since last night, right before she and Charley engaged in – what had Kitt called it? A public sex act. Perhaps that wouldn't seem like such a long time to some but for the past six weeks Evie had barely had a moment's rest from the torturous, repetitive thoughts surrounding her injury. Maybe if she could develop a habit of focusing on other things, she had a chance of getting past everything she had been through, and the scars it had left behind.

Charley pressed the button for the lift, and watched the digital display above as it counted down the floors.

'How are we going to go about this?' asked Evie, trying not to let her nerves sound in her voice. It might not have been so bad if Kitt, Halloran and Grace were here. But it was just the two of them, and if Percival tried to put up any kind of fight Evie didn't know for sure how it would turn out. Charley was strong; she worked out and trained hard as part of her job. But men had a brute strength about them that could be hard to match. Evie could only hope that when it came down to it, Percival would come peacefully.

'I don't know yet. I've got to get a grip on myself,' said Charley, tapping the wall with the palm of her hand.

'Is there anything I can do?'

Charley looked at Evie and her frown dissolved. 'You're here, with that bloody stupid bear, that's enough.'

Evie covered her mouth in mock shock and then put her hands over Hamilton the Third's ears. 'He can hear you, you know.'

Charley broke into a grudging smile and shook her head as the lift, at last, dinged to the ground floor. The pair hopped in. Charley hit the button for the twelfth floor at least three times and the doors thudded shut.

'Whatever happens up there, I'm here,' said Evie. 'Don't forget that.'

'I won't,' said Charley. 'But I can't promise you this is going to be pretty. I have no idea how Percival is going to react to being confronted. I can't believe all that he's done.'

'Neither can I,' said Evie.

'You do realize that he must have framed Ricci? All the stories he's told about her, I doubt we can believe a word of them. He made sure he stayed out of Holt's way at the station too so he wouldn't be made. He's manipulated every last one of us.'

'I know it's hard to believe. But there's a chance we can still handle it quietly. He probably won't want to make a big scene in front of everyone at the party.'

'Maybe,' said Banks, her mouth tightening as the lift

pinged to a stop and the doors slowly opened. Stepping out into the party, Evie looked around at the dozens of people of all ages, here to celebrate the career of a man who had betrayed everything he stood for. They were all turned towards a small platform where Chief Superintendent Percival stood elevated above the crowd, dressed in a fine grey suit and red tie, delivering his retirement speech.

Charley started walking towards the crowd when Evie caught something out of the corner of her eye. Something black and shadowy in her peripheral vision. She turned to see a side room off to her left. Inside, a broad figure dressed in black was hunched over the champagne glasses sitting on the table. There was something familiar about the figure, about the way they stood and moved.

Evie grabbed Charley's arm and whispered, 'Amira Buruk is here.'

'Where?' said Charley, her eyes widening.

Evie indicated the room where Amira was standing. Her back was turned to them so it was difficult to tell, but it looked as though she might be writing something.

Charley walked towards where she was standing. 'Mrs Buruk, stop what you're doing and turn around.'

Evie gulped as the woman turned. The hard lines of that square face took her aback as much as it did the first time. Mrs Buruk didn't look ruffled. She stood as though she had as much right as anyone else to be celebrating Percival's retirement, with a glass of champagne and a card in her hands.

'Can I help you, officer . . . Banks, isn't it?'

'What are you doing here, Mrs Buruk? This event is police and family members only. As far as I'm aware, you aren't related to an officer?'

'I just wanted to give your chief superintendent this card.'

'I can give that to him for you,' said Charley, 'and I recommend you leave these premises immediately.'

'I'm going to give it to him myself,' said Mrs Buruk, her civility evaporating. 'After all he did for my son.'

Charley looked Mrs Buruk up and down. 'I couldn't let you near our superintendent without searching you.'

'You don't have the right to search me.'

'Yes, I do. Hold your hands up, Mrs Buruk.'

'My hands are going nowhere,' she spat.

'They'll be going in my handcuffs for resisting an officer unless you do what I've asked.'

Mrs Buruk tried to stare Charley down but the officer held her gaze. First placing the champagne and the card on the table, Amira Buruk raised her hands and sighed.

Charley quickly patted the woman down, but stopped when she reached the inside pocket of the black jacket she was wearing. Evie covered her mouth as she watched Charley pull out a long, sharp kitchen knife.

'Can you explain what you're doing with this?'

'It's just a knife from the charity bake sale I was at this afternoon,' said Mrs Buruk, a smirk forming on her lips. 'We needed it to cut the cake.'

Banks stared at Mrs Buruk. 'What have you heard and more importantly, who from?' Mrs Buruk offered only a thin, bitter smile in return.

Charley turned to Evie. 'Quick as you can, tell one of the security guards who are supposedly on duty that DS Banks needs their assistance.'

Dropping Hamilton the Third down on the table, Evie half-ran to fetch the security guard standing by the lift.

'The force has been my whole life,' Evie heard Percival say over the microphone. He was still giving his retirement speech. He still had everyone under the impression that he was a model officer. Everyone except Amira Buruk, apparently, who must have learned that Percival was behind her son's death. From the unknown source that she mentioned back at the hospital? Evie shuddered at the idea that there was an officer loyal to Mrs Buruk feeding her whatever information she asked for.

By the time Evie returned with the security guard, Banks had handcuffed Mrs Buruk.

'She was carrying a knife. I've cautioned her but we need to keep this quiet until I can get someone down from the station to take her away. Don't want to ruin the chief superintendent's big moment.' Charley somehow managed to sell this, despite what she was going to have to do.

'We've got a secure room on the first floor of the hotel,' said the guard. 'I'll escort her down there and hold her until she can be transported to the station.'

The guard held Mrs Buruk's arm and guided her out of the room. She didn't resist, or speak. She didn't look in the least bit scared either. Evie had a sinking feeling that somehow she wasn't going to answer for her part in all this.

'C'mon,' said Charley. 'Let's do what we came here to do.'

Evie looked at Hamilton the Third sitting on the table. He was conspicuous but if she left him here she might not see him again. She snatched him up and held him in both hands behind her back as she followed the officer into the main hall. Hopefully, anyone behind her would think Hamilton was some kind of prank present for Percival.

'Without the important graft that I've dedicated my working life to,' Percival said to the crowd, 'I've got a terrible feeling that I'm going to become one of those people who takes up bowls. Though if my wife has her way, I think it'll be ballroom dancing, God help me.'

The room laughed and a few people let out cheers and whistles.

'No,' Percival continued. 'Joking apart, though, I know this is one of the hardest jobs out there. I've lived that truth for thirty years.'

Charley started to work her way around the back of the crowd, navigating her way slowly to the side of the stage. Evie followed, barely daring to breathe in case Percival got wind of their presence before Charley was ready. Exactly what she was going to do when she was ready, Evie couldn't say.

Banks settled on a spot to the left of the stage. She planted her feet, straightened her posture so that somehow she looked broader than Evie thought she was usually, and stared at Percival while he continued his speech.

'I have undying respect for you all as you continue this line of work – it takes a great deal of integrity to keep the public's trust.' At this point, Percival scanned the audience at the side of the podium and did a double-take as his eyes rested on Charley. Her dark eyes fixed on his; she didn't smile, she didn't blink, she didn't move.

Evie looked back at Percival to see him floundering. His mouth was open, but no sound came out. He looked over at Banks a second time and a pained expression crossed his face.

He knew.

A few members of the audience looked in Banks's direction to see what had distracted their speaker.

'Well.' Percival let out a short, nervous chuckle. 'I think I've rattled on long enough and we'd all like a drink. So,' he raised a glass of champagne he was holding in his hand, 'cheers to you.'

'Cheers,' the room echoed. Glasses clinked, people whooped and clapped and a quiet murmur of conversation gradually rose to a roar that filled the hall.

Evie was watching Percival almost as closely as Charley was. His hands were shaking. He downed what was left of his drink before turning towards where Charley was standing and stepping down off the podium.

Percival cleared his throat. 'DS Banks, what can I do for you?'

'I think you know, sir,' Charley replied. Her tone was unexpectedly gentle. Evie had expected Banks to take no prisoners but it seemed she had decided on a different tack. 'It's over.'

With an obvious effort he managed to meet her eye. 'Why don't we go out on the balcony?'

'After you, sir.' Charley gestured for Percival to walk ahead. She might be willing to keep this quiet but she wasn't going to let Percival out of her sight either.

Percival smiled and waved to several people who greeted him on the way to the balcony door. They were just about to slip outside when a woman in a black sequinned dress, with long grey hair plaited around the crown of her head, approached the superintendent. 'Noah, where are you going?'

'Marion,' Noah said, with a catch in his throat. 'I – I've just got a bit of last minute business to sort out with DS Banks here.'

Marion put a hand on her hip. 'You're a rotten liar, Noah Percival. You said your policing days were over as of this afternoon.'

This must be Percival's wife. A lump formed in Evie's throat as she thought how Marion would feel when she learned the truth about her husband. That all this time, she had been living with a murderer. Evie couldn't imagine what that would feel like. She wished there was a way of sparing the woman from that pain, but it was the awful truth. No matter how lovely his wife was, the truth could not be denied. Percival had impersonated another officer, framed two more members of his own police force, tried to extort money from Holt and killed two people along the way. Evie didn't know the why, but she knew the what and the who, and she also knew there was no way Charley would let Percival walk away from this.

'They are, pet,' said Percival. He drew Marion into his arms, squeezed her and kissed her forehead. 'It'll be over soon, I promise. You know I love you, don't you?'

'Well of course I do, you daft thing,' Marion said, frowning into her husband's eyes.

With that Percival let go of his wife and gave her a bitter smile before pushing open the balcony door. Charley and Evie followed.

At this height, it was even colder than it had been at ground level. A biting wind whipped around the corner of the building.

Percival made his way out to the edge of the balcony, resting his arms on the ledge, and stared out over the city.

'Noah Percival, you are under arrest on suspicion of the murders of Alim Buruk and Donald Oakes . . .' Charley started reading Percival his rights. He remained silent until she had finished and then turned to face her.

'I want you to know, I didn't ask for any of this.' There were tears in his eyes.

'I should hope you didn't,' said Charley, her voice low and dangerous.

'I was just trying to make sure Marion and I had a good retirement. She's been a patient wife all these years. She's only ever had what was left when the job was done with me. I wanted her to have more than that. And when I lost that money with the investment I made with Holt, I couldn't believe it. It was everything we had. And he didn't care. He didn't care what he'd cost us.'

'I think you should save this for when you get down to the station, sir.' Charley took a step towards Percival.

Quicker than either Evie or Charley could have expected, Percival manoeuvred himself up onto the ledge. 'Don't come any closer.' He swung his legs so they were dangling over the edge of a twelve-storey drop.

'Sir, there's no need for this,' said Charley.

'I didn't mean for any of this to happen.'

'If you didn't expect any of this to happen, sir,' said Charley, 'then why did you use DS Redmond's identity to make the investment with Holt?'

'Given the rate of return Holt promised, I guessed that there must be something about it that wasn't completely above board. So I used Redmond's name just in case. A fake ID and I was able to set up a bank account. It was just a precaution. Nobody was supposed to get hurt. All I intended to do was ensure my version of Miles Redmond made a very generous transfer into our savings account when I retired.

Then I was going to close the account and that would be the end of it. Nobody would ever know. But Holt scammed me. I lost everything.'

'Sir, come down from the ledge, you can put all this in an official statement,' Charley tried again, but Percival wasn't hearing her or anything else, so it seemed, except the voices of his own demons.

'I didn't want to kill Buruk,' said Percival. 'I knew Holt would have to do something underhand to get the money and was relieved when he chose to burgle the bookshop. It seemed a relatively harmless crime compared with some of the other things he was probably capable of cooking up. But Holt forced my hand when he arranged for Alim to be beaten. When he tried to frame you. Alim was going to give Holt up, and it was only a matter of time before that led back to me. Even with the care I'd taken to make Ricci look responsible, I knew you'd find me.'

'Why did you try and frame Ricci?' asked Charley. 'Why not Redmond, given that you'd already involved him?'

'Redmond's a sweet enough lad, but he's not believable as a criminal mastermind. Besides anything else, Redmond had worked with us for several years. Ricci was a new-comer. An outsider. The trouble coincided with her joining us. It seemed more believable, I thought. Especially when you two didn't hit it off and Holt tried to frame you for the beating. But I promise you, I didn't expect any of it to go this far. I just wanted to have something to show for all these years of work. But the situation just kept getting worse and worse.'

'Look,' said Charley. 'You'd lost everything and couldn't see a way forward, a jury will have some sympathy for that.'

'And Oakes, I didn't mean to kill him. I need you to know that. I need you to tell Marion.'

'You can tell her yourself,' said Charley.

'I went there, to the shop, in a balaclava and threatened him. I wanted to try and create someone – a fictional suspect – to pin the death of Alim on so nobody else would get hurt. I used the hammer so it would look like the same person who had attacked Alim also attacked Donald. But the bugger tried to run and when I caught up with him he started clawing at the mask. He got hold of it, he was going to see my face. He was going to know what I was doing. So I hit him. Harder than I meant to, and he didn't get up.'

Evie's eyes started to fill with tears. Percival had done some unforgivable things but all of them, it seemed, were born out of desperation. There was something profoundly sad about how unnecessary this had all been. Nobody had needed to die. It was just a big mess.

'Sir,' Charley said, her voice growing sterner. 'Get down off the ledge. We can work something out.'

'No, no, no,' Percival shook his head. 'There's nothing left for me now.'

And with that Noah Percival heaved himself off the ledge and a scream of terror filled the air.

THIRTY-SEVEN

'Noooooo!' Charley screamed out. She leaped towards the ledge and a moment later her whole body shunted forward against the wall. She shrieked in pain and remained bent double, leaning over the edge.

Evie dropped Hamilton to the ground and ran forward. To her astonishment, Charley had managed to grab Percival's wrist. She had both hands clamped around him but her fingers were white from the strain of holding the weight of a full-grown man as he dangled above the river twelve floors below.

'Let me go,' Percival screamed up at Charley. 'Let me go, Banks, it's what I deserve. You know it. I know it. Just let me go!'

Evie tried to reach for his other hand but Percival swatted her away, jerking his body and causing Charley to cry out again with the pain of holding onto him.

'Let me die, please,' Percival pleaded. 'Let me die, I'm

begging you. I can't go on. I can't go on after what I've done. Just let go.'

Tears were streaming down Charley's face and her teeth were gritted.

'Let me die, please, let me die,' Percival continued to beg. To her surprise, Evie thought she saw one of Charley's hands relax enough for Percival to drop an inch from her grip.

'Charley, no,' Evie screamed, grabbing Percival's wrist.

'He wants to die,' Charley said through her tears. 'He deserves to die, doesn't he? I've already saved his life once today. Do you think Amira Buruk would have left him alive?'

'You're not her,' Evie said. 'Charley, listen. I know that after all he's put you through, letting go of his hand would be the easiest thing in the world, but your job isn't about what's easy. You aren't about what's easy. You're about what's right.'

Slowly, Charley's eyes met with Evie's.

'If you let go of him, if you let him die, you will regret it. I know you will. Because I know who you are. You couldn't live with that any more than I could.'

Charley scrunched her eyes shut as though trying to concentrate hard on something.

'Trust me,' Evie said. 'I need you to trust me.'

Charley opened her eyes then and a frown crossed her face. Using the ledge as leverage she began to tug Percival back up. Evie grabbed hold of Percival's other arm; he tried to break free but Evie clung on for all she was worth and heaved and heaved. Still his body hung part way over the balcony and no matter how hard they both pulled he wasn't budging.

'Evie!' Kitt called, from somewhere behind them.

'Kitt,' Evie shouted back. 'Help! It's Percival.'

Just a few moments passed before her friend was by her side, and Grace was with her.

'Oh dear God,' said Kitt looking down at Percival.

'What happened?' Grace gasped.

'Bit of a long story,' said Charley. 'Perhaps we could drag the man back over the ledge and answer questions later?'

Kitt reached down and managed to grab the waistband on Percival's trousers while Grace grabbed the back of his shirt.

'Isn't Halloran with you?' asked Evie. 'His help wouldn't go amiss right now.'

'He's on his way up,' said Kitt. 'In the meantime, let's do what we can, eh? One . . . two . . . three . . .' The four of them pulled and pulled until they heard Percival's limp body thud down onto the paving stone. The second he was back on solid ground, Percival hunched over and wept. Both Evie and Charley were bent double, panting with the effort of saving his life.

Evie couldn't have said how long it was, a few moments or five minutes, before the balcony door burst open and Halloran and Redmond appeared.

'What happened?' Halloran asked, rushing over and putting a gentle hand on Kitt's back. 'Are you all OK?'

'He just tried to take a skydive off the roof without a par-achute, but I'm OK,' said Charley. 'I've read him his rights – where've you two been?'

'I were a bit late tut' party as it was,' said Redmond. 'And when I got 'ere I 'ad to deal with a crisis on the first floor.'

'As did I,' said Halloran.

'Oh no,' said Charley. 'Amira Buruk?'

'Apparently she escaped custody,' said Halloran.

'What?' said Charley. 'So she's in the wind?'

'We'll track her down,' said Halloran. 'The security guard she attacked is on his way to hospital but his wounds are mostly cosmetic.'

'Bloody hell,' said Charley, exasperated. 'I had her.'

'You've had a lot to deal with,' said Halloran, his eyes riveting on Percival.

'I hear you've been doin' all you can to send me down for yer crimes, sir,' said Redmond, as he placed a pair of handcuffs on Percival.

Percival looked up at Redmond. 'I'm sorry,' he said, as more tears fell. 'I'm so, so sorry.' With the help of Halloran, Redmond heaved Percival off the ground and walked him back through the balcony door.

Charley watched after him, wiping tears from her cheeks as she did.

'Is Holt going to testify against Percival?' asked Charley.

Halloran nodded. 'Is he! He practically fell over himself

to cut a deal with us. A slimy good-for-nothing if ever there was one.'

'You are talking about the man I could have been betrothed to,' said Grace with a smirk.

'If he did offer you a ring I'd check it against the database for stolen valuables,' said Halloran.

Grace giggled. 'Lucky I was here to help pull Chief Superintendent Percival back over that balcony but then, I was sure that if I went along with Kitt something crazy would happen; she lives life on the edge, you know?'

'Grace,' said Kitt. 'Do you not think I've been put through quite enough for one day without the added teasing?'

'You know you secretly love it. You know you couldn't live without me. You know your life would just not be the same without Grace Edwards.' Kitt's assistant made a dramatic show of putting her hands on her hips in much the same way the superheroes did in film posters.

Kitt closed her eyes and shook her head.

'Percival says he lost lots of money to Holt in an investment,' said Charley.

'Holt doesn't know how Percival found out about his affair with Olivia but given that he and Olivia have hardly been discreet around that pub on the Wetherby road I doubt it was difficult information for Percival to come by.'

'What will happen to Ricci now?' asked Kitt.

'Well, if what we think is correct, and Percival has been framing Ricci all along, then she'll be released,' said

Halloran. 'She has vehemently denied all of the allegations, and her version of her trip to the hospital to see Alim, among several other details, differs greatly from Percival's and Wilkinson's. According to Ricci, it was he who was left alone with Buruk.'

'That's why Percival didn't invite Wilkinson into our covert investigation,' said Kitt. 'He was the only one besides the suspect who knew the truth about what happened at the hospital.'

'I dread to think how Percival would have kept Wilkinson quiet once he learned Ricci had contested that part of the story,' said Halloran. 'Ricci also claims she had no intention of getting a patio put in.'

Kitt shook her head. 'All this time we thought he was helping us crack the case, and he was pulling the strings. Remember when he sent us to Bootham Bar Books and told us to look out for anything odd – he knew the bookcase would stand out to me. He put it there to cover the blood spatter and then led us to it to pin it on Ricci.'

'According to Ricci, the scarf we found at her house covered in blood went missing a few days ago. The likelihood is Percival stole it so he could use it to frame Ricci,' said Halloran.

'But what about the man who used Alim's credit card in Helmsley?' said Grace.

'It could be an accomplice of Percival,' said Charley. 'But I think it's much more likely that Kitt was right about that being a disguise. Percival was quick to dismiss that theory. There probably was no accomplice. Just him wearing a ridiculous moustache. We'll know more in the coming hours though.'

'I hope so,' said Kitt. 'But before we get off this rooftop and in out of the cold, I do have one more question.'

'What's that?' asked Evie.

'What the hell is that thing?' Kitt said, pointing to Evie's bear, which had been cast to the floor in the fray.

'That,' Evie said, 'is Hamilton the Third and you are rude.' She went over to where the bear was lying, picked him up off the ground and rested him on a stray chair sitting near the doors to the balcony.

Kitt looked at Charley askance. 'You took her to the Teddy Bear Tea Rooms, didn't you?'

'I might have, aye.'

'Oh dear, oh dear, oh dear,' Kitt said, shaking her head as she walked towards the door. 'This is going to be the start of a slippery slope.'

Evie turned back to Charley and ran a hand through her hair. 'I'm so proud of you,' she said and leant in for a kiss so deep it made her heart feel like it might thump its way out of her ribcage. As her tongue met with Charley's, Evie knew some of the others might turn back and see but she was far too lost in the magic of kissing her new girlfriend to care.

'Ahem.'

Evie and Charley broke off their kiss and turned to see Halloran standing in the doorway.

'I hate to interrupt, Banks,' Halloran said, 'but you do realize the last person back to the nick is buying the drinks?'

Charley frowned at Halloran. 'Oh don't be so childish, sir.'

The inspector smirked and turned to go back inside. The second he was out of earshot, Charley turned back to Evie. 'Grab your bear and make a break for the stairs. If he makes it back before we do we'll never hear the end of it.'

Giggling, Evie reached for Hamilton the Third, took Charley's hand in hers and ran back inside, out of the cold.

THIRTY-EIGHT

Misty fields scrolled past the window as the Middlesbrough train juddered along the track towards the small market town of Thirsk. There, Evie would disembark, leaving Kitt to travel another thirty or so miles north solo. It had been a week since the showdown on the rooftop of the Ryedale Hotel and the pair were travelling home for Christmas. Though Evie could have driven back to Thirsk in Jacob alone, she much preferred to spend the journey with her friend. After recent events this was truer of this year than any other.

'Is it really necessary for the bear to sit with us?' asked Kitt. 'There are luggage racks overhead, you know?'

'Hamilton the Third is not luggage,' said Evie.

'Fine,' said Kitt. 'Just so long as you don't expect me to address it directly.'

'You address Iago directly,' said Evie, nodding at the cat carrier that was sitting on the table between them.

'Iago is at least animate, if unfriendly . . . aren't you darling?' Kitt said, looking down at the yellow eyes peeping between the plastic slats in the carrier. A disgruntled hiss, likely due to the uncouth manner in which Iago was being forced to travel, was all she received in return.

With a faint smile Evie watched the scenery roll by the window and put her head in her hands. 'God, what a couple of weeks it's been.'

And it had. According to Charley, every member of York police station had breathed a collective sigh of relief when Superintendent Ricci was forgiving about her wrongful arrest. She had, however, been understandably keen to get all the paperwork in order as quickly as possible to officially charge Chief Superintendent Noah Percival with the blackmail of Holt, alongside the murders of Alim Buruk and Donald Oakes. When a pair of sunglasses matching those worn by Percival's alleged accomplice were found in a bin outside his home, he had no choice but to confess that it was he who had bought all those suspicious items from the shop in Helmsley in order to frame Ricci.

Evie was distracted from her thoughts by a high-pitched rendition of 'I Saw Mommy Kissing Santa Claus'. She looked across at Kitt's holdall, where something inside was twitching in time to the music.

'For goodness' sake,' said Kitt, unzipping the bag and setting the dancing Christmas tree Grace had bought her down on the table until it had finished its performance.

'Why did you bring that with you?' Evie asked with a chuckle.

'If you worked with Grace, you'd soon learn there comes a point when you'll do anything for a quiet life,' said Kitt. 'She made a big thing about me taking it home with me to "enjoy" over the festive period.'

'God, what is she like?'

'There's not enough time between here and Thirsk to answer that question. It's good to see a smile on your face though. I hope you're going to be able to enjoy your Christmas, after everything,' Kitt said, eyeing her friend.

'I'm going to do my best. Have you been sleeping?'

'The nights have been fitful but I have had some sleep. You?'

'Not really,' said Evie. 'I might sleep a little easier if they'd caught up with Amira Buruk.'

'I know – who knew there were people out there more slippery than Jarvis Holt?' said Kitt.

Evie chuckled. She wasn't surprised to learn that Holt had cut a deal for all charges against him to be dropped in exchange for his testimony against Percival. Grace, who had spent the week pretending that she was going to visit him in prison so they could reminisce about the 'good times they'd shared' was disappointed when that charade had had to come to an end. For Evie's part, she wasn't convinced there was any situation that man couldn't weasel his way out of. Percival, on the other hand, would not live out his sentence if he didn't get parole. Given that Percival was responsible for two counts of murder, perhaps that was as it should be but Evie couldn't help but feel a little sad about it all. Percival had had a noble career, until the very end.

'Cheer up, love,' said Kitt. 'At least poor little Wilkinson's off the hook, eh?'

'That's something. Although, we never did find out who Amira Buruk's police source was.'

'You're suggesting it might be Wilkinson?'

'No,' Evie said, smirking at the idea. 'But I'm just saying, there's still a chance there's someone at North Yorkshire Police we can't trust.'

'Mal has been fixated on that point too, and I'll tell you what I told him: Amira Buruk is the kind of person who'll say whatever suits her when it suits her to say it. She probably just wanted you to believe she had an officer in her pocket to rattle you. I wouldn't be surprised if the whole thing was fiction.'

'If that's true, how did she find out about Percival?' asked Evie.

'I don't know,' Kitt admitted. 'Possibly by having someone follow Holt, or us ... for all we know she's bugged Holt's home. After everything, I'm not sure if I'd put anything past her.'

Evie shuddered. 'I prefer to think that maybe Ruby just read the tarot cards for her.'

'Oh don't,' said Kitt. 'Ruby was in the library yesterday

connecting the cards she read to what had come out in the press about Percival's arrest. She was only there an hour but it was impossible to get any work done while she was.'

Evie chuckled. 'I bet you enjoyed that. To be fair, there were some parallels between her case and the reading.'

'Yes, on a very non-specific level,' Kitt said with a grudging smile. 'Which is why, no matter how much she begs, I'm never going to let her tell me her twisted version of my future with Mal.'

'I can't entirely blame you for that. But I'm sure Halloran appreciates having you around to comfort him at this difficult time.' Evie teased. 'I'm surprised you're not taking him home to meet your parents this Christmas.'

'Do you ever listen to a word I say?' said Kitt. 'I told you, we're taking it slow.'

Evie laughed at how quickly Kitt had risen to the bait.

'What about you, anyway, how are you feeling about going home?'

'All right,' said Evie. 'A bit nervous.'

'You don't have to tell your mum so soon, you know, about you and Charley. If you wanted, you could wait a while.'

Evie shrugged. 'That's the thing, I don't want to wait.'

'I'd say that's a very good sign,' said Kitt.

'I think so. In a weird way, I feel like I've been waiting for this all along.'

'So you're going to tell your mum, about the special someone you've met?'

Evie sighed and smiled out at the view. In the near distance she could see the White Horse of Kilburn, a limestone figure that was carved into the hillside many years ago. It was just a few miles outside Thirsk and whenever she saw it she knew that she was almost home again. The motion of the train always made it seem to her as though the horse had broken free of its restraints and was galloping along the terrain. She watched it canter, wild and untethered. Unapologetically itself in the moment without any fear of what tomorrow might bring.

'Yes,' she replied. 'I am.'

ACKNOWLEDGEMENTS

Much gratitude is due to my agent Jo Swainson who continues to steer me through the experience of being an author with the grace and good humour so dearly required. I consider myself very lucky indeed to know you and work with you.

Heartfelt thanks also to my editor Therese Keating who has masterfully offered both sincere encouragement and a critical eye as needed; the very things an author requires to be the best they can be.

Appreciation is also due to my specialist readers: Hazel Nicholson for advising on police procedure, John Leete for explaining the ins and outs of hospital life and Matthew Tyson for his seemingly boundless knowledge of vintage cars. A huge thank you to all of you for supporting me in achieving a certain level of authenticity.

There are those also who have read chapters and segments on the way to spur me on through the writing process: Ann Leander, Claudine Mussuto and Dean Cummings. To be in touch with creative spirits such as yours is a great gift that I treasure and always will.

When it comes to the support of my family and friends I am a very fortunate soul. Thank you to Mam, Dad, Elaine, Sheena, Steven, Phil, Barbara, Ray, Christine, John, Tom, Gigi, Janet, Peter, Katie, Katell, Jackson, Maria, Louisa, Ian, Nigel, Matt and Esther for all of the times you've asked how things are going with my writing and for not pressing me too hard over my non-committal answers.

Lastly, thanks to my husband Jo for his patience with my writerly ways, for loving the strange bundle of contradiction that I am and for reassuring me that I should keep putting pen to paper.